FROM THE DEPTHS OF HELL...

They are male and female, young and old—victims of a crazed and limitless power. Once alive, now not quite dead, they stalk, hungry for new prey, thirsty for fresh blood. Wrapped in the corruption of the darkest soul, they will rampage and destroy without bounds.

TO THE HEIGHT OF TERROR

Nothing can protect the living. Not the marvels of modern technology. Not the age-old prayers of religion. Not the most deadly weapon nor the most brilliant strategy. A wickedness beyond all imagining has possessed the skyscraper—and its fury will reign until hell has been given its due.

TOWER OF EVIL

James Kisner

JAMES KISNER

TOWER OF EVIL

LEISURE BOOKS  NEW YORK CITY

A LEISURE BOOK®

May 1994

Published by

Dorchester Publishing Co., Inc.
276 Fifth Avenue
New York, NY 10001

Printed in the United States of America.

TOWER OF EVIL

Prologue

Wednesday, 22 November:
03:30

Thump, thump, thump. . . .

The revolving doors at the end of the lobby had started spinning on their own, gaining speed with each revolution. They were supposed to be locked.

Shannon jumped, then forced herself to be calm and rose from her seat. She walked carefully across the marble floor of the lobby, moving uneasily between the twin banks of elevators to investigate. As she passed the mirrored doors, she was suddenly spooked by her endlessly multiplied image, which seemed to walk along with her. She wanted to turn and run, to hide somewhere. But there was nowhere to hide. And it was her job to investigate. She couldn't let her apprehension keep her from her duty, even though she felt she had already done more than her duty for one night—much more.

She paused just beyond the elevators, listening. One set of doors had stopped temporarily. The other doors continued to spin. She strained to see. It hurt her eyes to try to focus on the doors themselves, because beyond them—outside—there was only snow and blackness, creating a stark contrast with the interior of the building.

As the howling wind assailed her senses in ragged counterpoint to the noise the doors made, she took another step forward. Her view shifted to the floor in front of the revolving doors.

The thumping sounded wet because something was caught in the doors, preventing them from moving smoothly. Something that the doors continued to batter—a head. One Shannon almost recognized.

Each slap of the doors mangled the disembodied head more, rendering the features on the face less familiar. Shannon was drawn closer, her morbid curiosity aroused, part of her still not convinced what she saw really was a head.

She jerked back as a spray of blood jetted from the revolving doors, splattering her. Suddenly the head was jolted loose and spun along the floor, tumbling over and over until it came to rest in front of one of the elevators. Its hideous image was multiplied in the mirrored surfaces of the elevator doors, reflecting an infinity of heads.

Shannon coughed and covered her mouth with her hand to hold back the churning bile burning her throat. She looked away from the head and focused on the revolving doors, daring them in her mind to do anything.

As if taking the dare, both sets of doors began spinning again, accelerating till they were virtually a blur. Each turn splattered Shannon with more and more of the bloody residue left by the head on the edge of the circular frame. She was showered in blood. She would have screamed, but she knew that was what they wanted. They wanted her to admit defeat, to let them take over her mind completely. They wanted her to believe they were real! But she was too tough.

She muttered a curse and turned away from the doors, clamping her hands over her ears to muffle the whirring sound the doors made as she started to return to her post at the security desk.

Nothing anybody could do would make her admit defeat. She was stronger than anybody! Her resolve made her feel a little better. Then the head spoke to her.

Chapter One

Tuesday, 21 November:
08:05

Shannon Elroy yawned widely when her relief arrived to take over for the day shift. Her body ached. She had been working third shift at the bank tower downtown for almost three months, but she had not yet convinced her body to accept night for day.

The fact was—as she told herself many times—she was getting too old for this shit. She was no longer as adaptable as she had been back when she was in the service and her daily shift of duty varied. Now, out in the real world, where she sought the kind of normalcy everyone else seemed to have, she worked twisted hours that kept her from reassimilating herself into society as a normal person. To approach that, her various biological clocks demanded a more regular cycle.

Her relief, Stan Cork, was only 22 or so. He could still screw around with his body rhythms without too many ill effects. He was also a silly kind of kid, still more adolescent than adult, and he didn't take anything very seriously.

At 28, Shannon felt ages older than Cork. She didn't look any older, despite her strained, odd hours, but she felt it inside, where it counted. She had learned to put on a good front for the few people who saw her: applying fresh makeup no matter how shitty she was feeling; wearing a crisp, clean uniform; pinning her badge exactly perpendicular to the button of her left shirt pocket; and minding her posture, never allowing herself to slump into what she felt, never letting any of what was going on inside her show on the outside.

It was quite an accomplishment to look good in the Jones and Malone Security Company uniforms. They were plain dark brown, with short-sleeved shirts and trousers and cheap-looking plastic buttons—for both men and women. They were also made of pure polyester, which was not even finished to resemble wool or any other natural fiber. People could tell the uniforms were synthetic from half a block away, Shannon imagined, and that often made her feel self-conscious. Polyester was, after all, the cloth of the lower classes—the cheap-grade, petroleum-based fabric that marked the division between the classy and the classless. Its only virtue was that it never needed ironing. But among its many disadvantages were its tendency to snag easily and its ability to make the body clothed in it generate unbearable heat. Shannon often felt as if she were sitting inside a plastic bag in her uniform, especially under the hot lights in the bank's lobby, which burned 24 hours a day. At least she didn't have to wear a damn tie—not on this assignment, anyway.

Cork came up to the security desk, leering, as usual, as if everything was a joke. He had a wide face with a sprinkle of freckles over the bridge of his nose and stray specks of them on his cheeks. His hair was the color of red Indian-corn kernels, and with the stuff he put on it—some kind of styling gel, the smell of which reminded Shannon of embalming fluid—it seemed more like a lacquered wig than real hair. He was tall and thin, his frame not yet having acquired any real masculine attributes. It didn't seem possible he would ever be fully mature, either physically or mentally. Cork was, as Shannon often told others, a dork.

"Morning," Cork said, licking his lips with a lewd sparkle in his eye.

A dork like him couldn't have any balls, Shannon often thought. Cork the Dork, the ballless rent-a-cop. A summary. A job description. The lip-licking, she knew, was the prelude to some sexist and/or sexual remark, which would be the Dork's way of hinting how much he would like to see more of her.

His lust for Shannon was quite understandable. Just about any man who met Shannon wanted her. She was an attractive woman, taller than average, with a wonderfully complex and overt sexuality, which she tried to suppress, usually unsuccessfully. Her breasts were not large, but rounded and firm with a youthful bounce. Her hips were disproportionately wider than her torso, but the effect was akin to that of the sirens of the old movies, like Mariyln Monroe or Sophia Loren. Such hips, complemented by long, muscular thighs, were an invitation for the entire male universe. She could be both a mother and lover to mankind if she ever chose.

Her eyes were magic blue, arresting, the lids suggestive of an Oriental slant. Her hair was naturally medium blonde, wavy and long. Although her face was oval with a small pointy chin, she had a wide mouth and full lips, behind which hid slightly irregular but very white teeth. Her skin was very pale, but under closer scrutiny, revealed an underlying Mediterranean or Hispanic cast, though she claimed Indian blood in her lineage accounted for the tint. Her bright pink nipples seemed to belie that explanation, but since few had ever seen them, she rarely had to argue over her racial heritage.

"Morning," Shannon replied flatly to the Dork with a disapproving glance, and Cork's leer became more pronounced. Without looking back, Shannon reached behind her for her thermos and the canvas bag in which she kept various necessities. "What's that shit-eating grin on your face for?"

"You're out of uniform," he said.

"What the fuck you mean?"

Shannon had learned to punctuate her language with obscenities while in the service. She no longer noticed she used such words more often than most other women did, and if she did notice, she would not have cared. She rarely went anywhere where the niceties of language were observed, except her mother's house, where even damn was considered improper language.

"Your top button is unbuttoned." Cork grinned.

Shannon glanced down at her shirt and saw that the top button had come undone again, which happened with this particular shirt just about everytime she moved. The buttonhole was too large and she hadn't had time to mend it. Many of the uniforms were getting old, threadbare, and loose, and they needed replacement, but the company was too damn cheap to order new uniforms.

"So what?"

"I think your pink-nosed puppies may get out."

Shannon frowned and realized Cork was leering because her shirt was half open, and her deep cleavage and the lacy edge of her black bra were showing just enough for a clown like him to act half stupid. Shannon pulled her shirt together, shifted the button in place and glared at Cork. "You get your jollies looking down a woman's shirt?"

"Maybe."

"Well, you didn't see fucking anything."

"Hey, I've seen a lot more than that, anyhow."

She stood up behind the desk and pulled on her leather jacket, which had been draped over the back of the chair. "I think you're a virgin and you probably whack off at night watching Madonna videos." She picked up her thermos and bag and stepped away from the desk.

"Who doesn't?"

Cork slid easily into the chair and set a cup of coffee from the local Burger King at his elbow. He was never ruffled by Shannon's tough act; he considered their interchanges a game, though Sannon sometimes seemed to take things a bit more seriously than he did. Her hostile reaction made it even more fun to tease her whenever possible.

"Thanks for warming the chair for me," he said, shifting on the seat and smiling.

Shannon shook her head. "You dick."

"Hey, don't be so uptight. You take everything too serious."

"Your problem is you're not serious enough."

Cork smiled widely. "I can be serious about some things."

"Like what?"

"Like showing a woman a good time."

"I don't want to hear about it."

"You might be surprised, Shannon."

"Not by you, I wouldn't. I'd know exactly what would happen. Nothing."

Cork's smile remained in place. He didn't reply. He was done playing for the moment. It was time to get to work. He glanced down at her paperwork as he always did when he came on duty. "Anything happen last night I should know about?"

Shannon hefted her bag on her shoulder and started toward the back door. "Nothing I didn't write down," she answered wearily. "Just another long, dull, quiet night. A couple of workaholics came in and went up to twenty, then left. That was the highlight of the night's festivities."

"Check," he said and started filling out the top of his own duty report for the day.

Shannon paused at the back door, glancing down the lobby as the first of the morning crowd of office workers came in through one of the revolving doors. Then she leered.

"Forgot to tell you, dude—you're out of uniform, too."

"I am?"

"Your barn door's open, chump."

Cork cast his eyes to his fly, his face reddening. It was not unzipped.

"Made you look!" Shannon said and bounced out the door, wiggling her ass just enough to be sassy.

She loved to get the last word in.

08:36

Shannon arrived at her apartment after stopping for a Sausage McMuffin at the McDonald's on Michigan; she had half consumed it before she hit the door. She was still chewing as she stopped just inside and dropped her bag. She tossed her thermos on the sofa, peeled out of the uniform, undid and dropped her bra. She sat on the floor, resting her back against the sofa and rubbing under her breasts where the bra had bound her. She reveled in the freedom of not being in uniform and not having to be presentable or polite to anyone.

In the hierarchy of respect among the high-rise's workers, a security guard was hardly a notch above the cleaning people who came in to swab the toilets at night. Yet a guard was expected to be perfect and friendly and helpful and all those other boy-scout things. But in reality, a security guard was a nobody—a nonentity most people looked on with disdain. The pay sucked, too: five bucks an hour, no pay for holidays, and overtime only when she went over 40 hours, even if she worked a double shift two days in a row. And, of course, there were no fringe benefits of any kind.

Actually, Shannon was just a baby-sitter for the building. She didn't even wear a sidearm. So it was a job with no respect, poor pay, and crappy uniforms. There was absolutely nothing to recommend it—except that it was the first job Shannon had applied for in the last six months where the company was willing to hire her, and she needed the pay, small as it was.

Jobs of of any kind were hard to come by in the present economy. More and more companies were laying people off and shutting down plants; companies that advertised even bad jobs were swamped with applicants. She had had to take what was available and be glad of having that.

What frustrated Shannon the most was that she knew she was much better than the job. Her training in the service had provided her with many skills, none of which were being used in her security job. She had applied for the city police force, but once they selected Shannon as a candidate, it would be two months before they could even schedule a written test. She had even completed an application at the county sheriff's office, but nothing had come of that so far, either. She was stuck where she was, with no real hope of change in the near future.

She sighed, rubbed her mouth with a napkin, and tilted her head back to stare at the ceiling. Just above her, there was a brown stain that seemed sometimes to change shape. Right then, it was as unmoving as her own life.

She closed her eyes and fell asleep quickly, succumbing to the cumulative exhaustion of working three nights in a row.

Chapter Two

Tuesday, 21 November:
09:03

One of the elevators was stuck on the twenty-third floor of the bank tower. That was not an unusual occurence. The elevators had been installed by the company that had submitted the lowest bid, and Luxem had cut corners in order to meet the bid. In order to keep their costs down to meet their bid, the technicians from Luxem had used circuit boards in the electronics that didn't perform exactly according to the specifications the architects had written in the building plans. Luxem got away with this simply because few inspectors could tell one circuit board from another.

Usually, the nonspecification equipment presented no real problems, because the traffic in the building was such that the elevators rarely had to perform in any way out of the ordinary. Occasionally, however, there were more people using the elevators than normally. At times like that, the electronic control system first went haywire, then eventually overheated and rebelled, leaving at least one elevator sitting somewhere.

This morning was different. The traffic was normal—if anything, lighter than usual. The elevator car—number six in the bank that served the lower floors—had simply stopped for no apparent reason.

A troubleshooter was called. And in less than an hour, a technician from Luxem arrived to check the situation. Otis Travers knew that his company had used cheap electronics in the elevators, and he always patched them the best he could. Since Luxem charged $200 an hour for emergency service, the company was gradually getting back the money they considered they had lost on the low bid.

Such was the way of American business, and everyone accepted the practice, even the management company that operated the bank tower. No one saw anything unethical about it, certainly not Otis. He was paid well, and his job was usually simple, requiring him either to replace a circuit board or reset the system.

But when he arrived that morning, he could not discover any malfunctioning circuits. Usually the trouble was located in the circuit boards above the elevators—on the twenty-fourth floor for the low-rise cars—but Otis's test meter detected no faults of any kind, which meant Otis would have to get into car six and test the electronics on board.

He was a short, balding man, pushing 60, who had been working on elevators for over 30 years. He had taken courses in electronics to keep up with all the new developments in technology. He wore a crisp green uniform with his name on his left pocket and rushed about to sustain the illusion that repairing elevators required such great concentration that he couldn't be bothered.

He hated elusive problems, such as the one that car six presented today. He expected to come to the tower, unplug a circuit board, and plug another in, then hide out or pretend to be doing something for at least two hours—the minimum time Luxem had declared it would allow for any service call. The job was supposed to be easy, and it usually was.

Otis sighed heavily. Just to make sure the problem wasn't mechanical, he inspected the gears and cables above car six, but saw no signs of malfunction. So he picked up his red toolbox and went down the stairwell to the twenty-third floor, where car six awaited his ministrations.

He stood in front of the elevator, muttering unintelligible curses as he fished a special key from his tools. The key was actually a rod with a joint; when inserted in the round hole high up on the elevator door, it allowed the door to be opened manually. Since the elevator was malfunctioning, Otis could gain entry to it in no other way. He popped the odd key into the hole, twisted, and pulled the doors apart.

The electronics were more screwed up than Otis had anticipated. The main panel indicated that car six was on the twenty-third floor, but in reality, it was someplace else. Glancing down the shaft apprehesively, he didn't see the car. He couldn't make anything out in the darkness of the shaft.

When such a problem had happened before, Otis had merely closed the doors and checked each floor until he found where the elevator was hiding. However, the doors wouldn't close.

Otis gulped. It wouldn't do to leave the doors open. What if a tenant came along and tripped? There would be a big-time lawsuit.

He tugged at the metal doors again. They were supposed to shut easily and lock safely in place with little effort. Otis was sweating now and becoming angry.

He grasped the left door with both hands and pulled with all his strength. At that instant, he felt something warm wrap around his legs. He looked down, but saw nothing. It was probably air coming up through the shaft.

The warmth became substantial, like an arm. It squeezed his legs together, then pulled Otis into the shaft. Otis screamed as he fell, but the sound was lost among the noise of the other elevators suddenly moving up and down, their cables screeching as they wound around the massive gears at the tops of the shafts. It almost seemed deliberate—the way the elevators were moving to cover up Otis's scream. He had just enough time for that thought before he reached the bottom of the shaft and was impaled on a huge spring intended to act as a brake.

He didn't suffer since his heart had exploded in his chest milliseconds before he hit the spring. Seconds passed as blood oozed out of Otis's broken body, spiraling down the spring to splat on the concrete below.

No one came. No one had heard or noticed anything.

The elevators stopped moving, becoming silent. Then the doors on the twenty-third floor shut quietly on their own, and elevator six resumed normal operation.

Chapter Three

Tuesday, 21 November:
14:23

Shannon's eyelids popped open. A dog was barking down in the courtyard outside her window, and though she normally slept through any kind of daytime racket, she had been startled awake by its yapping. Her eyeballs felt as if they had been rubbed with sand-paper.

"Christ on a crutch," she mumbled, bending her head back to stretch and limber up her neck. The nylon of the sofa cover felt scratchy, and she got to her feet, wincing with the effort. "Goddamn dog."

She grimaced as she tasted leftover grit from her breakfast in her mouth and bile burned the back of her throat. Working the graveyard shift screwed up all her body's systems, playing special hell with digestion. It seemed her stomach was always growling, grumbling, or burning. She gulped back the bile and went over to the window.

Shannon peeked through the blinds at the courtyard below. The animal making all the noise was a big mongrel, part German Shepherd probably, barking at a cat in one of the stubby, barren maple trees in the middle of the yard. The cat was safely perched several feet above the dog, its tail twitching with displeasure as it watched the mongrel make a fool of itself. Cats knew dogs couldn't climb trees, but dogs were apparently too stupid to realize cats were aware of this fact and so refused to be intimidated.

Shannon turned from the window, deciding she didn't have the energy to go down and chase the dog away. Someone would come along and do it eventually. Or the dog would get tired. Or the cat would jump on it and claw its nose. She needed more sleep—deep sleep, the kind that rested the body and refreshed aching bones and tired flesh—the kind of sleep she craved but rarely enjoyed.

She shambled wearily across her small apartment and entered the bathroom. She opened the medicine cabinet and took down a large bottle of Rolaids, opened it, and popped half-a-dozen tablets, chewing and swallowing them quickly to kill the acid in her stomach. Then she brushed her teeth and considered taking a shower, but decided bathing would wake her up too much. She could live with her own stink until she had to go back to work.

She stripped off the rest of her clothes, leaving them in a pile near the toilet, which she used and flushed. Then she went to her bedroom and climbed onto the bed. She crawled under the covers, lay on her side, and pulled a pillow over her head to muffle the sound of the dog.

She yawned and shut her eyes, watching colors converge and patterns dance on the insides of her eyelids. It was like looking through a kaleidoscope. Gradually the patterns and colors were replaced by velvety black, and she tried not to think of anything, encouraging sleep to come soon.

Fifteen minutes later, Shannon sat up as if struck by electricity. She couldn't sleep. Her body screamed with exhaustion, and her brain was mush, but she just couldn't let go and relax.

It was going to be one of those terrible days when she would have to push herself near to physical collapse before she slept. That kind of day happened often to her since she worked all night. Her body demanded day rhythms occasionally, even if it was exhausted. The adrenaline kicked in and she got so hyper even a short nap was impossible.

"Damn it," Shannon moaned. Suddenly she felt uncomfortable, mostly sticky and smelly. She rolled out of bed and returned to the bathroom to take the shower she had denied herself before.

She stepped into the tub, pulled the shower curtain closed, and turned the water on as hot as she could take it, until steam was billowing all around her. She closed her eyes and ducked her head under the shower, reveling in the pleasurable sensation of hot water soaking her hair and running down her body. After a few seconds, she grabbed the soap and lathered herself, scrubbing vigorously until her flesh was almost red. Then she rinsed herself and turned the water off. She stood in the shower for a moment, allowing the lingering steam to permeate her sinuses.

Stepping out, she took a pink towel from the rack and rubbed her body dry. She brushed her teeth again, seeing only a vague image of herself in the steamed-up mirror.

She felt marginally better, so she put on a robe and went out to the kitchenette to fix her lunch. On her way, she noticed the dog had finally stopped barking. Maybe she ought to try going to sleep again.

Her stomach's growling was insistent, however. She made a sandwich of bologna and cheese on wheat bread and ate it with a glass of milk, followed by a handful of cookies. Then she made herself a cup of tea and lounged on the sofa to watch television. Oprah was on, and the show featured a trio of Satan worshipers pitted against three born-again Christians. There was a great deal of name-calling and lively comments from the audience.

Shannon yawned. All this talk of Satan reminded her of her childhood, when her mother warned her concerning all the possible ways the devil might get into her heart. As a young girl, she had taken what her mother told her seriously, but when she had reached 18 and gone off on her own, she soon decided blaming Satan for one's own actions was a cop-out people used because they wouldn't accept responsibility for what they did on their own.

She followed no accepted religion. Traditional religious beliefs bored her, because they seemed designed mainly to take the fun out of life. Don't drink. Don't smoke. Don't have sex without love or procreation. To Shannon's analytical mind, none of those edicts made sense. Why had God bothered to give men and women senses if they weren't meant to enjoy them?

Shannon changed channels and watched a couple of music videos on MTV, including a new one by Michael Jackson she hadn't seen. It was pretty good; she liked Michael Jackson's music, as well as most modern music, except for heavy metal. The other video was an ancient one by Billy Idol; in it, he sang on top of a tall building as zombies climbed up after him. The visuals had nothing to do with the lyrics of the song, as happened so often in videos. It was just flash and glitter.

Bored by the next video, Shannon scanned the other cable channels and found nothing that interested her. Her eyelids felt heavy again. She switched the television off and made her way back to the bedroom. After flopping on the bed quickly, she luxuriated in the softness of the pillow against her head. Sweet sleep was imminent; she was sure of it. All she had to do was let it happen.

When the phone rang three minutes later, Shannon's mind was halfway down a well, crawling toward unconsciousness. She wanted to let the answering machine get the call because nothing was more important than sleep. But the phone kept ringing, and the answering machine didn't come on.

"Fuck!" Shannon screamed and jumped out of bed. She ran to the phone in the living room and picked it up. "Hello!"

"Shannon, honey," her mother said.

"What do you want, Mom?"

"Don't talk to me in that tone of voice, Shannon. I'm just calling to see if you're okay."

"I was okay until the phone rang. I was almost asleep."

"It's almost five o'clock. Why would you be sleeping in the afternoon anyhow?"

Shannon rolled her eyes toward the ceiling. Day people just didn't understand. "I work all night, Mom. When do you think I get my sleep?"

"You've had plenty of time to sleep."

"I couldn't get to sleep until just now."

"Well, if you're going to be snippy, I don't want to talk to you."

"Fine."

"But you could come and visit me a little more often."

Shannon sighed. Why did her mother insist on laying the same old guilt trip on her every time they talked? Shannon was a grown woman. She didn't need to see her mommy every day of her life.

"All right, Mom. I'll come to see you this weekend. I promise. We'll go shopping or something," Shannon said, hoping to cut the conversation short.

"What about church?" Mrs. Elroy refused to accept her daughter's disdain for religion, considering it a temporary aberration.

"I work on Sunday."

"You could still go to church. Your sister always goes."

"That's Linda, not me." Her younger sister was always so perfect. She was probably still a virgin at nineteen.

"You should go."

"I don't want to, and you know it."

"You need something to hold your life together, honey. Christ is the answer."

Shannon resisted the impulse to say, "What's the question?" as she had done a couple of times with her mother. But she knew all it would get her was a lengthy lecture. Instead, Shannon said,

"Maybe. Maybe I'll make it someday when I'm not so tired."

"This Sunday?"

"I don't know. Don't push me."

"You're getting snippy again."

"I'll call you tomorrow."

"You be careful down at that bank. The television says there's going to be a big snow tonight."

"I can take care of myself. All right? I'm a grown-up. Now let me go back to sleep."

"See you Saturday?"

"Yeah, sure."

Shannon hung up, disgusted. Wide awake again, she glanced at the clock. She had only about six hours left before she had to go to work again.

"What a bummer."

She went to the window and glanced out. The sky was darkening and little wisps of snow were already swirling in the air. She turned and went to the answering machine, which was set up on a table next to the sofa. The red light that indicated it was on was not lit. She bent down and saw the cord had come loose from the machine and pushed it back in. The machine lit up, the tape wound, then rewound, and the red light began to blink.

"No more phone calls," she vowed.

She made herself a bowl of chicken-noodle soup and watched more television, getting through a couple of reruns before her eyes started aching again.

She leaned back on the sofa, her eyelids dropping until she was watching a show through a fuzzy-edged slit. She didn't get through the first 15 minutes.

From a great distance, there was a buzz, like a fly or an angry wasp caught in a bottle. Annoyed by the sound, Shannon opened her eyes slightly. The television was off, though she didn't remember turning it off herself. She grunted and shifted her body. The distant buzz persisted.

She rolled on her back and stared up at the ceiling through her eyelashes. The brown stain up there seemed to be moving. She squinted and tried to focus on it, but the stain wouldn't become sharp in her vision. It was becoming something vaguely reconizable, like a demonic face that seemed to open its mouth and reveal brown-stained fangs.

Satan was out to get her!

Shannon yelped involuntarily and sat up, her eyes wide open. She glanced at the stain on the ceiling again and it was the same as always—just a shapeless spot.

No longer groggy, she recognized the buzzing. It was the alarm in her bedroom, set for ten o'clock—22:00—as designated in the military timekeeping the company used. Time to get ready for work.

"Goddamn great," she said. Since it was time

to go to work, she was really sleepy.

The bed called out to her, and she considered phoning in sick, but she had done that already so often on short notice that she could lose her job if she did it again. Besides, she reminded herself, she needed the money. She was slowly saving up the down payment for a different car, because her old Ford Fairlane had over 100,000 miles on it and needed just about every part replaced.

She yawned, sat up, and cursed. Then, she hustled herself off to the bathroom for another shower before she got dressed.

Christ, it was going to be a long night!

Chapter Four

Tuesday, 21 November:
08:10

Stan watched Shannon leaving through the back door on the video monitor. As always, he appreciated the lithe, musical movements of her body—the way her breasts bounced and her legs seemed to curve into each step, generating sensual electricity in spite of the unisex uniform she was obliged to wear—and he wished he were a bolder man.

It was easy to make sexual jokes with a woman, especially one who was not grossed out by anything he had to say. But it was not very easy to get her to take him seriously as a man, not just another coworker.

He didn't think he had a chance in hell of making it with Shannon. It was obvious she considered him only a kid. And although she wasn't that much older than him, she was apparently vastly more experienced, not only in sex but in dealing with the world and people. She even swore better than he did, more like a man, more like his father and the other working-class men Stan had grown up with.

Stan realized he did not do much to impress her with his maleness. He had to admit to himself his behavior was pretty childish around her. She seemed to bring out his immaturity in him by dismissing his masculinity as if it didn't exist.

He had yet to determine exactly what her idea of a man could be. But the way she defined maleness was probably an ideal he could not hope to live up to. He probably didn't even come close. She was, no doubt, the type who liked men with lots of muscles and body hair—beach gorillas or gym jocks or even truck drivers—none of which he ever aspired to be. His physique was average, and he could never get a real tan because his pale skin tended to burn when exposed to the sun. He hated to work out because he was too impatient. His muscles refused to firm up or assume texture like the well-delineated lines of a body builder. And driving a truck was for mindless grunts, not for anyone with any functioning brain mechanism.

Stan sighed. Maybe Shannon would give him a tumble if she knew what he was really like, deep down inside. He was really courageous when he wanted to be. He needed courage to face every day in the bank tower. Dealing with fickle and capricious women, stupid tenants, and idiotic people tried his patience. Sometimes, he was tempted to just walk off the job and let the tenants and management stew in their own juices. Let them try to run the building without him on duty!

He wondered if Shannon knew why he required such courage she might somehow be more attracted to him. But how could she possibly be aware of the things he had to face, of the things that affected the way he acted? How could she know the amount of courage he needed to deal with his own conscience, for example?

Shannon would not understand. She was smart—street smart and brain smart—but she would not consider him courageous. She would judge him to be a wimp who couldn't endure the reality of what he had done in the past and couldn't own up to his deeds—or misdeeds—like a man.

He knew he should quit his job, leave behind the awful memories it raised. But he couldn't yet because his heart ached for the brief moments when she was close enough for him to smell her perfume or her overnight sweat—which was like another kind of perfume, a musky odor that made him tingle all over as he imagined grappling with her in a bed. Her perspiration would be one of the lubricants of love his manipulations would cause to flow.

He was forced to love her from afar, always hoping somehow he would get through to her how he really felt. But she remained oblivious to his feelings. How much longer could he bear it? If only he had a woman of his own, Shannon might not mean so much to him. But he was alone, still living with his parents, unable to break free because he didn't make enough money to do any better. Nor did he have any immediate hope of improving his lot in life.

Besides, it was unlikely Shannon would ever go out on a date with another security guard, unless he had something special to offer her. Since he couldn't impress her with his tacit love, the possibility she would ever notice him was remote.

He hated himself for his fecklessness. He was unable to do anything positive, unable to change his situation, unable to make anything happen. He could only continue to languish in torturing, unrequited love, hoping for a miracle.

15:45

The day had dragged by, and when Jack Landers, Stan's relief, arrived—early as usual—Stan was ready to run for the door. He had dealt with so many problems, so many petty gripes, so many stupid people that he was about to go off on someone, and such a violent outburst would cost him his job.

Jack Landers resembled the stereotype most

people identified with security guards. He was past retirement age, almost 70, and he had a potbelly. His hair was thin and very white, and he sported a bushy gray-and-black moustache that always needed trimming. When he talked, his upper dentures clicked, making his presence even more obnoxious. He was given to blustering and had a self-important attitude, as if he were a real cop instead of only a security guard with no more power than the average citizen. He was also hard of hearing, or else he didn't listen to anyone but himself. It was difficult for Stan to tell with old guys; he thought they lived in their own little world.

Stan started finishing up the paperwork for his shift as Jack hovered around the desk, apparently impatient to get to work, though Stan believed he just wanted to sit down.

"Well, Jack, the place is yours," Stan said as four o'clock approached. "Don't let any bums come in and take it away from you."

"Is that supposed to be funny?" Jack had almost no sense of humor. He also often ranted about the possibility of terrorists coming in to rob the bank, and he knew they always killed the security guards first. He expressed this fear almost every day, though that day he was too grouchy to pursue the topic, despite Stan having given him an opening.

"No," Stan said, yawning. "Forget I said it. Keep an eye on the cleaning guys so they don't steal any computers or toilet paper."

"Don't I always?"

"Yeah, sure." Stan surrendered the desk chair to the older man, pulled on his jacket and started for the door. "You're a better man than I am, Gunga Din—or Gunga Jack, in this case."

Jack ignored him, which was just as well since Stan had no further brilliant repartee to offer.

Before he left, Stan remembered some news he need to pass on to Jack. "Watch out for that Luxem guy, Otis. His truck is parked in the garage, but we can't find him anywhere."

"Maybe the truck broke down," Jack said.

"Maybe. Probably no biggie. If he shows up, just make sure he calls his office. You got that?"

"I'll remember. You don't have to remind me." Jack looked offended.

Stan resisted the temptation to remark on how Jack often did need reminding. Along with everything else, his memory was rapidly deteriorating, and if specific instructions were not written down for him, he would forget. But Stan didn't feel like hanging around any longer to write a note about Otis. If Jack forgot, it wouldn't make that much difference.

Stan turned, darted out the back door, and headed for his his car, a tan Subaru station wagon he had rigged up with a megabass thumper, extra woofers, and a monster amp that required a second battery to power it.

Suddenly, he felt disgusted with himself. The changing of shifts made his thoughts turn to

Shannon and their encounter that morning, when he had again played the fool with her, guaranteeing he would never gain masculine status with her. He would remain the kid she could barely tolerate. He smacked his forehead with anger and jerked open the door of the car, calling himself names as he tossed his tote bag in the back.

His next reaction was also part of the routine. He shifted his anger to focus on her, personally. She was the unfeeling bitch in this situation. She was the one who had no heart or understanding. She was the one who did not see how much he lusted after her, who did not see how much he needed her! Stupid cunt!

He slid into the driver's set and stuck the key in the ignition, then pounded the steering wheel.

Goddamn her to hell!

"Hey, buddy, spare some change?"

Stan twisted his face to confront a raggedy old bum who smelled like a compost heap. The man was leaning in the window, which Stan had rolled down so he could wipe moisture off his side mirror. He was extremely thin and pallid, and he had wispy gray hair sticking out from the edges of a battered brown fedora. He wore a fake leather bomber's jacket that had stains all over it, and when he spoke, his breath reeked of alcohol and tacos. He was utterly disgusting.

"Go away," Stan said as evenly as possible.

"Hey, man, just a quarter. Just a fucking

quarter. I got to git sumpin to eat. I ain't eat in days."

"Go to the mission."

The man looked indignant at the suggestion. "I ain't no fucking charity case. Now give me a goddamn quarter!"

Stan rolled up his window, turned on the ignition, and cranked up the stereo full blast. Six eight-inch woofers in the back shook the car and drowned out any further demands from the bum, who was shaking his fists at Stan.

"Fuck you!" Stan yelled and shifted intro reverse, spinning his tires as he backed out into the alley without checking for oncoming traffic.

The man dropped his arms, shrugged his shoulders, and headed out of the loading-dock area, apparently looking for someone else to put the touch on. Stan knew he couldn't upset these old rummies. Their leathery skin was as thick as an elephant's hide.

Stan hated them nonetheless. His feelings of hatred for them was almost as passionate as his lust for Shannon. They were worse than scum in his eyes; they were not even human beings. They ought to be driven out of town or, even better, exterminated like the vermin that infested them!

His anger stoking almost to the limit, he popped the car into drive. Then he floored the accelerator, making as much noise as possible as he pulled away into the alley, oblivious to any pedestrians passing by.

Driving home, Stan's anger at the bum subsided. As his stereo blared "Let's Talk About Sex, Baby," his mind drifted to images of other women he lusted after.

Shannon might be the main object of his sexual desires, but she wasn't the only one who made his zipper tight. There were a lot of sexy babes working in the various offices in the building during his shift, clearly half of whom were worthy of his attention. Some of them made him ache with displaced hormonal angst just by walking by his desk.

Of course, sexual liaisons with these women were even more improbable—make that impossible—than with Shannon. They all looked down at him. He was just a security guard—a man in a cheap uniform whose main function was to keep the riffraff out of their way as they tapped on their high heels through the lobby, the cheeks of their asses rolling and. . . .

He had to stop thinking about all the women he saw. They were unattainable. He would never get into any of their pants in a billion years. Not if he were trapped with one of them on an elevator and they had only minutes to live. Shannon was his only hope for the immediate future. Aside from the strip bars he went to on occasion, he didn't go anywhere else where he could meet women.

Shannon—damn her anyhow.

He recalled when she had first started and they had had different shifts. She used to relieve him when he was coming off the evening shift that Jack currently had. A few times she had failed to show up, causing him to pull a double shift. He hadn't forgiven her completely for those past transgressions. Hell, she owed him at least a blow job to make up for those extended hours.

He allowed himself to dwell on the image of Shannon down on her knees, wetting her lips before wrapping them around his swollen penis. He could just about feel those full lips on him, and he became aroused in reality as well in his imagination.

She probably gave incredible head. Her face was built for it. And she'd get on top of him and ride his stick, or maybe he would come in her mouth. It didn't matter—he just wanted to get off in her.

No! He was just being nasty. He didn't mean to reduce his needs to sex. He had real feelings for Shannon. He could actually care about her. It wasn't dirty, he insisted to himself, vaguely feeling that maybe Shannon—whatever she was doing right then—might be able to read his thoughts.

He did care about her. He sometimes worried about something happening to her while she sat in the building all night long, when all the weirdos and creeps were out. What if she stepped outside for a breath of fresh air and one of those damned old homeless geeks came at her? Who would protect her? She was only a woman. One hell of a woman, though.

Stan turned the stereo up louder to drown out

his thoughts. He was tired of fighting himself, tired of trying to figure things out. He longed to be home, where at least a hot meal and a warm bed awaited him. They were small comforts, but more than Shannon had ever provided him.

Interlude One: Festering Evil

Nameless and unnameable, something quite irredeemably evil—something that had waited to come into being until one moment in the time that people counted—had found a foothold in reality. Its hour had arrived, and it would manipulate and use reality in ways unreal.

It would terrorize and feed. Drive all the people it touched insane and feed on the insanity, too. It would feed on the hatred in human hearts. Then it would kill and feed some more. It would make the dead walk again and perhaps make them dance. And the dead would kill the living.

Then there would be even more dead to do its bidding—hordes of the dead advancing against fewer and fewer of the living. That would be fitting. Death gave the evil life, and the more blood that flowed—both before and after death—the more strength it would gather.

The first bloodletting that morning, when it was testing its newfound strength and awareness, felt especially fulfilling, almost like a first orgasm. Taking life from human things was its destiny, and the first one whetted its appetite for more. It promised to be a great day for more, too, because the cold was upon the human beings, and that weakened them and made the killing easier.

The killing was itself exquisite. But before the blood actually flowed, there was the terror and the fear and the abrupt horror when a human being knew he was going to die. All those sensations were exceptionally satisfying and nurturing to its essence.

Before, when it had stretched out and make things happen, it had festered in its metal prison, where it had been born when a man not quite a human being—or so he was regarded by one of his tormentors—was murdered and cast into the confining space of the prison. The act of a coward had helped to invoke evil.

The evil had festered without form, without substance—an impatient embryo that was not aware of its purpose and so could not act. But a change had befallen the evil because its invisible tendrils of horror had finally reached out and found a place to grow. When it had sufficient substance to think in its twisted, bestial way, it understood quite well its purpose for being—to kill and keep killing.

And the environment that the human beings

had created for themselves invited the growing evil, welcomed it, made a home for it. There was much around it that echoed its own basic nature—much that dwelled within human souls that would make it bigger and more dangerous than people could imagine or envision in their most fearsome nightmares. Indeed, the evil would use nightmares against people, tearing their innermost dread contemplations from secret hiding places in the dark corners of their minds. Anything that resembled evil or touched on evil or substantiated it in any way was fodder for its burgeoning presence.

The essence of the evil was present in every direction the tendrils tested: in the cold air; in the concrete and metal of the building behind which its prison sat; in the hearts and minds of all the men and women inside that building.

The bank tower had been erected over a portal into hell itself. It reached up into the sky, defying God and man. But soon, everyone in the tower would know what true evil was—and then, no one would escape their last end.

Chapter Five

Tuesday, 21 November:
16:34

It was a frigid fucking day. Willie could attest to that. He had spent most of his adult life out in the streets, and though he had learned to cope with most weather, extreme bitter cold, such as that day offered, was beyond even the most weather-wise veteran's level of endurance.

He needed shelter, but he didn't have a place where he had to be taken in. That was what a home was, according to some poem he had been forced to read—it seemed like centuries ago—in school.

He didn't have a home of any kind. Maybe a lot of people would say that he didn't want a home, that all homeless people chose their lot in life. Maybe, Willie figured, on some level he did choose. He had made the series of bad decisions that had brought him to his present state of existence. But he didn't choose to continue that way. At least, he didn't think he did.

The trouble was that he didn't know if he really could think about much of anything anymore. He had numbed or obliterated most of his brain cells with alcohol whenever he could beg enough money to get a bottle, and among the cells he had lost were those that dealt with such niceties as how to be gainfully employed, how to maintain a home, and how to be who he was. Oh, he knew his name, and his gender, but most of the other details of his identity had vanished into the black hole of his consciousness.

He didn't think he was a Vietnam vet, like a couple of his cronies. He didn't recall going to war and wasn't sure if he was old enough to have been part of it, though he thought he was pretty old. It was hard to tell. He didn't keep track of the years anymore. He didn't know what day it was unless someone told him or he happened to glance at the newspapers in the vending machines. And he rarely looked at those because the news was always so depressing. The troubles of the world didn't mean much when he was worried about eating and sleeping and waking up alive and intact the next morning.

Willie had the street pallor of most bums. He resembled a creature that lived in darkness. Only his eyes, which were a liquid gray blue, and his nose, which was a combination of magenta, pink, and red, showed any real color. The rest of his face was like newspaper bleached by the sun. He was probably close to six feet if he could be straightened out, but hunching over—trying to shrink into himself and be invisible—had cut nearly half a foot from his height. His hair was the color of straw in a broom that was ready to be thrown out; his hair even had dust and dirt in it. On his chin and jowls grew a perpetual stubble that never seemed to reached beyond a certain length. His body was thin, though he would be described as big boned by most who cast a critical eye on him.

He wore a lightweight jacket over a faded denim shirt and tattered woolen trousers he had purchased for a dollar when he'd had one to spare. He carried all of his worldly possessions with him. In his pockets were a rusty pocket knife, a disposable cigarette lighter, a corkscrew, one AAA battery, two or three cat's-eye marbles, a small pocket tin of aspirin with only one tablet in it, some pennies and nickels, a snot-encrusted handkerchief, and two keys. He couldn't remember what the keys belonged to; maybe he had just found them.

Under his arm, he usually carried a grocery sack that contained an extra change of clothes, though he had only a pair of trousers in them at the moment. His spare shirt had been stolen, he suspected, by one of his fellow street denizens.

The only other baggage Willie had was his monumental stink. Body odor was a rare aroma to be savored compared to the stench Willie had acquired. It would take a week's scrubbing and a few gallons of ammonia to even get down to the odor produced by his skin. He smelled more like a ripe garbage heap out in the summer sun at the city dump, with overlaying odors of shit, piss, snot, vomit, mildew, tooth decay, mold, fungus, and various other effluvia, the pungency of which would classify a skunk a rank underachiever.

Fortunately, Willie could not smell his own aroma. His olfactory senses had been rendered numb not only by his own odor, but by constant exposure to places where rot and mildew festered, and by hanging out with others of a like fetor.

The stink was both a weapon and a tool. It could fend off most street kids, and getting away from it was the primary reason most people would give him a quarter or even a dollar.

Cold days diminished his odor to a small degree, so he wasn't doing too well using it as a tool to gather money. Many people's noses were stopped up or frozen. Willie just presented a visual nuisance that was easy to ignore as the few hearty souls out on the streets had done steadfastly all that afternoon, leaving him broke.

He found himself on the corner of Delaware and Market Streets. The wind whipped down the street and struck him, making his teeth clatter and his spine ache. He hustled himself to the alley behind the Metropolitan National Bank building and turned in. He could find some shelter from the wind and the cold in the loading dock of that building if he wasn't run off by the security guard. He'd have to chance it. It was too cold to stay out.

He walked to the dock and decided to hide out between the trash compactor and the big dumpster back there. He slipped in between the two and managed to quit trembling once he was out of the wind. Then he crouched on the cement, hugging himself to keep as warm as possible.

A nap would feel good, but he reminded himself sleeping could mean he'd freeze to death out there, especially when the temperature dropped even lower as night came.

He finally stopped shaking and decided to fish around in the dumpster for something to keep him warm. Maybe he'd find a nice box or a piece of carpet. He stood up and started to climb into the huge metal box. He was about to scramble inside when he heard a voice.

At first, he thought it was the security guard, but he looked in both directions and saw no one. Besides, the voice had a raspy quality to it, and he could not understand it.

Maybe he was getting the DT's. It had been a while since he'd had a drink. He lifted his right leg up over the edge of the dumpster and a voice called his name.

"Who's there?" Willie asked, letting his leg down and turning around.

"Willie, you know me."

Willie still saw no one anywhere. "Where are you, man?"

"In this thing."

"The dumpster?" Willie pulled himself up and peeped into the trash. "Where?"

"Not there. Over here." A thumping noise came from the large trash compactor, a monster longer than the dumpster, ten feet high and twelve feet wide.

"Jesus, not in there. You crazy? You'll get mashed up with the trash, man. They don't even look when they turn that damn thing on!"

The owner of the voice laughed. "Ain't afraid of that, Willie."

"Why the fuck not? You must be crazy then?"

"Who ain't crazy, Willie? We're all crazy, you and me and everyfuckingbody. It's a crazy world, and it's a shitty place for folks like you and me."

"You ain't making any sense."

"I don't have to."

Willie wondered if he was talking to himself. Could he be that far gone and not know it?

"No, you ain't talking to yourself. It's me, Ted."

"Ted who?"

"You never knew my last name, Willie, just like I don't know yours. I expect we both done forgot our own last names, man. Or maybe homeless people don't have no last names, because it don't matter who we are. But you and me used to hang out over on Ohio Street before the cops started rousting us. Remember that? Remember how you got me a pint of Jim Beam one day last July?"

Willie strained his mental aparatus. A vague picture came into view—a blond-haired guy who used to sit on the wall of the parking lot on Ohio Street along with Willie and two or three other regulars. Someone complained one day, and a big black cop came along and made them move. Ted, if he recalled correctly, was never seen after that. By anyone.

"Where you been, Ted?" Willie inquired, still trying to get a mental fix on how long ago it was he had seen the man.

"I been here all the time. And I'm tired of it. I'm ready to go out and make some noise and bust some heads or something. I almost got out this morning, but I could only get in the elevator shaft in that building there, and it wasn't enough."

"You don't mean you been in that trash machine all this time?"

"Sure have. Bummer, ain't it?"

Willie suddenly felt uneasy. The only way Ted could still be in the compactor was—no, that wasn't possible. Anything or anyone who was in there more than a few hours would be compacted with the garbage and trash bags. A person would be just plain dead.

"That's me," Ted said, intruding on Willie's thoughts again. "Dead Ted."

Willie's whole body started shaking uncontrollably. "Don't try to spook me like that, you son of a bitch! Where you really at? Under there somewhere? Come on out and quit your goddamn fooling!"

"Dead Ted, Dead Ted, Dead Ted!"

Willie clamped his hands over his ears. "Stop it!"

"Come over here!"

"I ain't moving."

"Come here now!"

Willie discovered he had to obey the odd voice. He uncovered his ears and walked slowly around to the other side of the compactor where the door was.

"Open the door, Willie."

Willie reached up and did as he was told, yanking the metal door open on its creaking hinges. Inside it was very dark.

"Hi, Willie." Dead Ted's voice echoed around the metal walls. "I've been waiting for a dumb fuck like you to come along."

"What?"

The compactor door slammed against the back of Willie's head, forcing it down hard on the sharp metal edge of the frame. The door opened and closed again and again, smacking Willie's head into pulp. Then it closed one last time, and his head came loose, but his face stayed behind, sliding down into the garbage inside the compactor, where his dead eyes stared into nothing but black.

Willie's body was thrown to the cement by an invisible force. Incredibly, he wasn't dead. He just didn't have a face. His hands reached up and confirmed that fact, coming back bloody and smeared with grue.

The next thing that happened was in the remnants of what had once been Willie's brain. Something in his mind descended into momentary hell, was extinguished, then replaced by a new thought entity that twisted the formerly buried resentments into desires for revenge. Revenge on anyone and anything.

The symbol of all his sorrows: the towering skyscrapers that held the people with money, the people he had to approach and ask for spare change or a dollar for a pack of generic smokes or a couple of bucks for a bottle of cheap wine or whiskey. The uncaring people, the people who looked through him, beyond him, as if he were not there at all, as if he wasn't a person like them, as if he was nothing but whitening dog shit on the sidewalk, simmering in the summertime. The people with their tailored suits and tight skirts and proud walks or frightened scampers.

Now, they would have to pay. He would take their skyscraper. He and the others of his kind—the others hiding out in the dark doorways down the ragged alleys of the city, choking back wine and whiskey and smoking cheap cigarettes and pissing in their pants. Together, they would be an army, and they would take away everything the proud people had, and they wouldn't scurry away or scamper or dart across the street to avoid Willie and his kind anymore, because those proud people would be dead.

He stood up, his limbs gathering power from a different dimension as he stretched them toward the snow-flecked sky and screamed through the opening in his head where his mouth had been.

But it wasn't really a scream; it was a cry of birth and triumph. Something new, quite different, evil, dread, and unpredictable lived within him. Dead Ted was in there with him, and Dead Ted had plans, which did not include Willie.

But before Ted could act on any of them, he ran into a temporary setback. Faceless, he flailed around, unable to guide himself without vision or other senses. He stumbled out into the alley, walking in front of a truck that struck him full force, bouncing him up into air. He sailed over the compactor and came down into the dumpster, landing on a metal wall stud that gouged his side open.

Then he slid down amongst the trash and debris, along with pieces of wall and ceiling tiles that tore his clothes. Cardboard boxes tumbled on top of him, hiding him.

The driver of the truck that took him out didn't even stop. He hadn't seen what he hit and figured it was a pothole. Indianapolis streets were legendary for them. He wasn't paying much attention to anything anyhow, because he'd been up all night highballing it from Nashville, Tennessee, to Indianapolis with a load of desks for some damn office building he had yet to locate.

The body that was now Dead Ted twitched as worms from a torn trash bag migrated to its bloody head, and he was powerless to do anything to stop them from taking up residence in his flesh. He shuddered and became motionless. He would not stir until much later that night. It would take him that long to build up strength in the battered body he had chosen. He needed much strength to kill again—to begin taking his revenge on the city and all the people who had ignored him.

Chapter Six

Tuesday, 21 November:
23:11

Shannon had been so distracted that evening she forgot to take her uniforms to the laundromat. Since she had only two—the company was too damn cheap to provide a complete wardrobe—she had no choice but to put on one she had worn before. If she'd had time, she would have rinsed one out in the bathroom basin and dried it with her hair dryer. But as it was, she was late.

Standing in her bedroom clad only in her panties and bra, she sniffed her two shirts, her nose wrinkling with distaste, and decided the one she had worn the night before was the least obnoxious. And she wouldn't have to transfer her badge, she noted mentally, from one shirt to the other one. She put the shirt on, buttoned it up hurriedly, and slid into the slacks without bothering to check which pair might be marginally cleaner.

"Fuck it," she mumbled and dumped perfumed talcum powder down the front of her shirt and slacks, then patted them, causing clouds of powder to sift through the air. She dabbed extra cologne on her neck and into her armpits. If she were to stink after all that, then whoever she encountered would just have to endure it. She sure as hell had to endure a lot of other people's stench down at the bank.

She glanced at the window and noticed the blizzard seemed to be getting worse. She had to get going before the mayor shut down the streets!

She pulled her black socks on, tucked her feet into the black shoes she was required to wear, and laced them up. Dashing out into the living room, she grabbed her tote bag, tossed in a package of potato chips and a soda, tugged on her winter jacket, and went out the door, locking it behind her.

Out in the parking lot, Shannon could barely distinguish her car from the others; they were covered with so much snow they all looked alike. But she remembered where she had parked the rusty old Fairlane and trudged through the snow toward it, wishing she had worn her boots instead of the regulation shoes. By the time she reached her car, her feet were cold and soaking wet.

"Great," she said under her breath. She tried to open her car door and found it was frozen shut, so she had to kick it a couple of times to free it. She pulled it open and threw her tote bag inside, started the car to let it warm up, then set about brushing the snow off the windshield and other windows. This task froze her hands since she had neglected to bring her gloves and didn't feel like going back up to her apartment to get them.

The car was slow to warm up, and when she finally got behind the wheel, the heater was just beginning to blow hot air. She held her hands in front of the panel vents, rubbing them vigorously and hoping they weren't frost-bitten. When it seemed that her blood was circulating freely again, she grasped the wheel, put the transmission in reverse, and backed out slowly, trying to avoid spinning her nearly bald tires. She levered the car into drive and edged toward the street, praying no cars would cross in front of her, because she didn't think she could stop very quickly. She was in luck. The street was deserted.

That's because normal people don't go to work in the middle of the goddamn night, she thought. *They stay home and watch TV when there's a fucking blizzard.*

Her headlights reflected sparkles of light from the swirling, powdery snow, so she could hardly see where she was going. She had to strain to see anything at all, and if she hadn't been so familiar with her route to work, she surely would have driven off the road or gotten lost.

Her wipers fought to keep the windshield clean. But like everything else on the old car, they didn't work that well, and one of them screeched where the tip of the metal blade touched the glass. She was definitely flying blind. She'd be lucky to get to work at all.

She considered turning back, going home to sleep some more, but that wouldn't be fair to the officer she was relieving. He had to get home, after all. Well, she didn't have to be fair, did she?

As she struggled with her conscience, she noticed the wind was picking up, howling outside the car as it splattered more snow against the glass. The snow in her headlight beams seemed to glitter. It was fascinating, almost hypnotizing, the way the snow had become a light show. It would be so easy to get caught up in the show, let it entrance her.

Then she saw something taking shape in front of her. At first she thought it was her imagination creating shapes in clouds. But this seemed different. She squinted and focused and saw—what was it? A man?

No, it was more like a ghost. Whatever it was, it moved with the car, keeping just ahead. Gradually, it assumed the shape of an apelike something loping in front of her car. Then it was joined by other creatures like itself, and they left the pavement and started dancing and twisting before her, their heads seeming to taunt her.

She suddenly remembered making snow angels as a child. Was that was she was seeing? Did snow angels come to life and go out into the world on a night like this?

Abruptly, one of the creatures leaped upon her hood and pressed its head against the windshield glass. It grew a face—a hideous ugly face leering at her.

Her wipers halted temporarily. The blizzard dumped snow over the creature and the wind buffeted it, but it held on. The creature opened its mouth to show sharp teeth in purplish gums. Shannon gasped as she realized its face resembled the demonic visage she'd imagined seeing on her ceiling.

Then the wipers started working again and hit the thing repeatedly until they sliced its face off. The thing roared through a jagged hole in its head and tumbled off the car. Shannon looked in her rearview mirror to see what had happened to the creature, but it was quickly obscured by the blizzard.

She turned her attention to the front again and saw the wipers were smearing slimy blood back and forth over the glass, reducing visibility to zero. She made a noise somewhere between a scream and a curse as she realized she had moved into the opposite lane somehow. A large box truck was bearing down on her; its driver leaned on the horn. She was going to be creamed!

At the last second, Shannon came to her

senses and jerked the steering wheel hard to the right, avoiding collison with the truck by a hairbreadth, while simultaneously running up on the curb and hitting a parking meter. The Ford died with a shudder, and the trucker kept on going, not even stopping to see if she was hurt.

She jumped out of the car, cast a glance at the truck disappearing in the snow, cursed its uncaring driver, then went around to examine the windshield.

There were no signs of anything having been on the hood, no signs of anything having hit the bumper. The only damage to her car was where the grill had met the parking meter. The meter was not even bent, but her grill, made of cheap chromed plastic, was cracked in several places. She only hoped the car hadn't suffered any mechanical damage, because there was already enough wrong with it to give any mechanic shit fits.

She grunted. Her situation was so outrageous it didn't even deserve a curse. And the accident had happened because her imagination had been conjuring up demons, which were probably a product of her lack of sleep.

She never got enough sleep, she reminded herself ruefully as she got back in the car. It was a wonder she didn't hallucinate all the time. As it was, her body rhythms were so off kilter that she had to concentrate hard just to remember what day it was.

Before she shut the door, she checked out her surroundings. Without realizing it, she had somehow managed to get all the way downtown. She was only a couple of blocks from the building where she worked. It didn't seem as if that much time had passed.

She crossed her fingers and prayed that the car would start again. It took a couple of tries, and the car's engine protested mightily, but it finally kicked over.

Shannon wrestled the Ford off the curb and guided it in a ragged but basically straight line to her final destination.

Wednesday, 22 November:
00:25

Shannon parked in the loading dock behind the building. The Ford rattled when she shut off the ignition, its engine refusing to come to a complete stop for almost a minute. Blue smoke puffed out the exhaust pipe as it died.

Slightly disoriented from the near head-on collision, Shannon took a deep breath of frigid air and watched the snow falling in the alley. The wind was blowing much of it up into the dock area, but the drifts never would not get too high in there, so her car might not be snowed in too badly.

She replayed the last few minutes in her mind. Looking back, she realized the strangest part of the experience was that she had never been scared by the imagined beast on her hood. She was mostly irritated by its presence, and maybe a bit fascinated. She wondered if she should tell anyone about what had happened. No, they'd want her to go see a shrink or give her a drug test. She was clean, of course. She'd seen too many whacked-out druggies during her tour of duty in the military to find any attraction in altering her body chemistry with dangerous substances. But she didn't like the hassle involved or the implications. If she was ever even suspected of doing drugs, her superiors would begin watching her so closely she wouldn't be able to breathe.

Having some degree of personal freedom was one of the few good points about this job. As long as she did her duty, no one from the main office came to check on her. She had no boss breathing down her neck; she was in charge. Of course, the pay sucked, but she had a job, and a lot of people couldn't say that since times had become so uncertain no one could plan the future.

She found herself wondering about the homeless on such a night. She had never really concerned herself with them seriously. Few of them ever asked her for a handout, after all, maybe because she was a woman. But she figured it must really be miserable trying to find shelter when the weather was this bad. There weren't enough facilities in the city to handle every one of the homeless, hopeless souls who wandered the streets. How many would freeze to death before the night was over?

She'd find that out in the morning, when newscasters reported how many elderly had frozen in their homes because they couldn't afford to pay their utility bills and how many street people had perished for want of shelter. It seemed the reporters conveyed this information every winter with glee, as if it were great fun to keep track of death and suffering in the world, which, of course, was much better than telling people about all the good things going on.

What good things? she thought cynically. *What's good about any of it?*

There was little she could do about the plight of other people, of course. She had her own life to lead, her own troubles to worry her. She couldn't afford to take on anyone else's burdens.

She had to get through the night herself. She would be safe and reasonably warm inside the building, and she had something to eat. So her situation wasn't exactly the same as that of the forgotten old and homeless.

So why did she feel guilty? She couldn't help anyone! She had to put herself first. She was the only one she could really count on.

Shannon turned around, and hauling her tote bag in with her, she headed for the back door, which led into the lobby. She heard the lock click as Jack Landers unlocked the door via the remote switch at the security desk. She pulled on the handle and stepped in, flinching involuntarily when the wind slammed the heavy metal door behind her. She went through the next door and was in the lobby, facing a glowering Jack.

"What's up?" she asked. It was her standard greeting—one that didn't require a reply.

"Where the hell you been? You're nearly half an hour late!"

Shannon glanced at her watch. More time had passed than she'd imagined. She returned Jack's angry stare with one of defiance.

"I've been driving through a fucking blizzard to relieve your sorry old ass. I should've stayed home and let you pull a double. You're lucky I got here at all."

"That ain't no excuse!" he said sharply, spittle foaming at the corners of his mouth as his dentures clicked.

"It's snowing outside, Jack, in case you didn't notice. It's a blizzard. It's winter!"

"You don't have to tell me twice," he replied. "I can see what's going on out there."

"Then you should know why I'm late."

"You should've started earlier."

"How the hell was I supposed to know how long it would take to get here?"

"Well—" He had no cogent response to that. Shannon could see he was merely talking to hear his teeth rattle. She wondered what that sounded like inside his head, or if he even noticed it.

"You'd better get going yourself," she said, coming to the desk with her bag and removing her jacket. "It's not going to get any better, and if you don't get a move on, you'll be stuck down here."

"I ain't supposed to leave for another hour."

Shannon rolled her eyes. "I know that, Jack. But in another hour, you won't be able to leave."

"I'm on duty till—" He seemed momentarily to have forgotten the hours of his shift.

According to the S.O.P. for the guard site, the third-shift guard was supposed to do rounds of the floors while the second-shift guard stayed over and watched the lobby. On such a night, however, Shannon doubted there would be any Iranian terrorists coming through the front doors. She smiled to herself about Jack's greatest fear—being offed by terrorists.

"Go ahead and leave, Jack. I'll do my rounds in short runs and keep coming down every five minutes or so to check on the lobby. If the Iranian terrorists show up, they'll get me instead of you."

He arched his bushy eyebrows above thick trifocals. "Don't you make fun of me!" he fussed. "I seen it in every one of them damn movies. First thing they do when them terrorists come in is blow away the security guard. Like in that movie with the battery name."

"*Die Hard,*" Shannon said, smirking.

"Yeah, that one. They don't even say anything—just blow your head off. Just like that." He reached to his side for a gun that wasn't there. "Goddamn company doesn't know how dangerous it is doing this work. They should let us all wear guns. Can't even defend yourself if some crazy sumbitch comes in."

"Why don't you get yourself some Mace?"

"Don't allow that neither. Don't allow a man to arm himself at all. Like this uniform and play badge is going to stop them crazy bastards!"

Shannon knew that, once started, Jack could carry on for hours. But she'd had enough fun and his denture clicking was starting to grate on her nerves.

"Okay, Jack, that's enough. You go on home to your old lady, and I'll baby-sit the building."

"Well," he said, his blustering stopping as quickly as it had begun, "I guess you're right at that. Probably take me a goddamn hour to get home."

He stood up behind the desk and allowed Shannon to slip into the chair; then he went to the utility room off to the left and brought out his winter coat and a lunch pail that looked as if it was almost as old as he.

"You be careful tonight," Jack told Shannon. "Weird things happening round here. One of them screwy nights when everthing goes wrong if it can."

"What do you mean?" Shannon glanced down at the monitors. She could barely see the loading dock on one screen since the blowing snow was obscuring the camera's view out there; neither her car nor Jack's truck was visible. The other monitor showed only the entrance to the service elevator, which was behind the main lobby.

"Just weird stuff. You know the cleaning people—most of 'em anyhow—are still messing around on the floors. So you'll have to put up with them. And they been reporting things like broken locks and weird smells. A couple of the toilets were stopped up something awful, and the alarm for the computer room on the twenty-first floor went off. When I went up there, nothing was wrong."

"The alarm system's probably frozen."

"Maybe."

"Well, none of that stuff is so weird. I can handle it."

Jack came a little closer, his expression becoming almost solemn, his eyes widening. "Something really weird, though, is what they say happened to the elevator man."

"Who?"

"Otis is his name. The guy that comes in once a week and checks out the elevators."

"I know the dude. What about him?"

"Sumbitch just up and disappeared," he said, elaborating on the knowledge Stan had given him. "His truck is still in the parking garage."

"Maybe he got drunk."

"Maybe something happened to him."

"Like what?"

"Something. I don't know." He zipped up his coat and headed toward the back exit. "It's a strange night, I tell you." He didn't go into detail. He often said things without following up on them.

When Shannon looked up to ask him why he thought the night was so strange, he was gone. She heard the outer door slam loudly as he departed at last.

"Old fart," she said.

Suddenly shivering, she started filling out the paperwork to begin her shift. It seemed the wind was somehow penetrating the stone-clad walls of the building itself.

Had she allowed Jack to upset her? Or was she still spooked over what had happened on the way to work? Or was she merely cold?

At the moment, however, she didn't have time to analyze what was bother her. She had things to do to take her mind off anything out of the ordinary that had already happened or might happen. She would concentrate on her duties as a guard, and with that to occupy her, she willed herself into an uneasy calm, trying to settle in mentally for the night ahead—or to be more precise, the rest of the morning.

It's Wednesday, she decided uncertainly, after a few seconds' thought.

Chapter Seven

Wednesday, 22 November:
00:31

Jack winced as he stepped outside onto the loading dock. He wasn't totally prepared for the murderously cold wind that greeted him, penetrating his heavy winter coat as if he had nothing on.

The loading dock was not technically a dock, as on most high rises. It was really the back part of the building, the area under the parking garage, which had been set off for trucks and other delivery vehicles that did business with the tenants of the building during the day. Its roof, which was the bottom of the multilevel garage, was constructed of countless tons of concrete reinforced with steel beams. The loading dock was made up of several hundred square feet of paved cement, on which sat a massive trash compactor and a 30-foot open dumpster. There was also an entrance to the basement level of the garage out there; it could only be accessed by tenants who had coded plastic cards and the money to pay for the expensive spaces reserved for the elite.

Jack had driven to work in his pickup truck, a late model Nissan with a cap over its bed, which he rarely made real use of. He drove a truck because it was part of his Midwestern heritage to do so and more manly than a car—even if it wasn't a full-size vehicle. In his less-than-perfect physical condition, Jack could barely lift anything into the truck's bed anyhow.

Snow was starting to collect in the corners of the dock area and was beginning to form deep drifts in the alley adjoining it. It was going to be a real bitch driving through the mess. Fortunately, the Nissan had four-wheel drive and new tires with heavy-duty tread, so it should maneuver through the nasty weather rather nicely. Jack could have mentioned that to Shannon, but she probably thought he would have trouble getting home because he was old and not as good a driver as a young whippersnapper like her.

Hell, he could drive as well as anybody. In fact, he was a damn good driver and always had been. It wasn't his own driving that worried him. It was the stupid assholes who didn't know how to drive in snow. There was always some cowboy who thought he could go faster than everyone else; that kind of driver invariably hit the careful, experienced drivers.

"Anybody puts a dent in my truck, I'll put a dent in his head," Jack muttered and trod toward the Nissan, hugging his ancient lunch box close to his body as the wind bit into his exposed skin.

He climbed into the truck, put the lunch box behind the bench seat, and fumbled for the keys in his pants pockets. He was sure they were in there somewhere. He had too damn many keys—for the house and storage barn, his wife Sue's car, and various file cabinets where he kept papers—and he kept them on four different rings. He also had change and cash-register receipts tucked in among the keys, making their retrieval a task to be reckoned with, especially since the arthritis in his hands was flaring up and his fingers were numb from the cold.

He was also still feeling testy over Shannon's behavior toward him. She was a snippy thing, a snot-nosed kid who thought she knew it all, and she got on his nerves with her uppity attitude. Women were too damn independent nowadays and didn't show a man—of any age—the proper respect. Hell, what was a woman doing being a security guard anyhow? It was a man's job. What could she do if terrorists decided to break into the building? Cry?

He chuckled to himself. That would be what a woman would do. She'd just curl up and cry like a puppy. Even if she had a gun, she wouldn't know which end to point and would probably blow one of her own titties off!

Dumb little bitch. Her sassiness reminded him of his daughter, who had never listened to anyone and ended up pregnant when she was a month shy of her sixteenth birthday. She had the kid, made him an early grandfather, then messed up her life by marrying the asshole who knocked her up. She sure should've listened to her daddy on that one. He could have told her when a man was no good.

He found the ring with his truck keys and tugged them out of his pocket, bringing with them a few dimes and pennies and a wad of pocket lint. Not bothering to pick up the change, he inserted the keys into the ignition.

Before he started the truck, Jack heard something. It wasn't the wind, he was pretty sure. He listened intently a few seconds and heard the noise again—a kind of metallic clatter that was vaguely familiar.

Considering only briefly, he determined the sound was coming from the big dumpster on the other side of the compactor. The noise sounded as if someone was digging around in there, and the racket was loud enough for him to hear it above the howling of the wind.

Why didn't Shannon come out and investigate? Because, he realized, she couldn't hear the noise, and all but one corner of the dumpster was out of camera range. Even if the entire dumpster had been in range, the cameras were almost worthless because of the snow.

Jack thought about going in and telling her about the disturbance, but he didn't think she'd care that much. She never had shown the proper concern for protecting the contents of the dumpster, which was a major part of her duty. Damnation, some wino or bum might be in there, and the post orders clearly stipulated such people were to be told to remove themselves from the premises. He'd have to do it. Technically, he was still on duty anyhow.

Grumbling as he replaced his keys in his pants and climbed out of the truck, Jack went over behind the compactor and stood for a moment watching the red dumpster. It was full of plasterboard, metal wall studs, and ceiling tiles that had been discarded during the process of remodeling one of the suites in the building. There wasn't anything of value in there. Even the studs had been so bent by workmen that they would never be useful again.

Seconds passed and the only sound was the wind. Maybe the wind hitting the dumpster had made the noise he'd heard. That explanation was plausible because the dumpster wasn't level. Besides, the night was too damn cold for him to check into it any further, and he certainly wasn't going to put himself to the trouble of climbing up on the dumpster's rim to look inside. So he turned to go back to his truck.

Then he saw a hand come over the edge. It

was badly bruised and bloody and had turned purple from the cold.

"Who's in there!" Jack demanded. He felt smug because he had been right about there being someone in there, and he intended to give the miscreant a thorough chewing out for loitering on private property.

The hand was joined by another hand that was also banged up. Skinny arms came into view.

"Come on out of there. This here's private property and you're trespassing and loitering!"

The hands gripped the metal edge of the dumpster, tensed, and pulled. A head and the top of the torso to which the hands and arms were attached slowly emerged from the rubble. Shreds of torn cloth whipped around the torso like ribbons blowing in a parade. A male nipple peeked from between the shreds. There was a gash in the side of the torso in which blood had coagulated and turned brown. But the form climbing out of the dumpster had no face.

Jack stared, his mouth dropping open, his upper denture hanging down to his tongue at an odd angle. The face looked as if it had been sliced off the front of the head, leaving behind only a mask of grue. Jack gulped and tongued his plastic teeth back where they belonged.

"Get away from me," he said hoarsely, his throat suddenly so dry he could hardly speak at all.

The faceless thing hefted the rest of its body over on the pavement, dropping in a crouch at Jack's feet. Jack's feet weren't there for long, however. They had started propelling him back to his truck as soon as the thing's overpowering scent singed his nostrils. It stank mightily—like something that had rotted for weeks before being discovered in the back of the refrigerator.

Jack was going for his gun. Though he wasn't allowed to carry a weapon while on duty, he kept a .38 Special in his truck under the front seat—mostly for protection when he drove home late at night. If he could just make it to the truck and get the .38, he'd put that thing out of its misery before it laid a hand on him. For it surely did not have good intentions.

Jack lost his footing in the snow and fell on his butt, almost sliding beneath the Nissan as he reached for the door. He grabbed the edge of the running boards, which were as functionless as the rest of the truck, but made it look sporty. He managed to pull himself up and open the door. Then he reached inside, yanked the gun from under the seat, cocked it, and spun around. But his pursuer was nowhere in sight.

Jack advanced slowly, retracing his steps to the dumpster, waving the gun unsteadily in front of him and not daring to speak or do anything else that might give the thing an advantage. Then something brushed the back of his neck, and Jack let out a gurgling croak and jumped around.

The thing was standing right in front of him.

Jack could see grubby-looking maggots crawling in and out of what little flesh was left on its half skull. Jack lifted the gun and pointed its barrel into where the thing's face should have been.

"I'll shoot you," he said, finding his voice. "I swear I will. I ain't afraid to use this."

He thought the thing actually shrugged. Jack felt his index finger squeezing the trigger, which was strange because he had not yet decided to fire. Something was controlling his hand. He tried to yell, but his voice had left him again.

After his finger pressed all the way back against the trigger, the gun fired a single round, and Jack was thrown on his rump again. It was amazing how the shot made so little sound. Was the wind really that strong or his hearing that bad?

He didn't have the chance to speculate further on the acoustic possibilities. He was too busy watching cracks spreading out from a hole in the concrete roof over him. He tried to get up and move, but the snow made the floor too slippery for him to make any progress.

There was no time anyhow. Powdery concrete sprinkled on his head, followed by small shards, and bits of the roof. Before he could look up to see what had happened to the faceless thing, a large chunk of the concrete—about eight feet in diameter—dropped on him, crushing the life from his body instantly.

The sound of the crash was muffled, too, as if only a gray cloud had descended on Jack

Landers. For a few seconds, there was silence. Even the wind made no noise, and the swirling snow blew around inside the dock as if animated by itself.

Dead Ted stood unsteadily, a wraith buffeted by the shifting air around it. Then he stooped next to the concrete slab that rested on Jack Landers's body. It had landed on him in such a way that one of his hands was sticking out on the side, and his head jutted from the end, almost separated from the neck. Blood soaked into the snow surrounding the area, turning it pink.

Dead Ted felt around until he located Jack's head, running his fingers over the dead man's features. He needed a face. This one would do.

Chapter Eight

Wednesday, 22 November:
00:40

Shannon had finished filling in her name, guard site, address, and starting time on the daily report. Though she was late, she had gone ahead and put down the time she would have normally started, figuring the company owed her that much for coming out in the snow. Old Jack wouldn't say anything, since he wouldn't even see the report. Besides, she noticed he had put down his normal departure time on his report. So he was stealing from the company, too.

That was not dishonesty; it was justice. Security guards had no job benefits and were expected to do a lot for small pay. When they could screw the company back a little, they had almost a moral obligation to do so.

It was time for her to do her security checks, which consisted of her rounds for floors 30 through seven since the first six levels were occupied by the parking garage. She also had to check the equipment up on the thirty-first floor, which was called the mechanical penthouse. There the suction pumps, elevator motors, heating and air conditiong units, and the other machinery that kept a high-rise building's systems going were located, and her job was to make sure all the gauges read in the safe zone. In the winter, there was rarely any problem. Summer heat was a building's worst enemy and most likely to cause malfunctions.

She placed the daily form in a clipboard and hung it on a peg under the desk. She would update it as needed throughout the night, noting any strange circumstances, disturbances, or other incidents that either the building management or her bosses might think were significant. If nothing happened, she would merely jot down that all was in order about every hour or so, if for no other reason than to show she was awake.

She yawned, then frowned. She didn't feel like doing her rounds yet. Nothing was likely to happen if she put her duty off for a few moments. She stood up, deciding to take a stroll through the lobby to stretch her legs and, she hoped, to work off some of her sleepiness. If she occupied her body and her mind sufficiently, she would get through the night and into the morning without dozing off.

She walked to the revolving doors and looked down to make sure Jack had remembered to lock them. The posts that slid into rings in the floor were fully engaged. Still, she pressed against the doors, testing them. Satisfied the doors were secure, she stepped to her right and gazed out through the 15-foot-high plate glass to the intersection of Delaware Street and Market Street.

The blizzard had not abated. The few cars parked on the streets were merely unidentifiable mounds in a landscape of snow. The traffic lights suspended over the streets by cable were taking a beating in the wind. It was surprising they continued to work at all, but they dutifully kept turning red, yellow, and green for traffic that was not there.

The streets were totally deserted. The city had not called out the snowplows because the weathermen had yet to predict an end to the storm. Their forecast was for the blizzard to last another ten hours or so, in which case the city would be virtually buried and immobilized. It would take days to clear the streets and make them passable, and new snow might fall in the meantime.

She found herself feeling sorry for Jack. She didn't like him that much, and he was an old fart, but she didn't think anyone should be subjected to the perils of freezing to death or driving off into a ditch. Of course, that could have happened to her too, but she felt she was stronger than Jack. She was more of an instinctive survivor. She had had to be to have lasted through her hitch in the service, where every man she encountered seemed intent on proving how unworthy she was to wear a uniform.

Well, she had proven them all wrong, but it had done her little good in the real world, where she was reduced to wearing the uniform of a security geek.

There would be time to change in the future, she assured herself—time to make herself better. Maybe she would become a nurse or something. Learn computers. Learn anything that would lead to a better life someday.

Watching the snow was beginning to depress her, so she returned to her desk and scanned the key sheet that the Clean Corps, the company that employed the cleaning crew, had provided for keeping track of the keys to the various offices and suites they cleaned every weeknight. She had to record when each key was returned, because the building management was paranoid that a cleaning person might accidentally take a key home, giving him the means to come back and break into the offices he had cleaned.

As far as Shannon knew, such a burglary had never happened. When someone's purse was stolen, or a piece of office equipment walked away, employees of the Clean Corps were always the first suspects, even though there had never been proof that one of them had committed any criminal acts. Next on the suspect list were the security guards, owing to their having access to virtually every room in the building. Most companies suspected their own employees as a last resort, though more often than not the employees were the criminals. Many of them had been caught stealing computers, fax machines, and even television sets.

Shannon had a grim expression as she thought about these things. They reminded her once again with what low regard security gaurds were held. She was no different in anyone's eyes from the other stiffs in polyester. She was not special. She was just another suspect when something went wrong.

Of course, she could steal a lot of things from the various offices with her knowledge of how things operated—such as which video cameras showed what, which suites had burglar alarms, and which were likely to have people in them. Indeed, if she knew where to fence things like computers, typewriters, and copy machines, she could probably make a lot of money for herself.

Despite her disregard for the company that employed her, she remained fundamentally honest. She was not a thief, and she was very careful not to do anything that would ever make anyone consider her one. She had ethics and moral standards—probably more than most of the people who occupied the various offices in the building.

After all, many of them were lawyers and bankers, and everyone knew both those professions had the largest group of crooks involved in legalized theft in the country. Neither could be trusted to give a straight answer about anything, and either would pick the public's pockets—by legal means, of course—without hesitating.

She directed her attention back to the key sheet. All but six keys were still checked out, meaning there were around 20 or so employees of the Clean Corps still in the building. They were running way behind tonight.

They would have to stay in the building too, unless they were fools. Few of them had cars, since most were recruited from the blacks who lived in the city's poorer neighborhoods and seldom had the means to own a car. Their wages from the Clean Corps certainly would not put them behind the wheel of anything decent. Shannon had learned most of them worked for minimum wage, and even the supervisor Sam Campbell made no more than she did, which really was awful since he had a great deal of responsibility.

But that was the way things were nowadays. People worked their asses off for small wages. Employers knew that most working-class folks were happy—or, as the bosses would say, lucky—to have any kind of job, and they used that fact to their advantage, firing people for the slightest infraction or hanging their jobs over their heads to whip them into shape.

Pulling herself from her bitter thoughts, Shannon scanned the after-hours registry on a clipboard lying on the edge of the desk. It indicated six people were working in some of the offices. They'd have to stay in too. Maybe nobody would go anywhere. Maybe they could all get together and have a party.

Shannon laughed to herself. That would be some affair—cleaning people, lawyers, a secretary or two, and a security guard. Unless they found some booze and got awfully drunk, there would be no mixing among the various classes these people represented.

She sometimes fantasized about weird sexual matches and imagined one of those straight, uptight, corncob-up-the-ass lawyer types—one of the morons with briefcases—getting involved with someone like Jerena, the black girl who cleaned restrooms on the twenty-first through thirtieth floors. Jerena was dumber than owl shit on a shingle, and she had tremendous jugs that jutted out firm and hard and inviting. She was a stereotype without knowing it, even down to the gold tooth in her mouth and the straightened hair.

Why, Shannon wondered, did people allow themselves to be stereotpyes? Was it because they didn't know they were doing it? Or was the line between racial pride and being a stereotype so fuzzy?

Anyhow, Jerena and a lawyer would make

a good match. Let Spike Lee make a movie about that!

She switched on the radio that was kept under the desk, hoping to shake her mood by listening to music. Radios were supposedly taboo according to company regulations, but most stations had one available to help guards get through the third shift. She tuned to a local FM station that played a variety of current music.

A song called "Rump Shaker" was playing. It was unusual for the station to play such a song; maybe the disc jockey figured it was so late that whoever might be offended by such a song would be in bed.

The song ended and the disc jockey announced, "Hey, that was 'Rump Shaker,' and this is Smooth Larry, hoping all the booties out there are shaking to my sounds tonight—and not that nasty old wind!

"Hey, all you night owls out there, how's your booty doing tonight? If you're outside, your booty be freezing. That's for sure. Because the weatherman says this stuff coming down on us is a full-blown, honest-to-God blizzard, and the winds are blowing harder than Shaq O'Neil slam dunks, which is around seventy-five miles an hour. In fact, dudes and dude-ettes, this here blizzard is already one of the worst ever to hit the city, and it's not even through hitting. The mayor, if he ever wakes up, might even have to declare this a genuine disaster. So put on your mittens, cover your booty, and watch out for ice, snow, and wind. And be sure to let the cat in, because nobody likes a cold pussy on a night like this."

Shannon switched the radio off. Smooth Larry talked too much and played too little music because he thought he was a comedian.

"About as funny as a sore dick," she said, remembering one of her former superior officer's favorite lines.

She glanced at the key sheet and after-hours sheet again. At least she wasn't all alone in the building. After the cleaning crew was done with their work, maybe they would keep her company. Some of them could actually carry on a halfway intelligent conversation.

She checked the time. She had put the security checks off long enough. She put a sign on the desk indicating she would return shortly, made sure she had her keys and beeper, then went to the elevators. She entered one, punched in the code for the thirtieth floor, and ascended quickly to the top of the building.

Chapter Nine

Wednesday, 22 November:
00:59

The 31-story tower in which Metropolitan National Bank was housed was considered an imposing structure in downtown Indianapolis, where the tallest building had only 48 stories. The people of Indiana had difficulty dealing with anything much taller. Since the state had so much wide open land, it always seemed more natural to spread out rather than up. Nor were there any physical obstacles, such as wide rivers or bays, to prevent the city's lateral spread.

The few tall structures in the center of the city clustered around Monument Circle, where a concrete spire had been erected to honor the Civil War dead around the turn of the century. These buildings formed a ragged skyline with more dips than points. The presence of any taller buildings at all was due to the influence of city planners. They thought a city the size of Indianapolis—with its population of nearly a million people—ought to have at least a passing resemblance to other major cities in the nation, even if it was a forced, unnatural one.

Indianapolis residents, most of whom had agrarian roots and still possessed the mentality of farmers, resisted the idea of their city resembling others of similar population. For they had long ago determined their city should be cleaner and safer than other metropolises; and to avoid juvenile delinquency, drug-related crimes, and the other ills that plagued such major Midwestern cities as Chicago, Cleveland, and Detroit, they did whatever they could to eschew cosmopolitanism, whether it was in culture or in matters as mundane as how one got from one side of the city to the other.

As a result of such thinking, Indianapolis folk did not use mass transportation much, there was limited parking in the downtown area, and most people preferred to go to the many malls in the suburbs. With so little traffic downtown, merchants shied away from starting new businesses, and many of the older businesses—including department stores that had been located downtown for nearly a century—had closed down. It was a matter of simple economics: there were too few shoppers to keep the old stores going and too many shoplifters to keep them open merely for nostalgia's sake.

Still, quite a few offices were located in the downtown area, since Indianapolis was the capital of the state, and there were many state and local government buildings downtown. As a result, lawyers, bankers, insurance agents, and accountants had settled in around the government facilities. The employees of the government and of the companies that interacted with the government formed the biggest group of people who came to the downtown area at all during the week. Some of them shopped in the few small businesses that remained open, usually at lunchtime, but most of them went home as soon as their workday was over.

The overall result was that downtown Indianapolis was an illusion that existed only briefly during the week, and hardly at all on the weekends. There was simply little reason to visit the area, except for business or legal reasons. Any mall on the periphery of the city provided much greater shopping variety, nominally more safety, and certainly more parking—which was also free. Downtown parking was either in expensive garages or at meters that provided two hours' time at most, so it was easy to get ticketed or, worse, towed. If the city fathers had actually planned it, they couldn't have made the center of the city more unappealing for modern, mobile Hoosiers.

Metropolitan National Bank was one of the most recent businesses to have located its main offices in the downtown area when the MNB Tower was built in the late 1980s—before state laws had changed and allowed out-of-state concerns to buy into Indiana banking institutions. Since that time, just about every other bank in town had been purchased by a banking giant from Ohio, and there were rumors MNB was itself available for sale.

Shannon had heard the rumors, mostly from MNB employees who feared for their jobs. When the Ohio firms bought one of the Indiana banks, they invariably cut back on personnel, often closing down several bank branches as well; or they fired Indiana people and had their own people migrate into the area.

But Harold P. McHenry, president of Metropolitan National, whose portrait Shannon beheld on the thirtieth floor of the building, would not worry about unemployment if he sold his bank. He and the other top dogs on the board of directors would go away from any such deal with a lot of money, or a piece of the action in the new bank, or both. They would not suffer at all.

"Asshole," Shannon spat, squinting at the portrait as if she might rip it to shreds.

Since she had become a security guard, she had come to respect big shots less and less. She had never held authority figures in high regard, especially after her hitch in the service, where she had learned that an officer was generally a prick with brass on his collar, and having seen how the big shots in the business world treated other people, she had developed a hearty contempt for any snooty son of a bitch who wore a suit and carried a briefcase. Shannon judged the lot of them to be heartless, uncaring thieves whose purpose was to make money and exploit other people.

Shannon looked away from McHenry's picture to regard the double doors to his nearby office suite, the interior of which she had seen only once. The week after she had begun working there, McHenry had ordered the locks to his digs changed so that only the cleaning crew could get in. He had become paranoid about such lowlifes as security guards coming in and looking around and possibly lifting one of the expensive collectibles or gauche knickknacks he had on display.

However, one look at his office had been sufficient for Shannon. She had immediately realized McHenry had so much money that he had trouble coming up with ways to spend it. His suite featured a private bathroom with a hot tub, leather couches and chairs, a big-screen TV with access to cable, a VCR, a powerful stereo system, and a desk long enough to seat a family of eight for dinner. She had been aghast at how much money it must have taken to furnish Mr. McHenry's suite, certainly much more than she would make in a year or two. It seemed so wasteful for one man to have so much just in his office. She imagined his home must be a palace, and if she ever saw it, she would probably puke.

The rest of the offices on the top floor belonged to various officers of the bank. They were not quite so lavish, but reflected wealth nonetheless. As she walked through them that night, testing various doors to make sure they were locked, her face bore an expression of grandiose distaste. Having been brought up in a lower-class household, she had been indoctrinated in the belief that there was something fundamentally wrong in having so much money and spending it so frivolously when there were so many people in the world, herself included, who had almost nothing.

The wasteful expense represented by the bank's corporate offices was almost exceeded by that of its lawyers, who required the next two floors of the building. There were no suites as outlandish as the bank president's, but the offices of the head honchos were well appointed by any standards—with overstuffed chairs and couches, wet bars, and lush plotted plants that required constant care.

The break room for the lawyers and their employees also reflected their status and wealth. It boasted a fountain soda machine and other such niceties as a large popcorn machine, a color TV and VCR—hooked up to cable, of course—a very well-stocked refrigerator, and a bank of vending machines offering the best in snacks, candy, and sandwiches. There were also several square tables with padded wooden chairs around them, a luxurious couch, and a marble-topped coffee table. The lounge was outfitted better than many small restaurants.

Shannon helped herself to a soda, drank it down quickly, and tossed the empty plastic cup in the trash before going on. She had only two doors to check in the attorneys' quarters, going from upper level to the lower level via a walnut staircase.

Next, Shannon took the elevator to another business that occupied two floors—an accounting firm that drew a lot of business from the bank and its customers as well as from other businesses downtown. The furnishings there were not quite so lavish, perhaps reflecting the general mentality of bean counters everywhere. Shannon rattled a few doors on the accounting firm's floors, checked in a kitchenette to see if any coffee burners had been left on, then started down the stairs to the firm's lower level, where she noted all the lights were on.

"Security!" Shannon shouted. She always announced her presence loudly when she thought anyone might be around, so she would not startle any late-working tenants.

"Who's there?" a female voice answered back.

"Security," Shannon repeated, heading in the direction of the voice. "Where are you?"

"In here."

Shannon followed the voice to a small office in the corner of the suite, where a diminutive redheaded woman was hunched behind a desk squinting at a computer screen.

"Hello," Shannon said. "Just making my security checks."

A plastic sign on the edge of the desk identified the woman as Cassandra Peters. She had a legal pad at her right elbow, which she glanced at intermittently as she entered figures on the keyboard.

"Kind of late, isn't it?" Cassandra said, looking up at Shannon only briefly.

"I got in late. The snow slowed me down."

"Oh, my!" Cassandra shivered and drew the collar of a pink fuzzy cardigan closer to her chin; the sweater barely enclosed the woman's breasts. A well-preserved 40, she wore only a modicum of makeup. "Is it snowing already?"

"It's been snowing for hours."

"And I still have so much work to do before tomorrow! The big bosses from Chicago are coming in and I just have to get this report done."

"Honey, there's a blizzard outside. I don't think those guys will even show up."

Cassandra pushed her half-frame glasses up her nose and paused in her work. "I remember the blizzard of sixty-eight. We were snowed in for days at my house. Couldn't get out to get milk for the babies! You think this is going to be as bad as that one?"

Shannon had been a child then and didn't remember anything at all about the fabled blizzard of that year, but she didn't want to admit her youth or ignorance to Cassandra. "I don't know if it's as bad as that one, but it's bad. You probably won't be able to get out tonight. It's still coming down and they haven't even called out the first plow."

"My husband will be angry if I don't get home sometime."

"Why don't you call him?"

"Oh, I don't want to wake him." Cassandra shook her head and sighed. "I guess I might as well keep working. Even if no one shows up I still have to finish this."

"Well, if you need some company or a break, you can come down to the lobby. I'm sure not going anywhere."

"Thank you." Cassandra turned back to her computer and resumed entering her data. "I'll keep that in mind."

Shannon turned away quickly and strode toward the elevator. She was glad she didn't have a job in a regular office, where the pressure was ridiculous sometimes. She couldn't imagine working all night long just because some big shots were coming. She would tell her boss to take the job and shove it if anyone tried to make her work like that!

She went to the next floor, where several different firms had offices, and checked their doors. Finding one unlocked, she duly noted on a pad she carried with her during her rounds. She locked the door and hurried to the next floor, where she encountered a young black man vacuuming in the hall between two offices.

"Hey, Turner!" Shannon yelled brightly.

Turner jumped, then swung around. He switched off the vacuum cleaner and smiled, revealing a gap in his top front teeth. "Shannon, you sneaked up on me again."

"You pretending to work or really working?"

"I got to really work tonight. Sam's breathin' all over our asses tonight."

"Sam's in the building?" Sam Campbell, the supervisor of Clean Corps, usually left as soon as he was satisfied his employees were fully aware of their duties for the night.

"He was the last time I looked. He's been comin' up on the floors and checkin' on everybody. Got a wild hair up his ass over somethin'. Maybe his old lady didn't give him none last night."

"I wouldn't give him any if he was my old man. He wouldn't appreciate it anyhow."

"You savin' yours, ain't you?"

"Hey, that's none of your business, dude."

Turned laughed and leered, but his expression didn't offend Shannon because she did not consider him a threat. "Don't save it too long, girl, or it'll grow together. I heard that happened to one old girl I knew."

"Bullshit," Shannon said, smiling. "And speaking of bullshit, I have to finish my rounds. Catch you later."

Turner nodded and switched the vacuum back on.

Shannon felt better for having encountered some people during the first part of her security checks. Knowing she wouldn't be all alone in the building all night made her job more tolerable. She got along well with the cleaning people because they seemed more real to her than the wage slaves who worked in the offices. She could be herself with just about any of the Clean Corps, but someone like that Cassandra woman would never communicate with her on the same level. Even if Shannon didn't wear a uniform, she wouldn't be considered in the same class as the woman trapped behind the computer; she was too coarse, too worldly, too likely to swear at an inappropriate time. And she knew she couldn't sustain a phony front for a boss or client very long.

Maybe that's why she was in security. She didn't have to put on airs very often. She had only to be polite, and her job was well defined. Few people expected her to do much more than sit when it was time to sit and move when it was time to move. She didn't expect to do security the rest of her life, but for the time being it beat being a secretary or clerical, even if the pay did suck.

The next ten floors of the building were occupied by more law firms and accountanting offices, additional bank offices, a travel agency, an insurance company, a couple of brokerage firms, and miscellaneous other businesses. She covered those floors rather quickly, shaking door handles, checking for hot coffeepots, and noting other security infractions with the efficiency of a person who had done the same task countless times.

She encountered a handful of office workers and most of the other Clean Corps employees as she continued. She chatted with each briefly, then hurried through the rest of her routine so she could return to her desk as soon as possible to sit and relax for the remainder of her shift.

She ended up on the seventh floor—the last occupied by offices, since the remaining levels made up the parking garage. After she rattled a few doorknobs, she paused to go to the bathroom. She never used the ladies' room down on the second floor, because it stank perpetually from overuse, and she genuinely feared she might catch a vile disease from a toilet seat in there.

As she was washing her hands, she studied her face in the mirror over the basin, examining her skin for wrinkles. She usually applied lotion to her face before going to work, but she had forgotten earlier and her skin felt dry. Her blonde hair looked okay, though it was mussed up a bit from rushing through her rounds, and she felt compelled to pat a few strands back into place. But there really was no reason to try to improve her appearance any more; there was no one she needed to impress in the building that night or any other night. Of course, she didn't want to appear too shabby. Who knew when her dream man might walk in the door?

That was a joke. She was as likely to meet her dream man on this job as she was to meet Elvis.

She laughed to herself, then bent down and splashed cool water on her face. Feeling somewhat refreshed and stimulated, she patted her skin dry with a wad of paper towels, then stepped into the hall.

Before she went any farther, she stood and listened. Something was not quite right. After a few seconds, she realized it was the way the building sounded. It was generally quiet, except for the sounds of office machines or water coolers bubbling occasionally, but she heard a loud noise coming from the ventilation ducts in the ceiling. Instead of the almost inaudible rumble caused by the heating system, she heard what must have been the wind howling through the ducts.

The noise sounded as if a lion were trapped up there, and Shannon was momentarily spooked at the idea of a wild animal being loose in the building somehow. She shook her head to clear it of the weird notion, making a mental note to check later to see if there was a break in the ductwork somewhere that was allowing the awful weather outside to intrude.

The building, she had learned rather early on, was not that tight. Many of the windows and doors to the outside leaked, and the overall workmanship was shoddy, demonstrating how most modern structures were the product of the lowest-bid mentality that determined which builders were awarded contracts. She would leave a note for the maintenance engineers anyhow, even though they were slow to fix anything she documented for their attention.

Shannon moved down the hall a few feet, heading for the drinking fountain to wet her lips and soothe her throat, which was dry from her having hurried through the last part of her rounds. No matter how cold or warm it was in the bank tower, she always worked up a sweat and a good thirst by the time she finished her nightly security checks.

Before she reached the fountain, however, it suddenly came on by itself, gurgling loudly. A chill sparked down her spine, though Shannon knew the fountains were set to go off on their own occasionally to keep the water fresh and the plumbing functioning. But the water bubbling out of the fountain's spigot seemed rather dark.

Her first thought was that sewage had backed up into the fountain somehow. But the fluid dribbling out wasn't just dark. It was thick and a deep red color. It looked just like blood. Shannon stopped and watched, her eyes widening. Though it made no sense, the fountain was spurting blood.

She approached the fountain cautiously, expecting to discover an optical illusion caused by all the pollution in the city's water supply. Maybe something wasn't working correctly because of the cold. The smell coming from the water was first like copper, then like stale meat.

When she reached the fountain, Shannon stared into the blood as it pooled around the drain and was sucked slowly into its openings. She put her finger into the liquid, expecting it to be cold. But it was hot—body-temperature hot.

The blood flowed over her palm. She jerked her hand away with a muffled shriek, as if she had been burned. Terrified, she started running.

01:57

Sam Campbell leaned against the security desk, waiting patiently for Shannon's return. He had seen the blizzard outside and knew he would be in the building for the duration, so his sense of urgency about leaving had dissipated. He had plenty of time to tell security what he had come down to relate.

Sam was in his mid-thirties, with dark blond hair cut short and combed straight back. His face was thin and round with very ordinary features, including dark blue eyes that barely shone under nearly black eyebrows. He was five foot eight or so and slender. He wore a navy-blue sweater and light gray work slacks. Pinned on his chest was a Clean Corps badge with his picture on it, identifying him as the Group B Supervisor.

He yawned, rubbed his stomach, and glanced around, making sure no one was present, then plunged his hand farther down to scratch his privates. Sighing, he wondered what his wife was doing at that moment—not that she would give any special attention to the slightly tumescent thing his fingers nudged. She was probably sleeping away, totally oblivious to the world outside. She wouldn't notice he was gone until the morning, if she awoke that soon. Without him there to prod her, she was likely to sleep half the day away.

She was fat and unattractive with a moody temperament that made Sam's hours away from her the most blissful of their marriage. She had been slim and attractive when they first met with the sex appeal many Virgo women radiated in their youth, but her attractiveness faded as she approached middle age.

Maybe things would have been different if they had been able to have children, though Sam didn't think so. Darlene was too selfish to give much of herself to anyone and would not be any better as a mother than she was as a wife. She would still be a lethargic fat ass who lay around the house expecting people to do her bidding, as if she were a queen and they were her slaves.

Well, at least she knew how to cook; it was the one domestic duty she performed without griping.

And Sam had children to tend in a way. He

regarded his employees as kids, and many of them were so simpleminded that he figured his acting like a parent toward them was highly beneficial.

He was getting down to some real serious scratching when he heard one of the elevator doors open. He yanked his hand out of his shorts and turned to peer down the lobby, expecting that one of the workers whom he considered children was coming to him with a problem.

But it was Shannon. He saw her virtually jump out of an elevator. She held her right hand in the air and rushed toward him, her full bosom heaving in the way that always made most men gulp a little, including Sam. What the hell did that woman have on her hand?

"Sam! Sam, you've got to come look!" Shannon thrust her bloodied hand into his face, causing him to flinch.

"Shannon, what did you do to yourself?" He attempted to examine her hand, but she pulled it away. "Let me get the first aid kit and—"

"Damn it, I'm not hurt."

His face registered a new concern. "Is one of my people hurt?"

"No, nobody's hurt. I mean I don't think so. It's—I don't know what the fuck it is or where it's coming from." She tugged on his arm without thinking, leaving sticky red stuff on his sleeve. "You'll just have to come and look. Tell me I'm not seeing things."

Sam seemed dubious, then glared at her hand.

"You messed up my sweater."

"Fuck the sweater. I'll get you a new one, for God's sake. You have to come and look. Now." She let go of his arm and started back toward the elevators.

Sam grimaced, then followed reluctantly.

Up on the seventh floor, Shannon pointed at the drinking fountain and gestured to Sam.

"So?"

"It was coming from there. Blood was coming out of it. Hot blood."

Sam edged her out of the way gently, then inspected the basin of the fountain. It was sparkling clean with no traces of blood whatsoever.

"This fountain?" he asked, his expression becoming more and more skeptical. "Clean as my mother's heart. And it smells fresh as springtime, too. Corey cleans this floor. He went out of his way to make it clean like a good boy."

"The hell it is."

Sam made a shrugging motion with his body, pushed the button on the fountain, and watched as clear water spouted out. He bent over and took a long drink, stood up, then smacked his lips. "Good stuff."

"Get out of the way!" Shannon growled, shoving him aside to press the button herself. Again, clear water flowed out. She was confused and embarrassed when she looked back at Sam. "It was blood, goddamn it. I saw it with my own eyes and I got it on my hand." She opened her palm to show him the blood again, but it was clean. At the same time, she noticed the blood on his sleeve had vanished.

Sam was silent a few seconds, then started to chuckle. "That's a good trick, Shannon. How'd you do it?"

"I didn't do it! You have to believe me. I saw blood all over the place. You saw it, too."

"Was this something left over from Halloween? I bet you used that disappearing blood kids get to make themselves up."

"I didn't do it, I tell you."

Realizing Shannon was genuinely mystified, Sam thought a minute and said, "I bet one of my people did it then. Pulled a trick on you. If I find out who did it—well, I don't think Corey would, but one of the others might."

"How'd he get it in the water?"

"I don't know. It wouldn't be a good trick if it was easy to figure out. Maybe I have an employee who's practicing to be a magician. I'll have to question them and get to the bottom of this. That's for sure." He became serious. "I'm sure he didn't realize how much it would upset you. You want me to fire him?"

Shannon was perplexed now. Maybe it was a trick. But it had smelled like real blood to her. Or was that part just her imagination? She was beginning to doubt the reality of the blood herself.

"No," she said calmly, "it's no big deal."

"Well, I'll give somebody a good ass chewing

anyhow when I find out who did it."

"Yeah, do that." She seemed distracted and a bit disoriented. She asked herself why things had to be so screwy that night, wondering if she should have checked her horoscope before coming in. She didn't really believe in that astrology stuff, but sometimes it seemed the stars definitely were not on her side.

"I guess we'd better go back down now," she said.

Sam smiled indulgently, mentally adding Shannon to his family of working children and vowing to watch over her more closely in the future. He'd had no idea how sensitive this child was!

The two of them returned to the lobby, where Sam pulled out a piece of paper and began reading aloud a few things that had malfunctioned, which he thought building maintenance should be aware of.

Shannon barely listened. Sam always found things he wanted the maintenance people to fix. It didn't immediately occur to Shannon that many of the things he mentioned shouldn't have broken down unless something was seriously wrong with the building's operating systems.

And though it did occur to Shannon that those events were slightly ominous, she hadn't a single clue as to what to do about any of them. She just recorded them on her report, doing what a security guard was supposed to do without comment.

* * *

Upstairs, the drinking fountain in the hall gurgled and coughed out fresh blood in uneven spurts.

No one was around to see it, but that didn't mean it wasn't happening.

Chapter Ten

Tuesday, 21 November:
20:31

Stan, the freckle-faced boy wonder. Stan the rent-a-cop. Stan, God's gift to women.

Stan Cork was drunk.

As he lay upstairs in his bedroom and felt sorry for himself as he thumbed through his collection of *Playboys* and *Hustlers*—gazing at yet more sexy women who were forever unavailable to him—he gradually became so depressed he felt there was hardly any reason to continue living. His ego, usually puffed up to sustain any of life's challenges, had fallen in upon itself, stripping away all vestiges of self-esteem. Stan couldn't bear any more.

As always, he pined for Shannon; that longing was usually enough to reduce him to a state of self-abasement from the depths of which he could hardly extricate himself. And his encounter with the bum that afternoon had cast him into even a deeper state of despair.

Since he had begun working downtown, he had become more and more disgusted with the so-called homeless, whose hordes seemed to him to grow daily. At first he had tolerated them, even given a few of them a quarter just to get them out of his face. But then he had had to chase them off bank property, roust them out of the dumpsters, and deal with them every time he went around the corner to get a sandwich and a soda. It was as if they were singling him out to pester. The accumulated effect of facing so many of them gradually turned his disgust into hatred. These people—if they were indeed truly human beings—were not homeless. They were shiftless. They were simply bums and panhandlers who needed to be removed from the streets altogether.

When Stan came to that realization, he had tried to deal with the bums in an adult way. He had called the police, but when they came, they usually just told the homeless to go away. Only if the vagrants were so drunk that they presented a physical nuisance or obstacle did the police take more serious action. The drunks were hauled away to dry out in a cell, then put back on the streets in a day or so. And once again, they were free to torment Stan.

Even the police knew the bums were vermin.

Stan remembered how shocked he was when he first saw an Indianapolis police officer put on latex gloves before frisking a drunken wretch who was passed out on the loading dock area. Stan's first thought was that the cop was being unduly fastidious; then he realized the cop was treating the bum as he would any disease-infested rat and protecting himself from possible infection.

If the bums were actually just human-shaped rats, why didn't they exterminate them as they would any pest? That notion festered in Stan's mind, becoming stronger each time he had to deal with another bum. After a while, Stan realized his hatred was making him irrational. He even started going out of his way to avoid his nemeses, for fear he might commit an act that was both irrevocable and rash.

Which, despite all his efforts to control his fury and passion, he eventually had done, and as a result, he didn't want to consider what the bums reminded him of. He couldn't handle all the implications and realities. He suppressed and subdued his conscience by an extreme effort of willpower and what he judged to be moral fortitude.

Shannon. If only she would come to know him and give him the love he yearned for and needed, she could keep his conscience in check forever. It all came back to her. Predictably. Inevitably. Why did he yearn for the impossible?

Stan flipped through a *Hustler* that was about

five years old, an edition published before the editors had started toning down the magazine's contents to avoid further boycotts by right- and left-wing prudes. There before him, with a spotlight seeming to shine on vividly pink, spread-open genitalia, was a woman who could have been Shannon's twin or body double. He imagined this was what dear Shannon's nude body looked like, right down to the florid areolae surrounding the straining tight nipples and the puff of gossamer blonde that was her pubic hair.

He ran his fingers lightly over the printed image, trying to believe he felt soft, yielding flesh responding to his touch with a chilled shudder. But the page was cold and hard like Shannon!

He threw the magazine across the room. Then he gathered up the others and tossed them in the air, catching and ripping some as they landed on his bed. Breathless, he pressed his face down on the sheets and pounded his fists on his pillow for a few minutes. His eyes watered, and he had to fight to keep his sobs from becoming so audible his mother might come from the living room to inquire about his tantrum.

He had to get a grasp on his emotions. He was no kid, even if everyone treated him as a child. He had to numb his feelings. After only brief consideration, Stan concluded the only solution to his present depression was to go out and get totally shit-faced, falling-down drunk, which he proceeded to do.

23:09

By late evening, Stan had achieved a state of intoxication that successfully benumbed all his senses and most of his thinking aparatus. It also restored his ego—big time. He had come to realize that Shannon had to be shown what caliber of man she was missing by ignoring him.

As he stumbled out of the Purple Pussy Lounge, where he had leered at strippers for the last few hours, he formulated a plan. He would go to Shannon and demand she put out for him. He would make that snooty, uptight bitch take his mighty member, and after she had had that wonderful experience, she would be his sex slave and beg to move in with him. Or would he have to move in with her? His parents probably wouldn't let him actually keep a woman up in his room. His besotted brain was unable to think the situation through logically, except for Shannon becoming his worshiper.

As he staggered down the sidewalk, the cold wind and blowing snow clawed at his face. And he became more determined to show Shannon what she really needed. He knew he must do so while his courage was bolstered by alcohol, or he would chicken out at the last minute.

Passing a doorway, he spied one of the bums he so detested hunched down in a doorway to avoid as much of the wind as possible. Stan made the mistake of establishing eye contact with the man, who immediately stood up and lurched out in front of him.

"Jesus, buddy, you got a dollar? I need a dollar real bad."

Stan stopped, though his body felt as if it were still moving somewhere. He could not focus his eyes on the bum's face, but smiled in his general direction.

"Yeah? Whatcha gonna do with a dollar?"

"Get a cup of coffee, I swear. That's all, some coffee so I can sit in the Steak 'N' Shake around the corner and keep warm."

Stan moved to and fro—or was the bum moving? Or was it the ground? Nothing seemed very steady. "Man needs a dollar," he mumbled as if he were talking to someone else. "Just a dollar. Hey, bud, I got somethin' much better."

"A drink?" The bum's rheumy eyes lit up.

"No, this!" Stan opened his fly and exposed himself. "You want some?"

The bum put up his hands and backed away. "You son of a bitch! Crazy drunk!"

Stan grinned widely. "Better than a dollar, fuckhead!"

"I ain't no faggot!" the bum yelled and took off down the street.

Stan let go of himself and laughed as he watched the man disappear from view. "Son-of-a-bitching wino. I showed him!" He continued a few feet, trying to remember what he had been thinking about when the bum had interrupted him.

Oh, yeah, Plan A: show Shannon what she had been missing in life, which he just happened to have in his underwear. It was a good plan, too. Lots of women just had to be shown before they went down. It was the wisdom passed down secretly among real men since the beginning of time. Too bad one of those strippers wouldn't have gone home with him. But, hell, that wouldn't work; he wanted Shannon, not some substitute. Where was Shannon?

He stopped and leaned on a newspaper machine. He didn't know where she lived. She wasn't even listed in the phone book; he'd tried to look her up before.

Plan A was developing holes, and there was no Plan B. He looked at his watch, squinting until he made out the time. It was almost eleven-thirty.

The bank! Shannon would be going to the bank, and he could sneak up on her there and surprise her. Yeah, that could work.

He suddenly became acutely aware of the cold, looked down, and saw he had not zipped up his trousers. He fumbled his prized appendage back into his underwear and zipped his fly. "Fuck! Don't wanna freeze it off! Gotta keep it warm for old what's-her-name—Miz Shannon Elroy."

He checked the street sign at the corner; he was about three or four blocks from the bank tower. He could walk it. Actually, he'd have to walk. He couldn't remember where he had parked his car.

Wednesday, 22 November:
00:04

It took Stan longer than he had anticipated to get to the building. Walking was a struggle in the blizzard, and he had managed to get lost, then was forced to circle one block twice before he regained his sense of direction. But he had made it to the front of the bank tower. He pressed his face against the plate glass and looked inside. Though his vision was bleary, he could see Jack sitting at the security desk, not Shannon. She must be late.

But that was even better. If he could sneak past Jack, he could hide and wait for Shannon and really surprise her! All he had to do was get inside. He could see the revolving doors weren't locked for the night. But if he just went in through the front, Jack would see him easily and spoil everything.

He waited a couple of minutes, trying to think of how to distract Jack without revealing himself. He had to do something quick, or he'd freeze. His ears already felt frozen. Maybe he could trick Jack into leaving—say he had been called in to replace Shannon for the night. That could work if Jack didn't notice Stan's breath or glassy eyes.

As Stan began to form yet another plan, one of the cleaning people came down on an elevator, said something to Jack, and the old guy accompanied the cleaning man back up on the elevator.

Seeing his chance, Stan entered through the revolving doors, walked as quickly as he could to the nearest stairway going up to the garage, ducked in through the door, and started up the stairs. He was in! That showed how safe the building was. Dumb security guard left it unguarded so anybody could get in. Stan almost giggled as he went up to the third level. His plan was working too damn easily. Must be a good plan.

Since the parking garage was open to the elements, snow had blown in, making the floor slippery and hard to negotiate, especially for someone who had had a few too many beers. It was cold up there as well—too cold for Stan to just hang out. He needed shelter.

He finally went around to the few cars on that level until he discovered one that was unlocked—a Buick station wagon, an older model, one of those big boats that would hold a football team. Stan climbed inside, crawled over the backseat into the cargo area, and snuggled up against the spare tire.

He checked his watch again. He hoped Shannon showed up soon. He closed his eyes, swallowed back a beer burp, and ignoring the need to relieve himself, fell asleep.

01:16

Stan awoke with grit in his mouth and watering eyes. He lifted his head to peep out the car's back window; it was still dark outside and the snow was blowing harder than ever. He managed to get the back door open and nearly fell out on the concrete, catching himself just in time. The abrupt movement required to maneuver himself made his head throb.

"Fuck!"

The lights in the garage had halos around them when he looked at them, and everything else was hazy. He put his watch up close to his face and strained his vision, but could only guess at the time. In any case, Shannon had to be in. She could've walked to work in all the time he spent in the car. As soon as he started feeling better, he'd be ready to spring his surprise on her.

His first imperative, however, was to take a leak. All the beer had gone straight to his bladder it seemed, and he didn't know if he could hold it any longer. Wind blew across his face, spiking his flesh with prickly cold snow that made the need to urinate overwhelming. Since he'd never make it to the nearest restroom, he decided to go behind one of the concrete pillars.

He shambled over to the nearest pillar, unzipped his fly, and started spraying a long stream of hot urine, which steamed in the cold air. To

Stan's delight, the neat effect was prolonged by the fullness of his bladder.

Stan was blissfully pissing as only a drunk could when he thought he heard something. He attempted to search for the sound, but seeing remained painful and uncertain.

"Shannon?" Maybe she was making rounds of the garage by now.

"No," a man's hoarse voice replied.

Stan caught movement in his peripheral vision—a blur of something around one of the other concrete pillars.

"Jack?" What the hell would Jack be doing up there? He should have gone home. "Jesus, can't anybody answer any fucking body around here?" Stan finished peeing and zipped up. He turned and found he was no longer alone.

"Jack?"

The figure before him had Jack's face, or most of it. It didn't seem to have any eyes. But it wasn't Jack. Suddenly Stan sobered up and his vision became sharper. He saw the ragged edges around the face where it had been cut off Jack's head.

"Not Jack." The lips worked, but like in a badly dubbed movie, the words didn't match their movement. "I know you," the thing rasped. Then it made a sound like a choking laugh.

"Get away!" Stan started to retreat and found himself backed up against the pillar. He smelled rotten meat and stale body odor; he realized the thing with Jack's face had the body of a bum!

And Stan recognized it. Maybe. Well, really all the bums looked alike if he got right down to it. But how would a bum get Jack's face? Unless Jack didn't need it anymore.

"Oh, God," Stan said softly. "Hey, just let me get out of here, whoever you are. Okay? I won't tell anyone that you got Jack's face."

"The name's Ted," the thing said. "Dead Ted to you. I've been looking for you, you little cocksucker!"

"Oh, no," Stan pleaded, "please don't do—"

"Shut the fuck up!" Dead Ted shouted, raising his voice above the roar of the wind. "You can't bargain with me! The only thing I want from you is—"

Dead Ted reached out and put his hands on the side of Stan's head. Stan pulled on Ted's wrists, then kicked out at him, but his feet wouldn't quite reach.

Dead Ted's grip was impossible to break. He pressed his palms so hard against Stan's head that Stan passed out and blood squirted out his nose, his mouth, and his eyes. Then his tongue protruded and his whole body shook. Dead Ted grunted, exerted more pressure, twisted, wrenched, then tore Stan's head off.

Blood gushed out of Stan's neck, soaking him, but Dead Ted didn't seem to mind. The headless corpse slumped forward, shooting dark red goo across the floor, where it splattered Dead Ted's shoes, then splashed beyond them on the tires of the nearest car.

Dead Ted held Stan's head up momentarily as if to examine it. Then a sudden impulse made the thing with Jack's face toss the head away. It sailed out through the space between the garage levels and landed on the sidewalk in front of the building, bouncing twice.

Dead Ted didn't bother to see where the head had gone. He grabbed Stan's body by the arm and dragged it across the floor toward the third-floor elevator access. He propped it up in a nearby closet for safekeeping, then took an elevator to the basement level. Some of Dead Ted's earlier kills would be stirring and waiting. They needed his leadership.

Chapter Eleven

Wednesday, 22 November:
01:45

Jerena Reynolds, the young black woman who Shannon had imagined as the star of a movie, was working on the tenth floor. She glanced at a clock on a nearby desk and sighed heavily. It was too damn late for her to still be there working, and what was worse, she didn't think she would be getting home for some time. She had seen the snow falling outside, and it definitely meant she'd be stranded in the building for who knew how long even after she was through with her job.

She hated this building. She had been working in it for almost two years and had grown to loathe her evenings there. But she couldn't seem to find any other kind of work. She had no schooling to speak of. She had dropped out of high school at age 16 when she had her second baby, and she didn't have much hope of learning anything that would earn her much more than the minimum wage she was making.

Jerena was in her early twenties; she had a full face, strong jaw, and bright, round eyes. She normally put on bright red lipstick and a little rouge, and her hair was bobbed and flipped under around the edge, so the oversize dangling earrings she usually wore were shown off better. She wore a red, loose-fitting Chicago Bulls sweatshirt that didn't do much to hide her large breasts. Tight jeans hugged her butt, which was big, too, but her waist was slender, so that her more noticeable attributes gave her a sexy figure.

Jerena shut her vacuum cleaner off and looked around her, trying to estimate how much more work she had to do before she was finished. The entire tenth floor belonged to an insurance company whose offices had a lot of desks and trash baskets and carpet. Emptying the trash baskets alone took almost an hour, and vacuuming the carpet around all those desks seemed to take forever. There were no shortcuts either—just work and work till it was done.

With about half the floor left to do, she figured it would be at least an hour and a half before she was done, if not longer. Then she had to haul the trash out to the service elevator, and finally, she'd mop the break room, which could take another hour.

She was just about exhausted. This was the second floor she had been assigned to that evening, since somebody hadn't shown up, and she'd been left to do his work as well as her own.

She was getting awful hungry, too. Thinking of the employee break room reminded her just how hungry she was. She had eaten a cheeseburger before she'd come into work at six, but she hadn't had anything except a Coke since then. Her stomach was growling and rumbling so loud even the vacuum cleaner didn't cover up the noise.

She shoved her hand into her pocket and pulled out a handful of change. She had almost two dollars in quarters, dimes, and nickels. Since she was going to be there another two hours, she decided she might as well go get a snack from one of the vending machines. When she got to the break room, she felt cold. For some reason, this room was always cold, no matter how high the heat was turned up. It was also too dark, so she flipped on all the lights.

The break room had a row of vending machines close to a kitchenette, where a microwave was available. Jerena wanted something good and hot to eat. One of the vending machines had ham-and-cheese sandwiches on buns that probably wouldn't taste too bad. She'd had tuna fish out of the machine once, and not only had it tasted lousy, but it also made her sick. Ham kept a long time, so she would take a chance on it.

She counted her change again to make sure

she had enough for the sandwich. She did, and there'd be some left over to get a drink. She dropped quarters and dimes into the snack machine, watching an L.E.D. total them up for her. When the price of the sandwich was reached, she pressed some buttons to choose her selection. A metal spiral turned and dropped the sandwich to the bottom of the machine, where a door had to be lifted to take out the food.

Jerena squatted, pulled on the door's handle, reached in, and felt around for the sandwich. She couldn't find it. She had seen it drop down, so she knew it was in there somewhere.

"C'mon, motherfucker!" She pushed her hand farther in and touched nothing but cool metal. She was beginning to get angry; she wasn't about to let the machine rob her!

Maybe the sandwich hadn't fallen all the way down. Jerena started to stand up, but she couldn't get her hand out of the door. Panicking only slightly, she used her left hand to press the door open a little wider so she could free her right hand.

The door felt as if it was going to clamp down on her left hand, so she jerked it away. Simultaneously, the door pushed back against the hand already in there, cutting into her wrist.

Jerena yelped. The damn machine was fighting her!

"You prick!" She yanked hard. The door was unyielding. She put her feet up against the machine and pulled with all her strength.

The door bit down on her wrist. Then Jerena pulled free, falling back on her ass. Her round brown eyes popped. Her right hand was still in the machine, and she had a stump where that hand was supposed to be. Blood pumped out of the stump, splashing all over Jerena's clothes. Screaming, Jerena got up and ran from the break room.

In the corridor, she met her vacuum cleaner. It was not plugged in, but it was running. The vacuum cleaner sounded mean, as if there were rocks caught inside, and it rolled toward Jerena menacingly.

She wrapped her bleeding wrist in the folds of her sweatshirt and rushed around the corner to the ladies' room. She darted inside and went to the sink. Outside, the vacuum cleaner kept bumping up against the metal door like a mad dog trying to get in.

Panting and sweating, Jerena bent over the washbasin and looked at her wrist again. She had to calm down and stop the bleeding. She pulled off her sweatshirt and wrapped it around the stump, hoping the pressure would keep her from bleeding to death.

Looking in the mirror, she saw she was covered in her own blood and almost choked. She took a deep breath and tried to think. Then she vaguely remembered that doctors could sew things back on nowadays. She knew a guy who had lost two fingers in a factory accident. His friends had taken him and his fingers to the hospital, and a doctor had put them back on good as new. She just had to get her hand back! There was still hope.

But she was light-headed from loss of blood and might faint before she could rescue her hand. And the vacuum cleaner was right outside that door.

Jerena suddenly realized the situation was just plain foolish. There was no way a vacuum cleaner could hurt her. She'd fool the damn machine.

She went to the door, jerked it open, and sneered at the vacuum. It backed up a couple of inches, then lurched forward, the nozzle grinding at the cloth of her jeans, then biting through to nick her flesh. The vacuum was trying to suck the meat off her bones!

She screamed and kicked at the vacuum until she freed her leg, but she was so befuddled by the new development she almost fell over. Thinking quickly, she reached out with her left hand, grasped the edge of the door, and regained her balance. Then she simply jumped over the vacuum, letting it rush in past her. The door closed and trapped the machine inside, where it made angry, metal-chewing noises.

Later, Jerena would sit down to figure out just exactly how that vacuum cleaner could run around on its own, but at the moment, she had to save her hand so the doctors could sew it back on for her. She returned to the break room and confronted the vending machine that had maimed her. Its lights seem to glow unnaturally, as if it were taunting her.

"I guess you want my other hand!" she said, thinking she was going crazy, talking to a machine as if it were alive. She looked around for a means of breaking the glass front of the machine. Then she could reach down inside and get her hand. The closest thing she could lift was a heavy metal coffeepot on the counter in the kitchen alcove. She tucked her stump up under her blouse and managed to wrest the coffeepot off the countertop. It was heavier than she thought it would be, but she could manage it if she held it hard against the mass of her breasts.

Gripping the coffeepot with what remained of her waning strength, she staggered over to the vending machine and used her body as a spring to heave the coffeepot into the glass.

Then another strange thing happened. Just before the coffeepot hit the glass, she thought she saw a face reflected there. It was a man's face—the face of a crazy man laughing at her!

Jerena whined and shut her eyes as the coffee-pot made impact and sharp shards of the glass front shot in every direction. One as large as a butcher knife lodged in her upper thigh. Another grazed her left cheek. Moaning, Jerena fell on the floor. She opened her eyes and stared at the piece of glass in her leg, not believing how much pain it was causing her.

Gritting her teeth, she plucked the shard from

her leg, thankful it hadn't gone up an inch or so and hit right in the crotch, and dropped it on the floor. Blood oozed from the fresh wound, and she felt more blood pumping out of her wrist again and running down inside her clothes.

She scrambled to her feet, paused to remove a small piece of glass from her butt, then approached the vending machine. Looking down inside carefully, she spied her hand lying there. She could reach it easily. Ironically, the ham sandwich was right next to it. Maybe she ought to get that, too.

She extended her left arm down and touched her severed hand. It was sickening to feel her hand not attached to her body the way it was supposed to be. Still warm, it rested in a small pool of blood. She fought back the impulse to throw up, wrapped her fingers around the hand, then pulled it out quickly yet carefully, not wanting to damage it.

For a moment, Jerena couldn't decide what to do. Then she remembered she had to keep something that was amputated cold until the doctors got to it. There was an ice machine behind her, next to the soft drink machine. Jerena turned around, lifted its door, and leaned down to place her hand inside—and the ice machine's metal door came down on her head, its edges like a razor-sharp guillotine.

Interlude Two: In the Basement

Illusions and reality and death. Delusions and unreality and murder. Dead Ted would turn everything inside out, upside down, topsy-turvy, and ass backward, and he would have his revenge not only on one man, but on the whole city—a city that was responsible for that man's action by allowing him to harass and harm him. He had determined everyone would pay for that. And the payback had already begun.

Dead Ted gloated and blustered. He patted himself on the back. He congratulated himself on his ability to set goals and reach them. For the moment, he had a sense of accomplishment he'd never had in life. In fact, he had discovered that in being dead he had more power to get things done than he had ever possessed as a living person.

He wasn't sure where the power came from—

not directly, anyhow. It seemed to him that it radiated up out of the earth itself, giving him inhuman strength and supernatural abilities. The power was warm, infusing his whole being with a feeling of grandiose possibilities. Accompanying the power was a taste for blood, evidenced in his newfound relish for committing evil acts, especially murder.

Every killing seemed to nourish him, even in the time before he escaped his prison and inhabited his old acquaintance Willie. For he could take over any living thing if he wanted. And he had discovered that meant things that were not alive, such as the bank building itself.

But a tall building was, in a way, a living entity. It had a circulatory system—a network of pipes, like veins and arteries, connected to various pumps. It breathed through heating, air-conditioning, and ventilation ducts. It had a central nervous system as well—the electrical and electronic devices that were connected to the other systems and told them how to run and what to do in various situations. It even excreted waste products, such as steam and smoke and ozone, as any living thing did. And anything connected to or housed within the living building was as under Dead Ted's control!

He had come upon this wonderful knowledge by accident, when he had first become conscious again. Even though he had been only a disembodied stray thought trapped in the metal prison, Dead Ted had reached out mentally, probing and finding he could get into the elevator's brain and control the movement of the cars.

At first, all he had done was cause a malfunction in the elevator system; then he had experimented and flexed his new powers to make the elevators do exactly what he wanted. So he was able to score his first victim—the man summoned to repair the elevators. That man's blood had provided his initial nourishment, giving him the strength necessary to possess Willie, then to go on to kill and possess the bodies of others.

What was fun about formulating and carrying out his plan for revenge was using people's imagination against them. He could get into their heads and make them see and hear things that weren't there, which made them easier to overcome, especially if he used something in the building to attack them. He was also having fun finding new uses for the building that its architects had never dreamed of!

When Dead Ted killed a person, he could still use him, and that was fascinating. Because his victims didn't have to stay limp and dead; he could reanimate them and manipulate them as if they were extensions of himself. He could even tap into their brains and use their own thoughts against others. Or he could let them run amok and just watch the results, taking over whenever he pleased.

Dead Ted's victims were crazy when they first realized they were dead, but then they discovered they could do things and not have to worry about paying the consequences. That was fun to watch, too. Everyone had some kind of evil festering in him. And that evil seemed to manifest itself more readily when the person joined the ranks of the walking dead.

Well, Dead Ted thought in his fuzzy way, they weren't exactly walking dead. Or even undead. Maybe they were moving dead, a new category of monster—though the bodies he had stored up in the basement at the moment weren't moving much yet.

Of course, that young security guard was useless at the moment. Because he had no head, it was difficult for him to navigate; and the older guard had no face, so he couldn't get around too well either. They were mere meat waiting for purpose. Dead Ted would find a use for them; he was finding he possessed a flair for using the things he could inhabit. Why, he even had an imagination!

In life, all that creativity and imagination had been suppressed. Society had made him a drunken, homeless person, a wretch whose brain was always numb. In death, he had a whole new life and boundless opportunities! Dead Ted had become someone at last—someone the whole world would have to reckon with if he had his way.

Of course, there were some obstacles to overcome. He had a few problems to solve before he gained total control over all the people trapped in the building. For one thing, Dead Ted needed more bodies to do his bidding. Fortunately, being able to inhabit the building meant he could be everywhere and see everything at once—like a god!

He exercised the ability and did a quick scan of the bank tower through its various eyes—cameras, mirrors, reflecting panes of glass, computer screens—and he had learned there were quite a few people on the premises that night. All he had to do was get to them.

But he would have to be more careful about maiming them so much, especially when it came to heads and faces. Things without sight tended to bump around too much. But decapitation and maiming were so tempting and enjoyable.

He could navigate for the body bereft of head or face, but it took energy away from controlling the building and the body he had adopted, and it was too much like work. And he never had liked to work.

Chapter Twelve

Wednesday, 22 November:
02:19

Sam had left Shannon alone at last, having gone off to monitor the progress of one of his crew up on the twentieth floor. She fervently wished Sam had not been in the building that night; he was an okay guy, but a little of his personality went a long way. And when he was in a fastidious mood—which was often—he could be a major pain in the ass.

Of course, after that episode with the drinking fountain, he thought she was crazy, and Sam was the type who, once having formed a particular opinion of someone, never forgot it. He would forever consider her a spacy woman who flipped out over the least little thing.

But she *had* seen blood in the drinking fountain, and it had seemed real—even if it had disappeared suddenly.

But he could be right. Maybe she was crazy—temporarily, at least. She was pushing herself too much, and she still felt sleep deprived. She might imagine anything. Yet Sam had seen the blood on her hands, too, so it couldn't have all been fantasy.

After thinking the situation over, she decided Sam was probably right about the blood being some kind of trick, a sick joke someone had played on her. Some of the Clean Corps people were childish enough to pull something like that. Corey, the guy responsible for cleaning the seventh floor, might have been hiding somewhere and watching her, laughing his head off over how freaked out she had been. He was only about 20—still a silly kid.

She would certainly be wary of any other such tricks from then on. If she ever found out who the practical joker was, however, she would tear him a new asshole!

Besides, it was over. There was no use dwelling on petty things that couldn't be changed. And she had things to do.

She turned the radio back on, and Smooth Larry was in the middle of a string of obnoxious jokes. She didn't have the patience to endure any more of his banter or his music. She tuned to an FM station that played a mixture of rock and comedy routines, deciding the tunes and the jokes would not get on her nerves. Good old rock 'n' roll—it had never let her down.

The night disc jockey reported on the weather, pronouncing it the worst, then played the Buster Poindexter version of "Hit the Road, Jack." Shannon liked the song, though she considered Ray Charles's original recording not only a classic, but more appealing.

With the radio playing, Shannon relaxed a little and started to fill out the paperwork for her security checks. She noted which doors she had found unlocked as well as other breaches of security so the building management could send out memos to the guilty parties—who would then become pissed off and blame the infractions on someone else. It was all a big game between the tenants and management. The tenants didn't want to be hassled, but they also wanted things to be secure. But no one wanted to accept blame for insecure conditions. And the security guard got blamed either way—for finding infractions or for overlooking them.

A buzz on the intercom interrupted her progress on the report. She glanced at the console and saw a red light illuminated over the button for the basement garage exit. She pressed the button to respond.

"Security. May I help you?"

"This is Richard Bowes. I was working late on a case, and I just realized I don't have my card for the garage gate. No one's upstairs in my firm's office, so I need you to let me out."

Looking at the man sitting in his shiny red Mercedes, Shannon almost laughed. Mr. Attorney couldn't get his car out. Wasn't it great to be a big-time lawyer with a private parking space! She'd have thought a guy with a college education could remember to bring in his parking pass.

"Just a minute," she said, barely hiding the sarcasm in her voice. She pressed a button to activate the exit gate and switched her monitor screen to watch the gate rise. But it didn't move. She pressed the button again with the same results.

"Hold on, Mr. Bowes" she said. "I'll have to use a key."

Bowes made a sound of impatience, which might have been a growl or a curse; static on the intercom made it unintelligible.

Shannon rode one of the garage elevators down to the basement, where she had to walk up the ramp to the gate. On her way, she noticed there were maybe a half-dozen cars down there, which didn't jibe with the number of privileged parking pass people she had counted in the building. Often, of course, the big shots refused to sign in at the desk, thinking themselves above such accounting of their whearabouts, so Shannon wasn't particularly surprised. She did, however, dread the prospect of having to deal with their comings and goings throughout the night, because just about all the people who parked in the basement were as asinine as Richard Bowes—whose scowling face and smelly cigar she had to confront at the top of the ramp. Fortunately, he had not stepped out of his car, so Shannon could keep her distance.

"Just a minute, sir," she said to him in a monotone, showing no deference to his profession. She wanted him to be quite aware she did not hurry for anyone, no matter how much status he might think he had.

She walked past him to the electronic lock next to the corrugated metal gate and inserted her master key. She turned it left, which action was supposed to override any other controls and raise the gate. But the gate did nothing. It didn't even make a noise. Shannon counted to ten, then tried again.

"Maybe it's frozen," she said.

Bowes was one of the younger attorneys associated with the bank, a tall, slim blond man who often stayed late, then came in early the next morning. A workaholic, he was trying to make points with his superiors in hopes of being promoted over others in the firm.

"I have to get out of here!" Bowes said in a commanding tone.

Shannon ignored his implicit command and only nodded, though she wondered where the attorney expected to go in such a rush during a major snowstorm. All the same, she wanted to get rid of him. She stooped down to inspect the bottom of the gate. There was no ice on its edge; the wind was coming through rather freely. But she gave the gate a good kick anyhow—which in the past had sometimes loosened it. Then she tried the key again. The gate refused to move. She turned the key both ways, hoping she might get the motor to respond, but she didn't even hear the click of the switch engaging.

There was one other way to open the gate—by hand. A chain and pulley apparatus was attached to the top of the gate for that purpose. It would take a lot of effort to raise the gate that way, but Shannon was willing to exert herself to get Bowes out of her face.

She removed her key, then reached for the chain. But the chain was not hanging where it was supposed to be. She looked up and saw only a short length of the chain dangling from the metal pulley.

"When the hell did that get broken?" she muttered to herself.

"What?"

"I said the chain's broken. I can't get you out."

"What the hell you mean you can't? I'm not staying in this goddamn place all night!"

Shannon assumed her efficient-security-guard pose. "Sir, I can't open it. I can only call the parking company and have them send a troubleshooter over. But with the blizzard outside, I don't think he'll show up very soon."

"Jesus H. Christ!" Bowes stepped out of his shiny red sedan, leaving the motor running while he took off his beige overcoat and stashed it on the backseat. Then he approached the gate, bent down, and tried to pull it up.

When he bent over, his shirt rode up and his trousers rode down, displaying the top of his rear end. Shannon tried to conceal her mirth. For a big shot, he sure had a hairy ass! He turned and glared at her when the gate wouldn't move. She was just able to change her grin to a blank expression.

"Can't I go out the exit gate?" Bowes asked.

"You could if it would work. But it's on the same circuit, and that's apparently burned out. Maybe. . . ." She glanced across at the top of the other gate. The chain to it was missing as well, and its absence negated her next suggestion. Both chains being gone was odd. When one of the chains was broken, the maintenance people were generally quick to repair them to avoid confrontrations such as the one Shannon was enduring.

"The only thing we can do is call for help," she said. "I'm sorry."

"Damn piece of shit!" Bowes said, chomping on his cigar.

Shannon told herself to note in her report that he had used foul language. Then he kicked the gate so hard he made a dent in the metal, and Shannon decided to make another notation about the damage to the exit gate. That would make for some fun later. Let management try to get money out of the sucker!

"I have to return to my desk, sir. I've done all I can."

"All right. All right." He returned to his car. "I'll be up there when you make that call. I want to tell them a thing or two."

"Yes, sir."

Upstairs, Shannon waited for Bowes. When he arrived, wearing his topcoat again as if he was actually going somewhere, she dialed the number of the parking garage's night man. He answered after only three rings.

"Morrison Parking. This is Chester." Chester sounded a bit out of breath. Shannon suspected he was answering a lot of calls that night and doing a lot of explaining about how weather could affect metal and electronics. But all the tenants were like Bowes and expected doors to open no matter what, because they were people with special privileges in life.

"This is Metropolitan National Bank plaza security," she continued. "Our basement exit gate is down."

"Yours and everybody else's. Everything is froze."

"I don't think it's frozen."

"Then use the manual control."

"It's broken. The chain is gone."

"Bullshit! I don't have no record on that."

"The chain's gone, man," Shannon said. "Why would I make that up?"

"Let me have that phone," Bowes demanded, then grabbed the receiver from Shannon. "I have to get out of this goddamn place tonight. Now haul your ass over here and get this gate open, or I'll sue your company and you!"

Shannon wished she could hear Chester's response. He was a burly ex-biker who didn't take guff from anyone. Whatever he way saying, it was making Bowes's face turn red.

"You son of a bitch! You can't talk to me like that. What's your name? I said what's your name? Answer me!" Bowes's whole body shook with rage. He held the receiver away from his face, then acted as if he was going to throw it. Handing the phone back to Shannon, he said, "The bastard hung up on me. Dial him again."

Shannon took the phone and held it to her ear. There was no dial tone. She flicked the plunger a couple of times, hung up, and put the phone back to her ear. "This phone's out."

Without asking, Bowes grabbed the phone from her hand to check it out for himself. When he realized Shannon wasn't lying, his face deepened to a shade of red that bordered on magenta. He looked as if he would truly explode if aggravated any further.

"I'll call him upstairs—on my phone." He almost threw the phone back. "Give me his number!"

Shannon dutifully jotted the number down on a slip of paper and handed it over to Bowes, who snatched it from her hand.

"What's his name?"

"Chester something."

"Chester. Well, old Chester is about to get into big-time trouble. Next time you see this bastard, he'll be out on the street begging for quarters!" Bowes did not wait for Shannon's reaction to his threat. He stomped off to the nearest elevator, jabbed the up button, and rode away.

"Ass," Shannon said. As soon as the attorney was out of sight, she leaned down and plugged the phone back in under her console. She had kicked the wire loose earlier because she had grown tired of dealing with Bowes. She chuckled at what a great show she had put on for him, pretending to be a dumb blonde when the phone didn't work.

It made her feel good to screw with people like Bowes, especially when he was unable to retaliate. Characters in his class did not realize how much bad service they received because of their attitude. If they would only chill out and not put on airs as if they were so damn superior to everyone else, they might get along easier. Of course, they never learned. They went through life perpetually pissed off at someone.

The phone rang soon after Shannon restored it. She picked it up and said, "Hello."

"Shannon?" a woman's tremulous voice inquired.

"Yeah, it's me."

"This is Sue, Sue Landers." It was Jack's wife. Shannon had never met her, but she had talked to Sue often enough because she usually called Jack every night before he left.

Shannon considered her a whiny old woman who probably drove Jack half crazy. "Is Jack still around?"

"Jack's not here, Sue. He took off early because of the storm."

"Oh. Why didn't he call me first?"

"I don't know."

"Well, when did he leave?"

"About an hour ago, I think. Maybe an hour and a half."

"Oh, my, he should've been home by now."

"Not in this blizzard. He'll probably show up. That truck of his is one vehicle that can make it through the snow."

"You think so?"

"Sure. He'll make it. It'll just take a while."

"I hope you're right."

"He'll be there. Now, if you'll excuse me, I have work to do." If she didn't cut Sue off, the woman would linger on the phone indefinitely, pestering her with endless small talk about things Shannon had absolutely no interest in, such as going to church and voting Republican.

"Sorry to bother you," Sue said, somewhat testily. "'Bye."

After Sue hung up, Shannon dialed the after-hours building management number to tell them about the problems in the garage. It rang two times, then clicked off abruptly, as if some-one had hung up as soon as he answered. The dial tone whined away to nothing as Shannon listened. The phone was really dead that time.

02:38

Shannon wrapped herself up and went out to the loading dock area to make sure Jack's truck was gone. Sue's call had piqued her curiosity. And she needed a little fresh air—no matter how frigid it was—to stimulate her and help keep her awake. The snow was still blowing into the area, making visibility virtually zero beyond a yard or so. Shannon shielded her face and started toward the area where Jack usually parked.

She passed her own car, which was draped in snow; then, not far away, she saw a blurry shape, which could be another vehicle. The only way to be certain was to trudge through the gathering snow and check it out for herself. Every step was difficult. The wind shook her whole body, threatening to tear her jacket off. Her hair streamed behind her, and she could feel snow collecting on her eyebrows and lashes. But she had to know what was out there. When she was within a few feet of the vague shape, she recognized Jack's Nissan pickup.

Suddenly alarmed, Shannon moved as fast as she could against the wind and snow. When she reached the truck, she saw the driver's-side door was open, and snow had blown inside. But there was no one sitting inside, dead or alive.

She leaned in and saw the keys hanging from the ignition. Then she brushed powdery snow off the seat and climbed in, shutting the door behind her. Shivering, she turned on the dome light and glanced around for signs of mayhem. Except for the snow, the interior was clean.

Maybe the truck had failed to start. She twisted the key, and the engine kicked over on the first try. She let the truck run a few minutes, turning up the heater to keep herself comfortable while she tried to figure things out.

The truck ran fine. She tested the gear shift, and it seemed to behave properly, which eliminated another possibility. There was no reason she could see that Jack had not driven away. Even if the truck had broken down, Jack would surely have returned to the desk to call home or a garage or someone. He wouldn't have just wandered away. He was ditzy, but not that ditzy.

What if someone had robbed him? There was a lot more violent crime happening downtown nowadays. Jack would be an easy mark. But surely anyone who'd rob Jack would've taken the truck on such a night—unless the thief was too stupid to drive it, and he had to be stupid to be out in the snow robbing people.

Shannon shut the truck off and got out. She walked around the truck a couple of times, looking for footprints or any other evidence of what had happened to Jack. But, of course, the snow had covered everything up.

She walked around a couple more times, increasing the diameter of the circle with each round. Then she stumbled upon what appeared to be a large snowdrift and fell forward. She shoved her hands out in front of her just in time to keep her face from hitting concrete.

"Christ!" She stood up and started brushing snow away until she uncovered a piece of concrete as big as a boulder. Pieces of metal studs protruded around its edge. She looked up and could see the hole in the ceiling from which the concrete had fallen; a little light from the parking garage leaked through. If a car had been parked on that upper deck, it would have been down there, too.

Shannon returned to the task of moving snow away until she discovered a shred of a coat sleeve and an area of frozen blood extending from the concrete. The piece of cloth looked as if it had come from Jack's coat. But where was Jack? And was that his blood?

Shannon dropped to her knees and attempted to pry the concrete up with her legs, but it wouldn't budge. It was dark underneath the gray mass, but she was pretty sure Jack's body would be visible if it were still under there.

Shannon was puzzled. Maybe the concrete had fallen and just grazed him enough to make him bleed. Then he had crawled away or. . . . But, then again, he would have gone back to the security desk if he had been able. Where else could he go?

She stood again and surveyed the area, her eyes searching for anything that might resemble a body. Any snowdrift could hide Jack easily. Or he might not be anywhere out there. If he had been hit in the head, he might have gone out into the blizzard without thinking. There were so many possibilities, and so few clues to guide her in any particular direction.

Time was running out. Half soaked from digging around in the snow, she became aware of the numbing cold again. If she stayed outside much longer, she might freeze to death herself. Yet if there was any chance she could save Jack, she certainly had to try. No one deserved to perish in the cold, except maybe attorneys and bankers. She knew she couldn't find Jack by herself. Whether he was alive or dead, she would need help.

"Jack!" she shouted. Her voice dwindled to a whisper under the roof. Her eyes were stinging and watering from the cold. The situation was hopeless.

She had to return inside and find someone who could assist her—maybe Sam or Turner—whoever she could locate the quickest. She didn't want to be alone any longer out in the elements, where she might get lost or perish herself. The few minutes it would take to find help would not make any great difference in what ultimately happened to Jack.

She pointed her body in the general direction of the door, took a step forward, and stopped when she stubbed her toe on something hard. Bending down, she uncovered Jack's gun.

It was no great secret that Jack usually kept

the .38 in his truck; he had told her about the gun more than once. The only reason it would be outside the truck was that he had been threatened.

She sniffed the barrel and realized the gun had been fired; inspecting the cylinder confirmed that a round was missing. Shannon could visualize Jack's fate. Someone had attempted to assault Jack while he was in the truck. Jack had taken the gun out and shot at his assailant. Maybe it was the criminal's blood under the concrete. Maybe Jack had missed the guy, too, and there was a struggle in which Jack lost his gun.

So where were Jack and the criminal? What had caused the concrete to fall? A bullet?

Suddenly, it occurred to her that someone might be using her car. It would provide enough shelter to prevent freezing to death. Jack himself might even be in there, slowly bleeding to death! She hurried to the Ford, gripping the gun tightly in her hand, her finger poised on the trigger—just in case.

She jerked open the door on the passenger side and thrust in her arm with the gun cocked and ready.

She didn't need the gun. The person sitting in the driver's seat posed no immediate threat. It was Jack. Or someone wearing his uniform. It was hard to tell which because the car's occupant had no face.

Shannon shrieked and ran toward the building's back door, falling down twice in the snow.

Once inside, she headed for the service elevator to get help from Randall, who ran the elevator for the Clean Corps.

Panting for breath, she pressed both the up and down buttons, then waited for Randall to arrive. He'd know where Sam and the others were. Maybe he could help her.

She slumped against the wall and watched the L.E.D. display the floor numbers as the service elevator slowly descended. Then she heard noise in the ventilation ductwork again. That time it wasn't a roar; it sounded like chains rattling. The racket made her drop the gun so she could cover her ears.

When the elevator doors slid open, Shannon shrieked again.

Chapter Thirteen

Wednesday, 22 November:
02:56

Audrey Masters thrust her pelvis hard against her partner, grinding in pace with his final spasms. Harold McHenry finished coming, disengaged himself from Audrey, and rolled off her. Lying next to her on the sofa bed, he gasped. His eyes were half open, and his face bore the extended grimace of orgasm.

"Mind if I smoke?" Audrey asked, reaching over the side of the bed for her cigarettes.

"No," McHenry said, though he was one of the most vocal antismoking proponents in the building.

Audrey lit up and blew smoke toward the ceiling in McHenry's darkened office suite on the thirtieth floor. She was in her mid-forties and very slim with small crab-apple breasts. Across her flat stomach radiated a web of stretch marks that seemed more pronounced both because of her tan and the flush of sexual frenzy she had just experienced. Her face was triangular with small blue-gray eyes and a pointed nose. Her mouth and eyes had many more wrinkles around them than would be expected for a woman her age; they were the product both of excessive smoking and excessive tanning, the latter of which had also made her skin leathery. Her frosted brown hair was cut short and tapered up her neck, giving her the appearance of an overage Peter Pan. But she was rarely compared to such nice characters; most people considered her a witch. The tenants of the Metropolitan National Bank tower certainly did; she was the property manager.

Pushing 60, McHenry had a square face with sagging jowls. His eyes were brown with flecks of green, and his nose was broad. His hair was thinning and gray blond. He was just over six feet tall, and his body was all pale flesh with no muscle tone to speak of. He was about 20 pounds overweight, but the presence of more flab than muscle made him seem more obese than he actually was, unless he was wearing one of his tailored suits. A dark gray, pin-striped suit lay crumpled on a chair nearby, along with a plain brown tie, an undershirt, and a pair of boxer shorts with large red polka dots.

McHenry slowly came to life, the afterglow of

his coupling with Audrey dissipating as if it were no more than flatulence. He reached and pulled a sheet up over their naked bodies. With the sex over, he didn't want to view either his own or Audrey's nudity. He found both repulsive—hers more than his, simply because she was not a pretty woman in any way. He didn't want to remind himself how much he had reduced his standards in the past few years, considering a woman with any tits at all as fair game.

Of course, he could have really pretty women. As president of the bank, he could choose from among many women. Money purchased no commodity more easily. But he found it more challenging and satisfying to pursue a woman and seduce her—or pretend he was seducing, since a man with money could never be sure exactly why a particular woman went to bed with him.

They all put out, he thought, remembering a catch phrase from his college days. *They really put out when you have power and money to offer.*

Of course, McHenry intended to give neither to Audrey. He would award her with nothing, except maybe the privilege of more sex later if he felt up to it. For the moment, however, he was used up. Though he knew he wasn't losing his potency as he grew older, he had discovered it sometimes took him longer to perform than he would have liked, especially when he was acting more out of compulsion than desire.

Sex that night was tedious, a ragged experience caused by various circumstances. He had brought Audrey up to his suite around 11:30, not bothering to sign either of them in at the security desk. He had silently dared the guard there to ask him to. The guard, having recognized the president of the bank, knew better than to challenge him.

The cleaning people had already finished the thirtieth floor by that hour, so when he locked his suite, he knew he would not be interrupted. Since he had forbidden anyone except the cleaning people access to his offices, he could pursue Audrey at a leisurely pace.

Audrey hadn't put up much of a struggle. So it must've been true what he'd heard about her: she was a pushover. He probably could have fucked her the second he had closed the door, as she sat on his desk with her legs spread wide open. However, when he saw her panties hanging down around her left ankle, and her pantyhose wadded up on the floor, he felt a bit queasy about taking her then. She was too easy, too whorish; she had no class whatsoever. Hell, for all he knew, she might even be diseased.

He had ignored Audrey's blatant display and told her he wanted to relax first. So they had gone through the ritual: had a couple of drinks, made small talk, pretended they were not there for sex, then started the kissing and fondling slowly.

Then he was repulsed again. That time by her

cigarette breath. He had been a smoker himself for many years and had quit only in the last five. But he had forgotten what tobacco breath really smelled like. He might have overlooked it if Audrey's body had been more enticing.

He hadn't said anything, though. He'd just gulped and pressed on, until he had opened the sofa bed he'd had put in his office to provide a ready place for seduction games. Then the two of them were fumbling naked on its mattress. When he had grown tautly erect and ready to plunge into Audrey's ample nether regions, he heard the clicking of the security guard's heels out in the hall. He shushed Audrey and fell quiet himself.

"Security," he'd whispered to her and slid off her without making a noise.

Audrey had had to catch her breath. The two of them listened for the guard to leave, but the guard had stopped for some reason. Finally, they'd heard a woman's voice say, "Asshole," and the noise of her retreating feet.

"Who's she calling an asshole?" Audrey had asked. "You think she knows we're in here?"

"Who cares? In any case, she spoiled the mood of the moment."

Then it had taken two hours or so—between bouts of his drinking and her smoking—before he was ready again, and he finally was able to come.

After they were finished, McHenry felt he should not have expended so much energy.

Audrey Masters was not that great in bed. His pride, however, would not let him send her away untouched, and of course, he could not have proven anything had he not carried their evening together to its logical conclusion. His inability to consummate their after-hours meeting would have given her power over him, and that could not be allowed.

He closed his eyes and let his right hand drift over to squeeze one of her small breasts. Her skin was oily from sweat. The room was filled with the smell of her musk, mixed with the acrid odor of her cigarettes. Touching her was repugnant, like putting his hands on a foul animal. He was doing it only to reaffirm the reality of what they had done.

McHenry had to figure out what to do with Audrey, and he prayed for guidance as to what to do next. In the prolonged quiet of the moment, he thought about killing her.

02:57

Snow swirled into Shannon's Ford, but its occupant didn't seem to mind. A quarter inch of snow had collected on his legs and hands before he fell forward on the steering wheel, the mass of blood where his face had been smearing the edges.

His body was motionless briefly; then it twitched like a marionnette with its strings being pulled. He leaned back and scooted along the seat toward the open door opposite him, being guided to the outside by the cold since he could not see.

He rose unsteadily out of the car. He was being summoned by a silent agency to the basement, where he belonged.

He followed the impulse planted in the remainder of his brain, making his way at last to the metal gates leading to the basement garage. He felt along the exit gate till his fingers found the bottom edge, inserted them, and pulled up, pressing the corrugated metal together like an accordion. He used so much force that he broke his right arm. That didn't bother him; it was merely a nuisance, just as having no face was only a minor annoyance. Neither condition caused him any pain.

He ducked under the gate and started down the ramp. He lost his footing after a couple of steps and slid the rest of the way, further lacerating the front of his head.

When he reached the bottom and fumbled to his feet, Dead Ted was waiting.

02:58

Richard Bowes's anger had not abated an iota by the time he reached his office on the twenty-ninth floor. If anything, the ride up had stoked his wrath to the limits. Were the object of his anger close by, Bowes would certainly have strangled him with his gloved hands.

As an attorney, he had no doubt he could get himself off for justifiable homicide. Anyone who caused him undue aggravation deserved to die.

Bowes sat in his leather swivel chair without taking off his overcoat, though he did unbutton the front and remove his scarf. He wanted to talk to the man who worked for the garage before he lost his momentum. He dialed the phone number and searched in his pockets for a cigar while he waited for someone to answer.

When no one answered the call, Bowes hung up in disgust and redialed. Having finally located another cigar, he stuck it between his lips and began looking for his lighter.

"Morrison Parking. This is Suzanne," a woman's musical voice finally answered.

"I want to talk to Chester!"

"Chester is on the other line. Can you hold?"

Bowes almost bit the end of his cigar off. "No, I can't hold. I want to talk to Chester now. You tell him Richard Bowes, attorney for Metropolitan National Bank, demands to speak to him!"

"I'll try, sir."

The woman put him on hold; canned instrumental music buzzed in his ear like a trapped fly. Bowes's face assumed a hue like a polluted sunset. He would have to make this woman pay, too. No one put him on hold!

While he waited, the seconds dragging by, he found his lighter in his inside coat pocket and brought it out, flicking it on and off nervously. After a full two minutes had passed he left the flame on and started to touch it to the end of his cigar. Simultaneously, a thin stream of liquid spurted out of the phone, splashing Bowes's ear.

"Jesus Christ!"

He jumped up, flung the phone on the floor, and grabbed his ear, which stung as if someone had thrown acid on it. But he soon forgot that pain when he saw the sleeve of his coat was on fire, and the flame was spreading both toward his hand and his face.

Fighting panic, he removed the coat and rolled it up to snuff out the fire. When the flames were stifled, Bowes smiled triumphantly; he was as good as any boy scout.

Then he saw that his pants were on fire. He looked down and saw the fire coming from the phone, which was spilling more liquid out on the carpet. The liquid ignited as soon as it came out. His nostrils twitched as he recognized the smell of gasoline.

He didn't have time to ponder how gasoline could be coming from his phone. He was too busy slapping his pants, trying to prevent the fire from reaching his crotch. He was so busy he didn't notice what was coming out of the heat vent behind him. Nor did he hear the chain as it snaked across the floor and wrapped around his ankles.

He was quite aware, however, of the chain pulling his feet out from under him, throwing his face right into the fire.

His hair caught fire first, the hair spray he used proving to be highly combustible. He rubbed his head frantically, trying to put the fire out with his hands even though his fingers were already blistered and half cooked. He tried to roll over to put out the new fire, but a second length of chain shot out of the vent and circled his neck, then cinched tightly around his Adam's apple.

Bowes panicked. His fingers found the chain and tried to pry it from his neck. But it continued to tighten until blood formed a necklace underneath his chin and dribbled down his smoking fingers.

Choking and gasping, he opened his mouth to scream, but that only allowed the gasoline to shoot down his throat. He thrashed and writhed on the carpet, now a plain of fire on which he was roasting. He squinted his eyes and looked up at the smoke alarm over his desk, wondering why it didn't go off and summon help.

His answer came when blood oozed, then streamed from the smoke alarm, sizzling as drops hit his burning body. The room smelled like scorched steak.

He continued to struggle as long as he had strength. Then his brain fried and Richard Bowes, attorney at law, was no longer among the living.

After Bowes died, the fire went out almost immediately. The residual smoke was sucked out through the vent. The chains came loose from Bowes's body and retreated down the vent as well.

A few seconds later, the smoldering, charred lump of flesh stirred and rose slowly. It placed a hand on the edge of the desk to steady itself, and two fingers, having been reduced to mere ash, fell off. Ignoring the loss, the burned corpse assumed its full height, found a cigar on the surface of the desk, jammed it between its bared teeth, and tottered out to the hall. There it waited patiently for an elevator to take it away.

02:59

Tongue on teeth, taste blood.

Snow falling.

Nose collapses, nothing smells.

Cold on ears.

Eyes roll right, eyes roll left. Blink.

Stan's head was awake.

Brain all scrambled.

Though it had been thrown some distance, Stan's head was not severely damaged. The only immediate problem was the one of detachment. Without a body, a head could do almost nothing.

Stan considered the possibility of locomotion with his tongue. His tongue might pull him along if it could get a grip on the sidewalk beneath the snow. Although tasting the sidewalk might be unpleasant, it would be better than just lying there.

But his head was on its side, and though he had tried to get it into a position in which his tongue would prove useful, he did not have the necessary muscles. They were in his neck, the majority of which remained with his body somewhere.

Stan was finding it difficult to think clearly, so he had to focus on one thought at a time. He momentarily put aside the problem of movement and tried to recall who had separated his head from his body. All he could conjure up was a blur that resembled Jack.

He didn't think Jack had any reason to behead him. So maybe he had not seen Jack at all—only someone who resembled him. That still left the mystery of who would want to maim him so severely. He didn't have any enemies who would go this far.

Since he couldn't figure out who had ripped his head off, Stan switched his thoughts to another imponderable topic. He was mystified by how his head continued to live without his body. He had never heard or read of any situation like this. Maybe, though, that sort of thing was not widely publicized; if people knew their heads had an afterlife, they might really freak out. When a person was dead—or half dead—he didn't want to think he would have to experience any of the nasty stuff reserved for his departed body. His head being alive made Stan speculate that maybe a person remained aware after death—at least long enough to be tortured when the undertaker worked on the remains. Unexpectedly revolted, Stan decided not to think about that disturbing idea anymore.

A wind came along and pushed his head upright, allowing him to look into the bank building. The plate-glass front was badly frosted over, so all he could see were occasional moving things that could be anybody.

"Shit," he muttered.

His expression became hopeful. "I can talk," he said, as if making an announcement to the world. The air whistling through the hole at the base of his skull provided the necessary element for speaking. He didn't sound exactly like himself, but he would be able to communicate if he ever encountered anyone.

Maybe he could coax someone to pick him up and help him find his body. Perhaps there was a chance of rejoining it and becoming whole again.

Or—he considered the only hopeful possibility in his present situation—he might wake up. His present situation could all be a dream induced by his massive intake of alcohol earlier in the evening. It might be a hallucination! It sure felt real, however, when the wind slammed his head into the revolving doors.

03:10

Dead Ted was starting to get the hang of the terror thing. He was learning how to make more efficient use of his resources, too—like using the gasoline on the lawyer. He'd found the gasoline in the auxiliary generator room in the basement. Making it appear to come from the phone was a good touch, too. But the best was the blood pouring from the smoke alarm.

Dead Ted was finding blood to be one of the most effectively scary props. It spooked everyone. He could make others see it when it wasn't there, or by taking blood from one of his victims, he could splatter others with real blood. By the end of the night, many people in the building would be wearing red!

So far, he had managed to kill quite a few people without being discovered. But the bodies were being found. Already Shannon had encountered one—that old security officer who kept wandering away—and she would find another quite soon. Of course, in order to keep her terrorized, he needed her to find the bodies.

Dead Ted didn't want to kill her or everyone just yet. Once they were dead, they weren't as much fun. He had to restrain himself and save a few people until he was ready to move on.

One thing in the last half hour had bothered him. For some reason, he couldn't get into the bank president's office to do anything to him or his companion. And Dead Ted so wanted to make the woman's pussy grow teeth or make the guy explode. But he could only watch them from the private rest room, where he had stretched up into the plumbing.

That he was unable to affect those two people posed a problem. What if he ran into other people who could resist him? That failure would make most of his efforts meaningless, for he had decided he would not rest until he had murdered every last living soul in the building. Otherwise, there was no point to what he was doing. He couldn't punish the city if some people could escape; it made him less of a threat. And it might portend the possibility someone had the power to stop him.

Maybe there was something about the room the man and woman were in that prevented his entry. If Dead Ted could manage to get them out of it, he might be able to kill them.

He'd have to create a diversion of some kind. If he had thought about it, he could have let smoke from the burning attorney go up to their floor. But it was too late. The attorney himself might make an impression on them, however. Or maybe he'd send up that cleaning lady and have her knock on the door to the suite while holding her head underneath one arm.

Dead Ted thought that was too corny. He liked spectacular effects, and he would think of one eventually. After all, he had a lot of raw material to work with.

Chapter Fourteen

Wednesday, 22 November:
03:01

At first glance, there was no reason for Shannon to be shocked by what she saw in the service elevator. Randall was sitting there on the chair he usually occupied while shunting the cleaning people to their various floors. That much was normal.

But there was a difference that night. Randall would not be performing his regular duties—his abdomen had apparently exploded, his intestines hung out of him like loops of sticky rope, and his blood covered the bottom of the service elevator.

Shannon was inclined to scream, but no sound came from her. She was too terrified to do anything but gape at what had happened. She would get no help from Randall. It was a silly thought, but she couldn't keep herself from thinking it.

Nor Randall from answering it. "I'll help you," he said, his voice hollow sounding and unreal. His eyes flicked open, and his dark brown face jerked in her direction. "But I got something better than help, baby. We all having a party soon, and you are invited!"

He bent forward as if he was getting up out of the chair and scowled when he saw the condition of his guts. Using both hands, he tried to stuff them back into his body cavity, but they kept falling out.

"This is a bitch," he said. "How am I going to party like this? Come on in here and help me, girl."

"No way!" Shannon shouted.

"That the way you wanna be, then the hell with you!" He pressed the button to the twentieth floor and the elevator doors shut.

As Shannon watched the L.E.D indicate Randall's ascent, she took a deep breath to regain control of herself. *Don't let this get to you,* she told herself. *There's an explanation. This isn't real. That's it—it's a joke—like the blood in the drinking fountain. They're trying to scare me. That's all.*

She bent down to retrieve Jack's gun, tucked it in her waist, and went out to the lobby, determined to find Sam and demand an explanation. It had to be his people who were playing the joke. Maybe he had even put them up to it, though she could think of no reason why he would torment her.

She removed her jacket and strode to the nearest elevator. Since Randall had gone to the twentieth floor, she'd go up there, too. Sam was probably on that floor planning his next little act for her benefit. She was ready to kill him and anyone else who was involved in the game. She'd show them a party all right!

The elevator opened and she got in, her face bearing an expression of such fierce determination no one would dare approach her. She pressed the button for the twentieth floor and blood squirted out around the edge, some of it hitting her in the midriff and the rest streaming down the polished metal elevator wall.

"That ain't shit," she said as the car started moving. She didn't even squeal. She wasn't about to let them—whoever they might be—have more fun at her expense. She didn't even bother to wipe the blood away. Then the elevator unexpectedly stopped at the tenth floor.

"Can you help me find my hand, Shannon?" Jerena asked, sounding like a little girl as she stood in the lobby and held up her stump. Her head appeared to be on her neck backward. She smiled, flashing her gold tooth. "You going to the party?"

Shannon hit the button to close the door before Jerena moved any closer. She was getting angrier; she didn't like to see Jerena used that way. Sam had taken advantage of the cleaning woman's stupidity to enlist her in his morbid little show. Well, he'd get an extra ass chewing for that!

The elevator brought her to the twentieth floor. She stepped out into the lobby and surveyed the hall cautiously. The office suites were in darkness, and all was quiet.

"Sam!" she yelled. She waited a heartbeat, then called his name again. "I know you're up here! What the fuck are you trying to prove?"

She decided to look for him. He was probably hiding out somewhere, waiting to jump out and laugh at her. Maybe Jack would be up there, too. He was probably in on the prank, pretending to be hurt when she saw him in her car. That old fart should have known better.

She moved quickly through the offices, having walked through them so many times on her rounds that she needed no light to guide her. Besides, maybe she would surprise somebody herself! Maybe she would show them Jack's gun and see how funny they thought that was!

Halfway around the floor, she bumped into someone in the dark—someone who wore strong perfume.

"Who's that?" she asked loudly.

"Just me," a woman replied. "I was working upstairs when the strangest thing happened. My computer blew up! Then it attacked me!"

Shannon felt around on a desk and turned on a lamp. The woman was Cassandra Peters, the redhead she'd met up on the twenty-fourth floor while doing her rounds. Cassandra still wore her sweater, and it was only partially open, revealing a wire dangling from Cassandra's chest. Around the same area was a dark stain. She wondered how Sam had talked the obviously straitlaced, uptight woman into playing along; maybe they were all bored because they had to stay in the building and had decided their charade of horrors would be a good way to pass the time.

"So what happened to you?" Shannon asked, pretending to go along with the new gag.

"Oh, it's weird. Don't know how to explain it." She opened her sweater to reveal that the wire was hanging out of a bloody hole in her chest. "It's my computer mouse. It jumped right into my chest, just like it really was a little animal."

Shannon studied the woman's eyes. They were glazed over, as if she had been drugged. Maybe the party Randall had mentioned was a drug party; Shannon knew he and some of the other Clean Corps people sometimes used drugs. They had even offered them to her before. She had refused, of course. She had seen too often what using drugs did to people's lives.

She wondered if there was some way they could have put drugs in a soft drink. Maybe she was hallucinating.

"I'm cold," Cassandra said abruptly.

No, she was clearheaded, and she was tired of being played with. Though the wire coming out of Cassandra looked real, Shannon wasn't going to fall for the hoax. She took hold of the wire firmly and jerked it out, bringing with it Cassandra's heart and a hot spray of blood.

"Jesus!" Shannon held the organ right in front of her face. It seemed to be pulsating, as if it were a real heart.

"Why did you do that?" Cassandra said, her expression one of dazed surprise. She pressed her hands over the hole in her chest; blood dribbled over her fingers.

"You people are sick!" Shannon yelled. She dropped the heart and ran away, leaving Cassandra behind.

At the elevator bank, Sam was waiting, his back turned to her.

"Sam, you son of a bitch! Why are you doing this?"

"Doing what?" he replied, turning slowly.

"You know what I'm talking about!" Shannon went up to him, and as he finished turning, she saw one of his arms was barely attached at the shoulder. And there was a large round hole in the middle of his forehead. "What are you guys doing? Why do you keep fucking with me?"

"I don't know what you mean, Shannon dear," Sam replied through bloodied teeth.

"Oh, I guess your people thought all this up on their own. I know they're not bright enough to do it. You came up with all this Halloween shit. Just tell me why, Sam. Explain the joke to me. That's all I want. And by the way, what are you supposed to be?"

Cocking his head, Sam managed to put on a

perfectly stupid expression that would convince anyone who didn't know him he was totally brain dead. "Got my arm caught in the elevator. Hit in the head with hammer. Hammer fly."

"Bullshit!"

"Hey, baby, I see you came for the party anyhow. Wanna do some lines?" Randall had come around the corner, awkwardly holding his intestines in place with his hands. "We're ready to get down, sister."

"I ain't your damn sister!"

"It's party time," Sam said, his voice shifting to its more normal sound. "Randall's right. We need you for our party."

Shannon glared at Sam, then at Randall, both of whom leered like schoolboys who had just seen a bare breast. "I ain't playing this shit," she said. "You can play whatever you want, but I'm going back down to work."

"No, we can't let you do that," Randall said, suddenly blocking the elevators on one side. "I ain't letting you leave."

"You can't go," Sam chimed in, blocking the other elevators.

"How about you mess with this?" Shannon yelled, pulling the .38 from her waist. "You want a bullet hole to go with that other hole in your head, Sam? How about a real shot in the guts, Randall?"

"Say what?" Randall appeared to be dumbstruck. But neither he nor Sam seemed intimidated by the gun.

"This is a real gun! It shoots real bullets that make real holes, and I just might use it if you guys don't get out of my way."

Randall edged closer to Shannon. Then a loop of his intestines shot out and wrapped itself around her arm.

"Jesus, get that off me!" Shannon hit the slimy intestine with the butt of the gun, and it came free, recoiling into Randall's torso.

"You sure a feisty bitch," Randall said.

"We just want to party," Sam said, his tongue rolling sloppily in his mouth, as if it were not fully attached. He drooled and dark red spittle sprayed from his lips.

"Screw you both!" Shannon screamed and darted into the hall, where she ran to a door leading to the stairwell. She jogged down two flights of stairs to the eighteenth floor, where she was able to get on an elevator without being blocked. She pressed the button for the first floor and rode down without interruption.

03:18

Before she returned to her desk, Shannon stopped in the rest room on the second floor to look herself over. She had blood on her uniform and on her face and hands. She even had some in her hair. And the blood didn't seem as if it was going to fade away. She wasn't going to wait anyhow. She filled her hand with liquid soap and began scrubbing her face and hands until all traces of the blood—or whatever the liquid really was—were gone. Then she combed the blood out of her hair and tried to get it out from beneath her fingernails, which was difficult because she had nothing to scrape them with.

But much remained on her uniform. Some of it had already started drying and was leaving a crust that didn't seem likely to disappear. There were large wet splotches under her arms from sweating, and there were a couple of small tears in her trousers. The uniform was a total wreck.

"Shit," she said. She would have to buy another uniform. The security company would not very readily accept her explanation for ruining that one. Her superiors would no doubt accuse her of nonprofessional behavior. If they found out people were using drugs all around her, she'd probably be accused of joining them. She might even get fired.

"Maybe I'll just quit and get religion," she said to the image in the mirror. "No job is worth this much hassle."

She left the rest room thinking of how pleased her mother would be if she really found God. Then, as she approached her desk, she heard a funny joke on the radio, and she automatically banished thoughts of religion from her mind.

"If a person has to find God, does that mean God's lost?" the comedian on the radio said. "Why don't you see His picture on milk cartons?"

Shannon's mother would go into a fit over a joke like that. Shannon might save that little gem for the next time her mother tried to shame her into going to church. It would be fun to watch the old lady explode.

Chapter Fifteen

Wednesday, 22 November:
03:28

The idea of killing someone was not altogether foreign to Harold McHenry. He had contemplated it many times before, and as often came naturally to a person with power, it occurred to him that, with his connections, he could contrive to get away with murder rather easily.

But though easily considered, murder was not something a man in his position would just do without provocation or meditation or, more pertinently, without some direct financial benefit.

McHenry considered killing Audrey Masters as he waited for her to finish showering. After they had lain on the sofa bed awhile, she had finally arisen to wash herself, and he had graciously allowed her to, since he had nothing more to say to her.

She was, at best, average in bed—no better than his wife and not even close to his secretary, a thrasher who would turn him every which way but loose in the sack. He had no desire to do Audrey again, not even to impress upon her how powerful he was.

Indeed, he was rather disgusted with her and had almost denied her access to his private bath, not wanting her presence to sully its beauty. If it was not a snowy night, he might even have kicked her out. But then he wouldn't be able to kill her, and though he had not totally convinced himself he would off the woman, he let her use the bath.

He listened intently to the sound of the water running and her moving in the shower. He imagined the lather streaming down her reedlike body, swirling around in the drain before being sucked down into the bowels of the building. It would be rather amusing and also fitting if somehow Audrey could be washed down into the drain herself in tiny pieces that wouldn't clog up the plumbing.

He toyed with the notion of going in and killing her in the shower. But that was too cornball—too much like *Psycho* and a million other slasher flicks. Besides, he didn't have a suitably sharp knife to cause her death that way. It was a pity the way the lack of implements could rob life of drama. He should have bought that samurai sword he had once seen in a catalogue.

When the idea had first come to him, it seemed so natural he hadn't question it. As the time and opportunity to act approached, however, he found himself questioning his motivation. Not on moral grounds, of course. It was a problem of practicality. Why should he kill her? She was a worthless woman, a lousy lay, and. a snooty bitch, but so were many other women he knew.

Since it didn't really matter in the scheme of the universe what he did, he needn't concern himself much about the why. Only the way. There were certain logistics involved, though the actual taking of her life should be rather simple.

Considering strangulation, he studied his hands—manicured, as soft as a woman's uncallused. Were they ready murder weapons? He was probably strong enough to strangle her. But that method seemed to lack class. Any idiot in the street could strangle a person.

He had no gun. Once he had kept a pistol in his desk, but someone had stolen it, and he had not replaced it immediately as he should have. He was sure most of the executive vice-presidents kept guns in their offices, but he didn't feel like looking for them.

So he was left to choose among objects that

were immediately available to him: vases, lamps, lumps of crystal. He could use any of them to bludgeon her. Yet none of those really appealed to him.

Was the letter opener on the desk sharp enough? Or could he smash her brains out with his secretary's computer monitor?

Wrapped in a towel, Audrey came to the doorway of the bath, interrupting his intense thought. "What's with you?"

"What do you mean?"

"You have a weird look in your eyes, like you're thinking about how to solve the world's problems."

McHenry chuckled. "The world's problems concern me only as they affect the bottom line."

"That's certainly philanthropic."

"I'm a businessman, not Mother Teresa."

Audrey gave him a look of mild disapproval, then went to the nearest window to peep through the drapes at the blizzard. "The snow looks strange up here," she said, shivering. "It just goes around and around, like it's going nowhere."

McHenry donned his pants and undershirt. He didn't feel like cleaning up just yet. He was waiting for something to happen—something that would turn his prior thoughts into action.

"The view is always fascinating from that window," he said quietly. "You ought to see it during a thunderstorm."

"That would be scary." She turned from the

window and went to the sofa bed. She took a cigarette from the pack on the floor, lit it, and sat on the edge of the mattress. "You still talking to those people from Ohio?"

"What?" he said with some surprise, though he knew exactly what she was referring to.

"I mean are you planning to sell the bank?"

McHenry's face grew dark. "You know better than to ask that. It's a big secret. No one knows anything about it."

"You mean nobody is supposed to know. I'd bet if you went out and found one of the cleaning people—pick the dumbest one you can find—she'd know something about it."

McHenry allowed himself a grin. "There are no secrets in big buildings, I guess."

"Maybe a few."

McHenry looked away from her. He was no doubt supposed to be intrigued by her referring to secrets that she alone might be privy to. But he wasn't. He knew everything that was going on, usually before Audrey did. And if anything escaped his attention, it either was not important or would come to his attention in time for him to act one way or another.

With quiet between them, he allowed his mind to clear itself out, and a sense of dread expectation came over him. He felt something strange happening to his body, as if his mind had disassociated itself from his flesh and become a separate entity that could only observe.

Panicky at first, he calmed himself immediately. He was not in bad shape physically, he could handle the strange sensation. He had willed himself not to let the physical aspects of his body intrude on his life. He was not an ordinary man. He had nothing to fear—certainly no guilt for what he contemplated doing to Audrey. Such remorse would bring on a heart attack for lesser men.

Then he realized something outside him was taking over, wrestling total control of his body from his mind and changing it. It was subtle at first, like his toying with the idea of murder. Then the change gradually became more dramatic.

He couldn't guess what the catalyst for the takeover might be. Perhaps it was the storm; perhaps it was Audrey and her tedious personality; perhaps it was the substantiation of his own hatred for people who got in his way. Whatever the reason, he had no choice but to let the power control him.

McHenry thought about the power a second and realized it was the power of pure evil unmitigated by any human sensibility overcoming him. Human feelings were for fools, after all. The great and the powerful, the people who made the world move, did not have to be governed by them. And if human feelings could be cast aside, was it not then logical that human form could be altered as well?

There was no reason to fight it. If evil gave him

powers beyond normal human beings, then he would take advantage of it. So he relaxed, letting the pure evil do as it would with him. He might learn something from the experience; maybe he was entering a totally new realm of awareness and power.

The possession of his body began with a tingling followed by a cold sweat. The skin on his face became tight; his vision altered as his pupils shrank to mere dots in his eyes.

"It's certainly no secret," he said, suddenly resuming his conversation with Audrey, "how Audrey Masters fucks like a mink!"

"What?" Audrey was stunned, as much by McHenry's abrupt outburst as by his words.

Quickly adapting to his new form, McHenry rose and came around to face her. His features were drawn, mimicking a Halloween mask of a demon. "I said everyone knows how you fuck like a mink. You'd fuck anyone!"

"Why are you insulting me?" she said, then noticed his fierce countenance. "My God, what's going on with you?"

McHenry's fingers lengthened and his nails turned dark as they became long and sharp. His eyes glowed brightly. He dropped his pants, revealing a new erection twice as big as the one he had displayed earlier.

Audrey fell back on the mattress. "Get away from me!"

"Now it's time for you to pay," McHenry said. He swiped at her with his clawed hand, ripping the towel away. Her skin was covered with goose bumps and mottled from the flush of fear. "You have good reason to be afraid. You are going to die!"

"No!"

He laughed and slapped the cigarette from Audrey's hand. Then he slapped her face hard, leaving a vivid pink welt on her left cheek.

She screamed and kicked out at him, aiming for his crotch. He caught her legs and held them apart. Audrey's eyes were drawn down again to his penis, which had grown even larger. To her horror, she saw the glans resembled his face. It even had a mouth and little green eyes. The mouth was working jaws filled with jagged sharp teeth. She thrashed against his grip, but her struggle did no good. He was not only stronger than she was, but more powerful than any human being.

Then he put the nether head into her, and it bit as it rode up inside her body. Blood gushed around it, splashing all over McHenry's crotch and stomach. His hands gripped her arms; his nails bit into her flesh.

She made a sound like a cat being torn to pieces. Her eyes looked down as McHenry continued to gorge himself on her innards. Seconds, later, with a squishing sound, the diminutive demon head popped up through her abdomen, chewing on shreds of her skin.

"This is the real me!" McHenry bellowed, and he realized that lurking in the pit of every great man was a monster that served its host well—just as his own was dispatching Audrey with an efficiency and flare he could not have managed on his own.

His eyes and the eyes of the thing sticking up out of her glowed orange. The nether head spat a combination of Audrey's blood and thick semen all over her chest and face. The thick fluid steamed when it hit Audrey, blistering her skin.

She coughed and choked as a glob shot into her mouth and burned its way down her throat. She kept choking as she fought for air. But her windpipe was effectively glued shut. Suddenly, she could no longer fight. She shuddered. Life left her quickly.

When she fell limp, McHenry removed the demonic penis and let Audrey's arms fall to the bed. He waited a few seconds to make sure she was dead, wishing he'd had a camera to record the brutal scene.

McHenry's body gradually restored itself—the skin becoming normal, the long nails receding, the fingers shrinking back, the voracious penis closing its dimming eyes and shriveling into itself. His scrotum ached fiercely. His eyes burned. When the transformation back to human was complete, he shook all over as if he had a bad chill.

Then the detached awareness that was truly McHenry settled down inside him again, and he viewed Audrey's corpse through a haze of strange sensibility.

Though he had only minutes before regarded her as another disposable person among millions, he was momentarily repulsed by the sight of her ravaged torso. Real gore, as opposed to imagined, had an effect on anyone, no matter how much he fancied himself above such feelings. McHenry had, in fact, never killed before. He had never dealt with the reality of a dead body. Nor had he ever killed in a demonic guise with a homuncular penis.

Or had he imagined that part of it? Had his mind constructed a special guise for killing to remove the reality of it from his primary awareness? Had he merely convinced himself he was something else long enough to kill her? Was that deception necessary to make the killing acceptable or merely to make it easier to accomplish?

Either way, how had he made the ragged hole in her abdomen? He glanced around quickly, looking for a possible weapon he might have used. He held his hands before him, scrutinizing them for possibilities. Could he have dug into Audrey's flesh with his fingers?

If he had not been hallucinating, then he would have to admit there was something supernatural involved. Maybe that was another revelation only the truly powerful ever experienced.

He looked down and noticed the entire front of his body was bloodstained, especially his crotch, his pubic hair matted in crimson knots. His penis shone with still moist semen. He touched his finger to it and the viscous fluid stung.

His mind did a couple of flip-flops. At least part of what had just taken place was real. But which part? Why did it bother him so much? Could it be he had a scrap of conscience?

He was not certain how to label his feelings and didn't have time to sort them out. There were pressing practical matters to worry about. What he would do with her body and the mess on the sofa bed? Why hadn't he thought that all out before going ahead?

Maybe he had been temporarily insane. There was no other explanation for this unplanned, unorganized act.

Could his lawyers help him? Or would he have to call upon the manifestation of pure evil again? Could he summon it again?

He knew he could not depend on potential help and suppositions. He had to act immediately. He would have to steel himself to get rid of Audrey's body on his own. Removal of the corpse was not something he could entrust to anyone else.

He gathered up the sheets around her and tucked them underneath her, flinching at the dead warmth of her body. When he was finished, she was quite a neat package until her blood started seeping through the sheets. He would need something plastic—trash bags or maybe the shower curtain. Either would just about fit. He could tape or staple the plastic together somehow, drag her out and—what? He couldn't just take her down in the elevator and stroll out the front door with her hefted over his shoulder.

What did people do with dead bodies? He thought about all the movies he had seen, and he could not recall one that covered that crisis. Of course, the screenwriters had time to figure those things out so there was always a convenient place to stow the body or dump it.

The only place convenient to the thirtieth floor was the roof. Maybe he could carry the defunct Audrey up there and toss her off. After she bounced off the side of the building a few times and landed on the concrete below, she'd be so battered the police would have problems telling what had happened to her. Maybe they'd think she was a suicide.

He glanced at Audrey's clothes. They presented another problem. At least there weren't many to bother him. He could destroy them later. He had better get the shower curtain before Audrey's blood made a worse mess. And on his way to the bath, he decided he might think better if he took a shower himself. Audrey could wait a few minutes while he cleaned up.

As he scrubbed himself under steaming hot water, he wondered again if he had somehow actually become a demon and not imagined it. Perhaps the transformation had been some kind of payback—exacted by agencies beyond his ken. He served no god, or so he avowed, but maybe evil was a force unto itself that was like a god who occasionally demanded something extraordinary from a human being.

That could explain a great deal about how evil worked in the world. Maybe he had discovered some deep, dark secret that he could put to use again sometime. Whether the demon was real or imagined, it had served his purpose. McHenry might not have accomplished anything at all if left to merely contemplate. The demon was necessary for action.

Could the demon be called upon to dispose of Audrey? He wasn't sure. He still couldn't figure out how he and the demon had co-existed or how he had effected the transformation.

Maybe the demon would eat her. But that was such a ghastly scenario, just thinking about it made him want to throw up, so he dismissed the notion entirely.

Sufficiently stimulated and feeling much better, he turned off the water and stepped out of the shower. His skin was almost raw from having been scrubbed so much. His image in the fogged-over mirror above the washbasin was almost red. It was as if he had steamed himself like a goddamn lobster.

He paused to pee, wondering if he could cut her into pieces small enough to flush down the toilet. But he dismissed that idea. He would need tools for that, and he didn't know where to find them.

He flushed the toilet, then unhooked the shower curtain and folded it over his arm.

When he came out of the bathroom with the plastic shroud, the problem of Audrey's disposal had become moot because she was gone. Only a bloody outline and faint impression of her body remained on the mattress. The door to the suite stood open, and moist red footprints led across the carpet out into the hall, where they suddenly disappeared.

Harsh laughter broke out, radiating all around him, as if it were coming out of the walls. He felt as if he were being watched. He also felt very foolish, knowing he had been manipulated by a master in a game that was new to him.

He would soon learn the rules. No one trifled with him with impunity! Harold McHenry was more than a powerful man. He was an absolute force. He did not allow anyone or anything to get the best of him.

Chapter Sixteen

Wednesday, 22 November:
03:25

Shannon realized she had been asleep. Very briefly, though. Perhaps only a few seconds. Falling asleep without being aware of it happened often after midnight. Moments were sucked into oblivion, and then she awoke, alert once again, often gaining her second wind just before daylight. A moment's rest could restore her, but that time she didn't feel particularly refreshed. She was so strung out, she doubted she would ever feel totally restored.

There wasn't a time in recent memory when she had really felt like her old self, like the young woman who had found the rigors of training in service a challenge. Since Shannon was approaching thirty, no physical exertion was challenging; it was drudgery. Life and making a living had become a treadmill in an endless nightmare. The only reward for that kind of punishment was feeling sorry for herself, which was ultimately pointless.

The challenges of the night were making her question why she had gone on in her job at all. There had to be something else she could do with her life.

Her thoughts turned to what had just happened with Sam and Jerena and Randall. Were they playing jokes on her as a game for their party? Or did they expect her to believe they were really mutilated?

Shannon could think of no reason why she should believe them. She also had an uncomfortable feeling that maybe those horrific charades weren't as simple as a party game. There seemed to be true malice behind them—a nastiness that was designed to either really frighten her or make her surrender to some kind of general madness that seemed to have infected everyone but her. Those jokes were the work of a sick mind, and after thinking about it, she didn't believe Sam was that sick. He was just a nobody with no imagination. By himself he couldn't have dreamed up things such as those she had seen earlier. Someone had to be helping him. But who?

Maybe she had pissed someone off, and the pranks were his way of getting back at her. That lawyer who had wanted to get out of the garage earlier was sure pissed, and being a lawyer, he would be ruthless in exacting revenge. But he hadn't had time to plan the elaborate ruse. And he couldn't have known how she had disconnected the phone on him. His anger had been directed solely at Morrison Parking.

Anyone who had conjured up such a scheme to terrorize her had to be holding a grudge. It had to be somebody who was childish and mean.

Stan.

He was a creep, and she knew how he would like to get into her pants, and he knew she wasn't about to let him. He was just childish and petty enough to try to scare her so he could feel superior and laugh at her later. And he had the mean streak, too. She had seen him treat homeless people like trash, instead of just politely asking them to move along. If Stan was the perpetrator of the evening's entertainment, then he was sicker than she had ever imagined.

But how in the hell would a kid like Stan get Sam and the others to go along with the gag? Surely none of them held any grudge against her. And Randall had kept talking about a party.

Maybe Stan threw the party and provided dope and booze enough to convince even someone like Sam to participate. He would, of course, just lie about his true purpose in setting up his perverse party games. But where would Stan have raised the money for that kind of party?

Shannon was tired of thinking about the

strange events. There was nothing weird happening at the moment; no one had dared follow her down to her sanctuary, the security desk. Maybe when they had seen that their bullshit wasn't fazing her, they had given up.

She yawned. There were a few hours before daylight, and she had to face the prospect—actually the likelihood—that she would be stuck in the building far beyond the end of her shift. She might not get home for hours. But she had the radio to keep her company.

The radio wasn't on at the moment, even though Shannon did not remember turning it off. She looked down and saw the radio's dial glowing, but there was no sound. She fiddled with the volume control, then the tuner, but couldn't even raise static.

She sat back up and the light over her desk suddenly hurt her eyes. Something wasn't quite right. Everything in sight was etched in sharp outlines, as if her sight had become so acute reality was too much to absorb. Her perception of time was severely distorted. It seemed as if time was standing still.

To confirm her strange suspicion, Shannon stared at the digital clock on her console. Its glowing digits were frozen. The colon between the hours and minutes was not even pulsating as it normally did. She studied the clock for what had to be two or three minutes, waiting for the last two numbers to change. But they didn't change. Then she lifted her wrist and stared at her watch. It, too, was caught in a snag of timelessness.

Shannon became aware that it was very quiet in the lobby. There weren't even any hidden sounds, such as the noise the vent overhead made when the heat was running. There was no hum from any of the alarm instruments on her console. There was no buzz from the fluorescent lights in the mail room nearby.

She slid off her chair and sucked in a deep breath before walking slowly down the length of the lobby, not knowing what she expected to find. She stood at the large plate-glass window, listening. She could hear no wind howling. And the snow was hovering in midair!

After glancing at her watch again and seeing it still hadn't changed, Shannon decided to use one of the phones by the front entrance to call the time and weather line. Maybe if she could hear a human voice—even a recorded one—she could break out of the stasis somehow. But when she picked up a receiver, the phone was dead. She tried them all with the same result.

She strode back toward her console determined to find a way to break free of the weird stasis. But she halted a few feet away, because sitting in the chair was an exact replica of herself. A piece of electrical wire was wrapped around the throat of Shannon's double, and her eyes were bulging, her tongue protruding and swollen.

"We're coming for you, Shannon. We're coming." A chorus of voices echoed through the lobby, vibrating in her head.

"Shut up!" she shouted.

"We're coming to take you to the party, Shannon. But you have to be dead *first!"*

"Shut up, you goddamn shitheads!"

"We're dead. Wouldn't you like to be dead, too?"

"Shut up, or I'll—"

"You won't do shit!

That time a single voice spoke from the direction of the security desk. Her other self was staring straight at Shannon, her tongue back in place, smiling malevolently.

"Be dead like the rest of us. Just believe in us and you can be dead, too."

Shannon ran toward the desk, her hands outstretched. She leapt over the top and her other self vanished. Shannon toppled over the empty swivel chair, landing on the floor.

Suddenly, the digital clock clicked to the next minute. The radio came back on. Shannon sat up and moaned.

03:30

Thump, thump, thump. . . .

The revolving doors at the end of the lobby had started spinning on their own, gaining speed with each revolution. They were supposed to be locked.

Shannon jumped, then forced herself to be calm and rose from her seat. She walked carefully across the marble floor of the lobby, moving uneasily between the twin banks of elevators to investigate. As she passed the mirrored doors, she was suddenly spooked by her endlessly multiplied image, which seemed to walk along with her. She wanted to turn and run, to hide somewhere. But there was nowhere to hide. And it was her job to investigate. She couldn't let her apprehension keep her from her duty, even though she felt she had already done more than her duty for one night—much more.

She paused just beyond the elevators, listening. One set of doors had stopped temporarily. The other doors continued to spin. She strained to see. It hurt her eyes to try to focus on the doors themselves, because beyond them—outside—there was only snow and blackness, creating a stark contrast with the interior of the building.

As the howling wind assailed her senses in ragged counterpoint to the noise the doors made, she took another step forward. Her view shifted to the floor in front of the revolving doors.

The thumping sounded wet because something was caught in the doors, preventing them from moving smoothly.

Something that the doors continued to batter—a head. Shannon almost recognized.

Each slap of the doors mangled the disembodied head more, rendering the features on the face less familiar. Shannon was drawn closer, her morbid curiosity aroused, part of her still not convinced what she saw really was a head.

She jerked back as a spray of blood jetted from the revolving doors, splattering her. Suddenly the head was jolted loose and spun along the floor, tumbling over and over until it came to rest in front of one of the elevators. Its hideous image was multiplied in the mirrored surfaces of the elevator doors, reflecting an infinity of heads.

Shannon coughed and covered her mouth with her hand to hold back the churning bile burning her throat. She looked away from the head and focused on the revolving doors, daring them in her mind to do anything.

As if taking the dare, both sets of doors began spinning again, accelerating till they were virtually a blur. Each turn splattered Shannon with more and more of the bloody residue left by the head on the edge of the circular frame. She was showered in blood. She would have screamed, but she knew that was what they wanted. They wanted her to admit defeat, to let them take over her mind completely. They wanted her to believe they were real! But she was too tough.

She muttered a curse and turned away from the doors, clamping her hands over her ears to muffle the whirring sound the doors made as she started to return to her post at the security desk.

Nothing anybody could do would make her admit defeat. She was stronger than anybody!

Her resolve made her feel a little better. Then the head spoke to her.

"Shannon, help me!"

The voice had a whistle to it, but it was definitely Stan's. The messed-up face resembled Stan, too, she realized.

Bullshit! That was what everybody wanted her to think. And the fact the face on the head was Stan's just about proved he was responsible for the night's goings-on.

"Shannon, help me!" Stan's head said again.

She sneered at the head, then kicked it.

"Jesus! Why'd you do that, you crazy bitch?"

Shannon was hopping around on one foot, holding the other in her hand. It felt as if it was broken. Stan had always had a hard head.

"Cut the crap," she yelled, looking around her, as if she expected people to come out of hiding and mock her. "This is the most stupid joke of all. Give me a break!"

"Shannon, just help me find my body."

"Stop it! Stop it, goddamn it. I've had enough already. It's not funny anymore. Never was funny, you moron." She let go of her foot and eased it to the floor, flexing her toes. None of her bones seemed to be broken.

She stooped down and, placing her palms against the sides of Stan's head, lifted it from the floor and held it at arm's length in front of her.

"Pretty good fake," she said. "Only Stan's head is uglier."

"That's not nice, Shannon."

"I don't know how you're getting your voice to come out of this thing—"

She suddenly realized something gooey was oozing from the head and dripping down onto the floor. The skin on the face, though badly torn in places, was detailed with freckles and pores. The nose had hair in it. There was stubble on the chin. Someone had gone to a lot of trouble to make the head convincing. In fact, it was too damn convincing.

Without warning, Stan's head shifted in her hands. His tongue snaked out and lapped at her right wrist, leaving a smear of blood and spittle on her arm.

"I could do that between your legs, too."

The face leered exactly the way Stan had the day before when he pointed to the bad button on her half-open shirt. The shock of recognition chilled her. Whether it was possible or not, she was half convinced she was holding Stan's head.

She dropped it to the floor, pivoted on one foot, and ran toward the back door. She would get into Jack's truck, take it as far as she could, maybe to the police station. Anywhere. Just so long as she got the hell out of there.

After passing through the first door to the rear, she came to the metal door that led to the loading dock and pressed the release bar. But the door didn't give.

She slammed against it with the full weight of

her body, to no effect. A heavy frost had formed along the bottom edge. Wind whined against it outside. Even if she could get the door open, there might be a large drift outside that would be difficult to get through.

She pounded the door with her fists, leaving bloody marks on its shiny surface. She had to get out! They—Stan and whoever—had driven her crazy. Why else would she imagine a head talking to her? Why else did she believe there was blood all over her hands? If she stayed in the building, they would keep tormenting her till they got whatever it was they wanted from her. Maybe her body. Stan might do anything to get a piece of her.

But Shannon wasn't licked yet. There were other ways to get outside the building. She could go out the front, then around the building back to the dock to reach Jack's truck. She wouldn't have to be out very long, so she probably wouldn't freeze.

When she returned to the door to the lobby, Shannon peeked out. Stan's head was nowhere to be seen. She could go right out the revolving doors. She had seen them moving, so someone must have unlocked them. Sam could have unlocked the doors with his master key. They'd probably used Sam's key to get Stan's head in.

Her jacket was was on the floor behind the desk, where it had fallen when she'd knocked over the chair. Though Shannon had only a short walk to the back of the building, the night was too cold to go without it. She'd grab it, sprint down the lobby, exit through the revolving doors, and be on her way out of that madhouse.

She approached the desk cautiously, just in case something new had been rigged to frighten her. When she was right beside the desk, she jumped around to the back, fully expecting Stan's head to be sitting in the chair, waiting. Fortunately, the chair was vacant.

Shannon picked up her jacket and pulled it on. Before she zipped it up, she took Jack's gun from her waist. She should have remembered it sooner. No one would stop her with a loaded gun in her hand. She closed her jacket and held the gun loosely at her side, as she walked briskly toward the doors, keeping her eyes straight ahead.

She was going to make it. Only a few more feet to go.

"Peek-a-boo!"

Stan's head dropped from above, landing on the floor in front of her, with a sticky splat that rained more bloody goo on her shoes.

Shannon didn't pause to guess where it had come from. She jumped over the head and dashed into the first set of revolving doors on her right.

She should have known the doors wouldn't move. They were also frozen solid, glued in place by the gore from Stan's head. She moved to the other set of doors and they were locked up as well.

Ignoring the lewd suggestions from Stan's head, Shannon tried the side doors, which were supposed to open if a person pushed the bar. But snow was packed up against them as hard as concrete.

"Can't get out, can you, Shannon?"

She spun around to confront Stan's head and aimed the gun at it. "How'd you like a slug between the eyes?"

"Like that would hurt me now!" The head laughed.

Shannon pulled the trigger and a small chip of the marble floor inches from the head flew away. The sound of the shot was amplified so much in the vast area of the lobby that it nearly deafened her.

"You're a lousy shot, Shannon. Give it up."

She adjusted her aim and fired again, this time cutting a small furrow across the left side of Stan's head, almost turning it completely around. Her ears rang from the second shot's echo.

"Christ!"

"So it does hurt!" Grinning with glee, Shannon took aim again, then halted. She had only three rounds left and there was no way to get any more ammunition. She was wasting bullets on the stupid head!

There was a much better use for what she had left. All she had to do was shoot one of the plate-glass windows out. The idea was so simple she had overlooked it.

She turned around, pointed the gun at the nearest window, shielded her eyes, and fired twice. She heard the echo again—her ear drums were aching from it—but no glass shattered. She uncovered her eyes and saw the two slugs had done no damage to the glass at all. They seemed to have melted and slid down the glass like water.

She was stunned. She started for the glass to take a closer look, but was distracted by a new nuisance. Stan's head had somehow made its way over to her feet and was nibbling at the hem of her slacks.

"Goddamn you to hell!"

"I'm already there, sweetheart!"

She was too rattled to think about anything except escaping the monstrosity. She decided to save her last bullet instead of using it on the head. She kicked Stan's head away from her and raced for the nearest elevator.

She jammed the up button, the door slid open, and she stepped in with no idea where she would get off.

Chapter Seventeen

Wednesday, 22 November:
03:00

Dead Ted lurked everywhere.

03:40

The last hour or so had been one of great activity for Dead Ted, and he was growing stronger with each passing minute. The more he excercised his power, the more power he seemed to have. His brain power grew exponentially as well, not only in the area of controlling his newly acquired minions, but also in the area of imagination.

He was proud of how clever he was. When there were almost no limits to what a person (he still had to think of himself with that term) could do, it fed the imagination.

Everything was subject to his commands, his little whims, his twisted sense of humor. So he was finding things to laugh about in everything he made contact with, physically or mentally.

He had never had such fun when he was alive. One of the biggest kicks of the evening so far had been the look on that banker's face when he had come out of the bathroom and seen the woman he had killed was gone. When the banker had realized she had walked away, Dead Ted was unable to conceal his mirth. Making that woman's body walk out of the room was a brilliant idea.

It had been great fun watching the banker and his woman go at it the first time, but with Dead Ted's help, their second round of sex had been truly unforgettable.

The power of suggestion was amazing. Dead Ted had only suggested to McHenry's subconscious mind that he might become a demon. He hadn't actually changed the banker. At least, he didn't think he had. McHenry wasn't dead, so his transformation didn't jibe with other things that had happened that evening.

But maybe people could do things like that if the circumstances were right. Before Dead Ted had been ressurected, it had never occurred to him that there were so many things a dead person could do. He was discovering live people could do strange things as well—under his influence.

Or maybe it wasn't entirely because of him. He knew the dead didn't rise, but he had; and the living didn't turn into demons, but the banker had done so. Maybe the whole world was screwed up tonight, and anything could happen to anyone. Maybe all the laws of the universe had suddenly changed and alive and dead didn't mean much anymore.

As far as Dead Ted was concerned, it really didn't matter so long as he had fun. Not everything had to be explained. When he was alive, Dead Ted hadn't had to know how whiskey was made to drink it. In any case, his power extended further than he could guess—and he was just realizing the extent fo which he could play around with living people.

He'd made the security guard woman go off pretty bad, by making her dream she was dead. That had set her up for being chased by that guy's head. And he could probably do more if he put expended some effort and his fun didn't become too much like work.

He had piled up quite a few dead bodies, leaving them in various places throughout the building. Playing with the dead people was great sport, but he had to leave some people alive, because scaring them was the best sport of all. There was no reason to kill everybody—not until he was ready to anyhow.

Besides, he should let some of the dead kill the living. Why should he do all the work? In fact, since he had a sufficient number of them, he would just let them run wild. And he would watch.

Or maybe, he would go off and do some mischief on his own.

A quick scan of the building showed him where everybody was. Some of the dead were dormant, awaiting his next command. Others thought they were going to a party somewhere. He touched each one, releasing him or her from his control. Then he told his victims to do whatever they wanted.

He'd keep a special eye on the banker—to see if he acted differently as a result of the release. Thinking about the banker made Dead Ted recall the session the old guy had had with that skinny woman and caused something to stir within him that had been dormant for some time during his life.

He felt horny. He immediately thought of who could help him with his condition, and of course, he knew where to find her. He could hardly wait.

03:41

Sam Campbell believed he was at a party. Then the party had just disappeared from his mind, and he found that he was actually alone on a dark floor of the building.

He experienced a fleeting sensation of wanting to do something really bad—such as kill somebody. But there was no one around to kill.

A cool breeze came from somewhere, and it seemed to be going through Sam's head. He touched his forehead and discovered a large bloody hole. He probed the hole with his fingers, not knowing what he expected to find. Extracting his fingers, he saw they were covered with blood. He stared at the mess on his hand a moment, then wiped it on his shirt.

He could not remember how the hole was made in his head, and his inability to do so frustrated him. He didn't like not being in total control of his mental faculties. A hole in the head was likely to disrupt them, though, so maybe his condition was not unusual. But he might be bleeding to death!

Frightened by that prospect, Sam started searching the floor for someone to help him.

03:41

Randall was sitting in the dark, watching the snow from a window on the ninth floor. He was glad he was not outside. A man would freeze in that kind of weather. It was good to be inside and safe, but he also had a job to do. He was supposed to be on the service elevator taking the cleaning people from one floor to another, and he was supposed to be collecting the trash to take out later. Why wasn't he working?

Then he remembered. It was because of that party he'd been hearing about. Where the hell was it?

He concentrated and conjured up a fuzzy recollection of Shannon, that fine fox of a woman who was the security guard, coming to the party. But when she'd showed up, she'd pulled a gun on him and his boss. Why would she want to shoot them?

Things were screwed up. Shannon was good people; she didn't go around pointing guns at her friends. He hadn't even known she had a gun. Where did she go? And where was Sam? Did they go to the party without him?

Randall started to get up, but an uncomfortable feeling in his abdomen made him sit back down. In the light reflected from the window he could see his guts were hanging out.

"Damn!"

He must have been in one hell of a fight. Maybe one of the dudes whose old ladies he'd been screwing had caught up with him.

03:41

Richard Bowes, a smoldering lump of baked flesh, had been pursuing a woman in the lounge on the twenty-eight floor. He was determined to catch her and set her on fire, because he was convinced she was responsible for his present condition.

All of a sudden, that conviction had left him, and he'd stopped in his tracks, while the woman, screaming, exited via the door to the stairwell.

Bowes examined his burned body and started

to cry. He had been such a handsome man before, and now he was doomed to be a freak. He had suffered emotional and physical trauma and possibly would suffer loss of income as well. In short, he had all the makings of a strong lawsuit against somebody.

Bowes collapsed on the floor and bemoaned his fate.

03:41

Otis the elevator repair man felt very tired and weak. Maybe it was because he had a giant hole in his chest and was impaled on a spring in the bottom of an elevator shaft.

That should cause considerable pain, but he didn't even seem to be hurt. His most pressing problem was figuring out how to get off the spring.

All he could do was twitch and squirm like a mouse caught in a trap. He opened his mouth to yell for help, but no sound came out. His throat was clogged with bile and blood.

03:41

Standing before a mirror in the rest room on the twentieth floor, Cassandra Peters brushed her hair and paid no attention to the gaping wound in her chest. She had to fix her hair and makeup; then she planned to return to work. Somehow she had become distracted from finishing the report for the big boys from Chicago, who would be in that morning.

She didn't want to get in trouble with her supervisor, a fat ugly hairy woman who she thought was a dyke.

03:41

Stan Cork's head was leaning against a marble wall in the main lobby. Inside that head, the brain still worked after a fashion, and his mind was preoccupied with getting his body back.

He needed it desperately if he were to carry out his original intentions for Shannon.

Since she had shot at him, he was even more determined to prove himself to her by forcing her to acknowledge his manhood. She needed some good, old-fashioned sex to tame her down and make her appreciate him.

03:41

Faceless Jack Landers, sitting on a bench in the basement, sensed he was alone. The others who had been with him had gone off, not bothering to offer him any assistance.

It was damned hard to navigate without a face. How did they expect him to get anything done? How could he drive home?

Sue must be worried sick.

03:41

As soon as Dead Ted's hold was released, Jerena Reynolds fell on her ass. She just sat there staring.

03:44

Audrey Masters came back into general awareness while sitting on the edge of a table in a lounge somewhere. Her eyes, at first clouded by a haze of transient pain, cleared slowly and allowed her to focus on her surroundings. She didn't recognize the lounge, though she was certain it was somewhere in the bank tower. If she had been outside, she would be half frozen.

How had she gotten here? On the elevator, she supposed. All she could remember at that instant was a voice telling her to get up and leave as soon as possible before she became food for the toilet.

Her brain felt numb. She tried to remember more—such as what had happened before she was told to leave. Only confusing, impossible images came to her in snippets like pieces of a torn-up photograph that were familiar but unidentifiable. She craved a cigarette badly.

She closed her eyes as a wave of nausea rasped through her body. It felt as if something was grating her flesh from inside. The feeling passed quickly, and the need for a smoke returned.

It was pleasant with her eyes closed, though. She felt somehow more secure that way. She let herself ride with the calmness, let her mind drift, hoping she would land someplace where things would be explained.

McHenry.

She had gone up to the banker's suite. She was going to stay only a little while, but it became fairly evident he expected to have sex with her. She realized she had provided tacit assent by going with him at all. Powerful men like McHenry had no understanding of the word no.

Well, she had been feeling a little deprived lately. So, even if McHenry wasn't the best in the world, he could scratch her itch.

Abruptly, vivid red jolted into her closed vision, blotting out the details. She winced. Something awful had happened. McHenry had been swearing at her. Then she remembered blood flying everywhere—*her* blood.

She concentrated hard on making the blood color go away until a different scene replayed itself. Back to his suite—when she urged him on by pulling her panties down. That was a rather whorish thing to do. But such a display didn't make much difference with a man like him. He probably didn't even appreciate the subtle approach. He certainly would not tolerate any coy, schoolgirl routine. When he wanted sex, he got it.

Her vision was shaded in crimson again. Then her memory was restored, and she wasn't spared one detail of McHenry's savage assault with his possessed penis. Her eyelids peeled back over eyeballs, which were aflame with the terror in the fragmented scenes she had replayed in her mind.

She realized she was still naked, and there was a big hole in her torso. Her skin was as crisp as bacon in places. There were bruises everywhere.

How had McHenry done it? With some exotic dildo acquired in a seedy adult bookstore and a Halloween mask? But if that had really happened, she should be dead.

You got it, baby!

She jerked her head in every direction, looking for the source of the voice. She trembled as she recognized the voice as the one she had heard earlier. She knew exactly where it was—inside her head.

She needed a smoke *really badly.*

03:47

It had been a long time since Dead Ted had availed himself of a piece of colored ass. He had never been a prejudiced man, favoring women of any color, parentage, or religious persuasion with equal lust in the days when he was able to feel such passions. He hadn't been with a woman of any color since his time in 'Nam, when he had paid ten dollars and some candy for a wild session with an Oriental whore.

Wait a minute, Dead Ted. You never went to no 'Nam. You missed that by about five years.

Dead Ted chided himself for his foolishness. One of the perils of shooting the shit was that he sometimes started believing his own bullshit yourself. Being dead made it more difficult to separate the truth from the lie, especially when the difference between unreality and reality had no meaning anymore—if it ever had.

But he knew for certain that he had not had his ashes hauled in ages by any woman. He hadn't been sober enough in the last few months to worry too seriously about having a woman. It was a big enough hassle to get money for booze and food without worrying about the fleeting pleasures of dipping his wick.

He knew some of his old buddies would sometimes scrape up a few bucks and go down the alley with one of the crazy women who lived in the street. Willie had told Dead Ted once that there were a couple of crazy women over on Illinois Street who would actually have sex for a dollar! Bargains could still be had, even in that day and age.

But Dead Ted, whether he was horny or not, had vowed to stay away from such women. A woman with standards that low had to have a killer dose of something. Although Dead Ted's personal standards had been low while he was living, and although he probably already had

had a dozen diseases from living in the streets with the rats and stray dogs, he couldn't bear the thought of contracting VD or the big AIDS.

But things were different. Since he'd died, there was nothing whatsoever to fear, and he could recognize all the horniness he had stored up and do something about it. For some reason, he felt the only way to assuage his condition was to get it on with a black woman. And Jerena, that sexy thing he had killed perhaps too violently, appealed to him.

Jerena was still on the tenth floor of the building. She was, Dead Ted realized and mentally shook his head, so stupid she could not find her way off the floor without his guidance. Maybe he'd show her the way out after he finished with her. Otherwise, she would probably sit on her ass forever.

He wondered if he could repeat the tricks he had pulled on that banker guy's head. Jerena might appreciate it more than Audrey had.

03:49

After getting dressed, McHenry had searched the entire thirtieth floor for Audrey's body without even turning up a clue as to what had happened to her.

Whoever had laughed at him had made sure he would not find Audrey. He could not imagine who had guts enough to taunt him. But the laughter had not seemed like that of a normal person, and it had sounded as if it had been coming from everywhere at once.

That was a good trick. His tormentor was a clever adversary. Tracking him down would be a challenge. But McHenry had to do it. He had to confront his new enemy and make him reveal where the body was. It wasn't something he could let slide.

There was not much of the night left, and even though the blizzard would keep a lot of people home, there were always some who managed to get to the building no matter what the weather was. If Audrey had been taken somewhere to be easily discovered, there was no doubt in McHenry's mind that his enemy had fixed it so that McHenry would be blamed for Audrey's death.

Maybe one of his competitors was responsible. The president of the bank across the street was a cousin of his who was jealous of his success and would love to see McHenry toppled. He probably had spies planted on McHenry's staff who were waiting for just such an opportunity to discredit him.

Or maybe there was something supernatural involved. McHenry knew little about such things, of course. He believed, in a grudging way, that there had to be things beyond the norm, and his experiences that night pointed to powers beyond the usual human ability. He had become a supernatural being himself, if he had not deluded himself somehow.

There could be rational explanations, however. His nemesis might have managed to put a hallucinogen in his drinks or food. McHenry himself was capable of orchestrating such nasty tricks, so it would not surprise him if his cousin or another powerful foe had decided to put one over on him—maybe to screw up the deal he had pending with that Ohio bank.

That idea made some sense. Business was business. All was fair in business and anyone could be a target. If that turned out to be the case, McHenry could play the game as well as anyone. Once he found out who was responsible, he'd show him how miserable his life could be.

It was even conceivable Audrey wasn't dead. She could have been offered a high-paying job, or a lot of money under the table, to double-cross McHenry and contrive to make him attack her. She might even have drugged him. She might even be hiding out somewhere.

That solution, McHenry realized, was only wishful thinking. Audrey might have been in on the plot, but she could not have foreseen that her involvement would come to such a violent conclusion. And viewing the bloody mess on the sofa bed, McHenry was very dubious about her survival. The blood was very real. He was clearheaded enough to determine that much.

He didn't have time to do a thorough clean-up job, so he wadded the stained sheets into a trash bag and folded the bed back into the sofa. There were a few dots of dried blood on the right arm of the sofa, but he doubted they would be noticed. He would find a way to remove or cover them up later. He locked the trash bag in a closet, then left his suite, locking the door behind him.

He had formulated a plan. He would search the remaining floors of the building, not for Audrey, but for his nemesis. He would destroy him before he caused more mischief in Harold McHenry's life.

03:52

Dead Ted was on the seventeenth floor when he recognized his acute horniness. He summoned an elevator and rode it down to the tenth floor.

Jerena was off to his left when he arrived. She was just sitting on the floor and staring off into the void that mirrored the state of her mind. Her expression didn't even change when Dead Ted went up to her. She didn't seem to notice him at all. He leaned down and waved his hand in front of her face. Jerena just stared.

"Hey, woman!" Though he was unable to speak, he could project his words into people's heads and make them think he was talking. He squatted down to face the staring woman. "Anybody home in there?"

Since he was so close, Dead Ted noticed Jerena's head was on crooked. Even though the lid to the ice machine had sliced it off rather neatly, the head and neck were not properly aligned. He blamed himself for the sad condition; he never should have let her put it back on herself. She just wasn't smart enough.

Well, he wasn't going to have sex with a woman whose head was not on straight. So he reached out, grabbed her by the ears, and jerked her head around till everything matched up perfectly. He thought he even heard a click when the two pieces came together.

Jerena blinked. Her tongue came out and licked her lips. "Can you help me with my hand?" Her voice was a monotone, yet it somehow retained the musical quality that made men melt.

Dead Ted would have smiled if he could control his borrowed face. Her inane innocence was almost touching. But he was horny, and his encounter with Jerena was probably the last opportunity he'd have to get relief.

He saw her right hand lying on the floor between her legs; she had not been able to put it back on at all. So he picked it up and twisted it onto the end of her wrist. He leaned back to study the effect. Though the seams on her neck and wrist continued to ooze blood, she looked fairly whole.

And she was still a choice piece of ass. He could barely restrain himself from ripping off her blood-soaked sweatshirt and diving between her oversize, outrageously firm breasts.

But he was not one to rush things too much. He stood erect and took her left hand in his. "C'mon, woman," he said. "It's time to get up."

She cast a look at him, her large brown eyes seeming to be both questioning and pleading.

"Who're you?" She allowed him to help her to her feet. Standing, she was about six inches shorter than he was.

"Ted's the name," he said, letting go of her hand and bowing slightly.

She cocked her head. "What'sa matter with your face?"

He had forgotten about his frightening visage and how it might not be too appealing. She didn't seem to be afraid, though, just inquisitive.

"I had a little accident," he said. "There's nothing wrong with the rest of me."

"What's going on round here? How come I so cold? How come you feel so cold?"

The poor woman did not understand she was basically—mostly, at least—dead, just as he was. He didn't think he could explain that to her and he didn't want to.

"We both had an accident," he said, hoping his simplified explanation satisfy her. "But now we can go have some fun. You know what I mean?"

Jerena was pretty certain what most men meant by fun, and she would have thought about it if she could have. But the words in her head were just beeping in and out and didn't make much sense. She didn't remember ever having a white guy; she didn't remember one ever coming on to her. But then, she didn't remember much of anything except that she had been feeling pain really bad for a while. Then it had stopped, and she was still in that big old building and didn't know how to get out.

She couldn't think of anything else to do with herself, however, and since this guy had been nice enough to fix her head and her hand for her, she guessed letting him slam her wouldn't be too bad a deal.

"Okay," she said at last.

Dead Ted said nothing further. He was glad she was cooperating. He could have taken control of her and made her do what he wanted, but he liked it better that way. He led Jerena over to the floor in front of a receptionist's desk, where the carpet was thick and soft. It would be comfortable enough.

She stepped out of her shoes on her own. Since his arms were more agile than hers, he decided to undress her the rest of the way. He pulled the sweatshirt off, its Chicago Bulls logo almost blotted out by blood, and let it drop on the floor. As her shining ebony breasts came into view, flopping with a resiliency he had to admire, the crotch of his raggedy pants immediately became tighter.

But there were more goodies. He unzipped her tight jeans and awkwardly peeled them down, revealing expanses of thigh and ass that would have made him catch his breath if he were still breathing. As it was, his main response was continued growth in the groin area. Finally, there were beige panties. The waistband of these was tattered, but they were clean enough. And he surely enjoyed pulling them down around her ankles.

The rest of Jerena might be cold, but her groin retained quite a bit of warmth. It was surprisingly hot and wet. Maybe the woman wanted Dead Ted as much as he wanted her. She didn't say anything. She moved a little, then moved some more, and soon she was riding his finger, emitting tiny sounds like a baby cooing.

Dead Ted disengaged his finger. Without being asked, Jerena lay down on the carpet, and waited while he took off his clothes. When he dropped his shorts, even he was surprised by the size to which he had grown.

It had been so long since he'd had any kind of sex, he was awkward at first. But once he was inside, she started bucking so fast and so hard he thought she was going to break his peter off!

As it was, her enthusiastic agitations made his face fall off. It dropped right between her heaving breasts with a sound like a wet towel hitting cement.

The unfortunate incident almost spoiled the moment. Jerena's eyes widened at the sight of his naked head, and Dead Ted thought she was going to stop altogether. He could hardly blame her. The face he had borrowed was an old one in the first place and not very handsome, but it had to be more pleasant than the gory, wormy mass left in its place.

Fortunately, it took him only a few seconds of fumbling to rescue his face from her cleavage and set it back in place. Then Jerena calmed down, and he was able to continue screwing her without losing his rhythm.

After a few more minutes of blissful grinding, Dead Ted felt himself tense, and he exploded inside her. He kept pumping and pumping until it seemed as if he was going to empty his insides into hers. He couldn't seem to stop.

Jerena had already climaxed about six times. Her expression was a combination of awe and alarm. She never had any man who could keep on going so long after he had come. But that man was something else. Ugly as sin, but definitely one dude who knew how to satisfy a gal.

Dead Ted kept on. His semen was already flowing out of Jerena, forming a pool beneath her. A few seconds later, it was coming out of the sides of her mouth. Then it spurted out of her nose and ears. Suddenly, Dead Ted feared he was going to kill Jerena if he didn't stop screwing her, and he sent her a mental message to stop her sexual ministrations.

Both of them were so wrapped up in their sexual free-for-all that neither had noticed a whirring noise approaching them. It was Jerena's vacuum cleaner, which had somehow escaped from the rest room. It shot across the floor, edged between Jerena's outspread legs and began to suck hungrily at Dead Ted's groin.

Dead Ted didn't feel much pain, but he could tell when a piece of him was being separated from his body. For her part, Jerena cleared her mouth to yell at the vacuum to stop. The vacuum, however, didn't recognize her as its master and continued to buzz Dead Ted, apparently intent on total emasculation.

Dead Ted realized that, when he had given up control of all the dead under his command, he had freed the building as well. Since Dead Ted had animated the building, bringing its various systems to independent life, he found a strange logic—according to the new unreality rules of that night—in the fact that mechanical things might go beserk.

Dead Ted had never considered that loosing his hold on the dead and the building that meant he would be attacked, and he became enraged at the very thought of the things once under his control turning on him. In the same moment, he discovered a new power. When he directed his anger at the vacuum cleaner, he not only made it back off, he made the damn thing explode. Vacuum cleaner shrapnel, peppered with the debris in the vacuum's bag, rained down on Jerena and him.

Dead Ted sat next to Jerena and the two of them picked pieces of metal out of their flesh. Extracting them left minor wounds that seeped tiny amounts of blood. There were no deep gashes to worry about. One piece of metal even proved to be useful. A three-inch shard had pierced the top of Dead Ted's secondhand face, nailing it to the bone beneath, so he left the fragment in place. He didn't want his face to fall off again at an inopportune moment. It would be an embarrassment.

Ready to move on, Dead Ted got up and put his clothes back on. He took a couple of minutes to help Jerena get dressed, since she still lacked complete motor control of her hands. Then, ever the gentleman, he bid her adieu with an unvoiced thought and left her standing there, her eyes staring straight ahead again.

Jerena's inactivity disturbed Dead Ted, making him worry about what the rest of the dead were doing. A scan of the building revealed most of them were so far not engaged in anything very imaginative. Without his guidance, they were fumbling around, committing only petty mayhem or feeling sorry for themselves or doing nothing at all, like Jerena.

Dead Ted was disgusted with his minions. He ought to make them all explode, except that extreme action would spoil the potential for more fun. It would be better to give them something to keep them occupied.

Suddenly inspired, Dead Ted devised a game for his continued amusement. The name of the game was Get The Security Guard—or, for that matter, anyone else who was still alive! Chuckling, Dead Ted ambled over to the elevator, pondering how he would cast the first die in that new diversion.

Chapter Eighteen

Wednesday, 22 November:
04:03

Shannon got off on the eighth floor, having remembered the seventh had the blood-spouting drinking fountain, which she wanted to avoid any further contact with. With dismay, she realized she had four hours to go on her shift. That was a very long time if the rest of the night went as the first part had. But it would be daylight before the end. If she could hold on to her sanity until the sun came out—assuming it did while the snow continued—she should be able to make it through the rest of the morning.

Shannon had not given up, however. She was shaken and unsure of herself, but she wasn't just going to sit on her ass those remaining hours and let things happen to her. She was by nature a fighter, and she would make life miserable for the tricksters who had chosen her as the butt of their jokes.

The whole horrible night would have been funny to her, too, if she weren't so strung out from lack of sleep. Maybe she would get into the spirit of it herself. But she had no access to stage props or fake blood, and she didn't think herself clever enough to rig anything up that would be even remotely convincing—not after what she had seen. It would take more expertise than she had to create something like Stan's head.

Shannon followed the hall, which encircled four elevators in a common lobby. Individual office suites occupied the eighth floor. She had jiggled the door knobs during her rounds, but she did so again as she went around, hoping to perhaps surprise someone before the next ghastly gag. After having checked all the doors, she returned to a small office close to the elevators and used her master key to gain access.

"Security!"

She waited a few seconds. Since there was no response, she assumed the place was empty. She locked the door behind her and stepped over to a desk. She picked up the phone on the desk, but it was dead. She checked the wires and saw they were intact. She went through a door into the main office area and tried every phone in there; every one of them was useless. The phones for the whole building were probably out because of the blizzard.

Other systems could go down, too—the electricity, the plumbing. If the heat went off, the building could grow cold quickly. It was a hell of a night for someone to be playing games.

She left the office and stood out in the hall. Since the phones were not working, her next plan was to locate someone who was not in on the game. She remembered there were several people listed on the after-hours sign-in sheet—about a dozen altogether. Some might have slipped out earlier without signing out, but some of them still had to be there. One of those people should be willing to help her. But she couldn't remember any specific names or floors they were on, and she wasn't going back down to refresh her memory. There should also be some Clean Corps employees who were not participating in the general madness.

Shannon realized she hadn't encountered anyone who was acting even halfway normal for hours—except that lawyer dude. He was probably still upstairs. She knew he would have had no luck getting anyone from Morrison to help him out, and she had not seen him come by her desk, which he would have had to do in order to get to his car.

The lawyer was an asshole, but that made it unlikely he'd participate in the so-called party. Maybe he would listen to her. If she left out the really crazy parts about the night's events, he might offer to help. He also might think she was some kind of maniac, the way her uniform was covered with blood. But she could think of no one else to turn to, and a dude like him probably had a car phone, which wouldn't be affected by the storm. They could call the police and get out. Why hadn't she thought about the lawyer before?

He'd be up on the twenty-ninth floor, maybe hanging out in the fancy lounge watching television. There was food and drink up there, too. Even if the lawyer wasn't around, the twenty-ninth floor would be a good place to hide out for a while.

Feeling somewhat more hopeful, Shannon called an elevator and went up in search of the lawyer.

04:14

When Shannon reached the twenty-ninth floor, she was nearly overwhelmed by the acrid odor of smoke in the air. It was so strong it should have set off the smoke alarms, which would have sent a signal down to her desk. Since no such signal had been sent, Shannon feared that the alarm system was malfunctioning.

She went looking for the source of the smoke and found Richard Bowes's office, where the aroma of burned meat hung heavy in the air as well. There was a general haze throughout the small room, making it difficult to see anything. Shannon waved her arms to clear some of the smoke away and saw a scorched spot on the carpet. Leading away from the area were sooty footprints made by the soles of a man's shoes.

Shannon didn't like the way her discovery made her feel. It was one thing to pull pranks, but quite another to cause real physical harm, assuming the pranks and the possible injury to Bowes were related. She examined the area further and found a melted wad of plastic that had been the phone. And she then detected a gasoline smell.

"Christ on a crutch," she muttered softly. Backing out of the room quickly, she bumped into a person and let out an involuntary shriek.

"Ah, the security guard," a man's voice said. "What are you doing up here?"

Shannon spun around. Despite his rather disheveled appearance, she recognized McHenry easily. She had seen his Cadillac down in the basement parking garage, but had not thought about him. He hadn't signed in on the after-hours registry, and she had not seen him all night.

"I'm looking for somebody who's not crazy," Shannon said, eying him with open suspicion and barely suppressed hostility.

"I don't think I fall into the crazy category," he replied, trying to appear as calm as possible, though he was actually quite frustrated. He had had the chance to search only half the floor for Audrey's body, and he had not yet decided what to do about Shannon's presence. "Have you found someone who does?"

"Does what?"

"Fit into the crazy category."

"I haven't found anyone who doesn't, except you. But one of the lawyers came up here earlier, and from the looks of his office, I think there was a fire. Maybe he was hurt."

McHenry looked past her into the vacant room. "Richard Bowes works in there."

"Not now he doesn't."

"I smelled something, too, when I got here. I hope Bowes is all right," McHenry said without much conviction.

Shannon sensed McHenry was putting on an act. He should have been more upset about the possibility of one of his lawyers being hurt, but he was not showing any emotion. Maybe the fire in the lawyer's office was the setup for another trick.

"What are you doing down here?" she asked bluntly, showing him how little she was impressed by his position in life.

Her audacity threw McHenry off guard temporarily. But he was quick to recover. "The same as you. Looking for somebody to talk to. We're stuck in this building."

"Your friend Bowes found that out. The doors to the garage are frozen shut."

"That's what I mean. We're all stuck here, so I came down to see if anyone was around."

Shannon didn't buy his story, but she could not challenge him without any evidence.

For his part, McHenry knew he wasn't convincing, but he didn't care. Still, he realized she could cause a stink if she found Audrey before he did—which would leave him no choice but to kill her as well.

"You said you're looking for people who aren't crazy," McHenry said, hoping to distract Shannon. "Does that mean you've found some who are?"

"That's an understatement," Shannon said. "Mostly it's the cleaning people—but some others, too—pulling Halloween jokes on me."

"What do you mean?"

"Pretending they're hurt, making blood squirt out of weird places, sending a talking head down to the lobby." She hadn't meant to reveal that last detail, but it didn't seem to upset McHenry. He accepted her examples so complacently she began to suspect he might be one of the pranksters, too.

"I don't know what to make of it," McHenry said honestly. "Why would they do those things?"

"If I knew that, I'd know what to do, I think. I guess they're bored or they think it's funny. But it stopped being funny a long time ago. That's why I need someone to help me find a way out."

"You don't intend to go wandering around in that blizzard, do you?"

"Do I look that stupid? One of the other guards—I think he got hurt for real—left his truck out on the loading dock. It has four-wheel drive. The keys are in it. The only problem is none of the exit gates will open."

McHenry's interest in what she was saying made Shannon become more wary.

"What did you plan to do with your gun?" he asked. "Guards aren't supposed to be armed in this building."

"I don't care if they are or not. I'm keeping this baby. I'll defend myself if I have to."

Unwittingly, Shannon had provided McHenry with a plan. If he could get the gun from her and kill her, all he would have to do was find Audrey, take her down to the truck, and dump her out in the storm somewhere. He could even dispose of Shannon while he was out.

He had to be careful before he acted. For all he knew, the woman was an expert shot who would put a bullet in his heart without hesitation. And Shannon had the look of desperation about her. Her clothes were stained with blood. She had scratches on her hands and face. She was not about to be toyed with, and it was clear she was not impressed by his status.

If McHenry could distract her, he might be able to get the gun away from her, then shoot her. "Let's get away from Bowes's office," he said coolly, being careful not to sound as if he was ordering her.

"Fine by me," she said.

The two of them went out to the reception area near the elevators. Once they were removed from the main source of the stink, McHenry noted that Shannon's aroma, though mixed with the smell of sweat and blood, was not unpleasant. She was also young, pretty, and voluptuous under the coating of dirt and muck she had accumulated. He wished he had not wasted his time on a dried-up old bag like Audrey when a prize like Shannon had been near. It was really too bad he was going to have to kill the desirable woman.

Maybe he could get his hormones worked up again. Seeing Shannon naked would certainly be more arousing than the sight of Audrey's barely female body. Of course, he would probably have to force sex on Shannon, but if he had the gun, he would have no problem.

"Now what?" Shannon said.

"Shall we search this floor more thoroughly or go down to the next one?"

"I don't know. Bowes must have run when—or if—he caught fire. Where would he run to?"

"To a bathroom?"

"I don't know. I don't have any fucking idea."

McHenry smiled. He liked women who swore. He had always wished his wife used more profanity.

"What's so funny?"

"Nothing."

"Well, are we going to sit here all night?"

"You like action, I gather." His eyebrows rose, and his eyes showed his increasing lust for Shannon.

The son of a bitch was coming on to her!

Shannon was disgusted. She needed help and the old bastard was thinking about getting into her pants. He didn't know her very well or he would have backed off pronto. She would put a bullet in him before she'd surrender to his advances. She was about to tell him that when he suddenly put out his right hand and tried to snatch the gun from her waistband.

"No way," she said, raking his hand with her nails.

"You little bitch!" He raised his hand to strike her, and for a second, his eyes glowed an unearthly mixture of green, red, and orange. The strange sight startled Shannon so much she hesitated before drawing the gun on him.

In that instant of hesitation, McHenry's hand started to descend, and she didn't see how she could avoid being hit before she used her last round of ammo on him.

But his hand never came down. Without warning, someone had come up from behind and smashed the back of McHenry's head in.

Shannon saw McHenry's eyes turn back to their normal color before they rolled back into his head. Blood shot from his nose and mouth, spraying her with a fresh coat. She also heard his skull shattering and saw brain matter flying out the back of his head as he dropped to the floor.

"What a mess!" Cassandra Peters said. She seemed to be genuinely dismayed by the brain-and-blood mess that had exploded backward after she'd bludgeoned McHenry. Cassandra still held the instrument that she had used to inflict the damage—a marble statue of a unicorn that was about ten inches high.

Shannon looked down at McHenry, expecting him to sit up and try to scare her. His killing could be another elaborate joke. But his chest was not moving, and the pool of blood beneath his head was growing rapidly.

Tightening her grip on the gun butt, Shannon glanced up at Cassandra. "You killed him."

"I certainly hope so," Cassandra said.

Shannon noticed that the bloody hole in the other woman's chest was caked with dried blood. There would be no point in faking that. There was no point in faking any of it. Yet it couldn't all be real. People could not walk around with big holes in their chests where their hearts should have been.

But Cassandra was apparently doing that, though that feat did not explain why she had killed McHenry so casually, as if it were something she did every day. Shannon was grateful that the woman had saved her, but Cassandra's lack of emotion over killing a man was perhaps the most disturbing thing Shannon had witnessed that night. Maybe Cassandra's mind had snapped during the course of the night's lurid activities. Maybe she was already unbalanced, and the gruesome games had put her over the edge, turning her into a homicidal maniac.

As if to confirm some of Shannon's speculations, Cassandra hefted the statue up over her head again, and said, "Stand still. I don't want to miss."

Shannon reacted without thinking, scooting out of reach behind the receptionist's desk. "Put that down!"

"I have to kill you. Don't you understand?" Cassandra came closer.

"No, I don't."

Cassandra hovered near the desk. The two of them went to and fro, trying to match each other's actions. Cassandra almost connected once, missing Shannon's head by half an inch.

Shannon yanked the revolver from her waist and pointed it at Cassandra's head. "Goddamn it, don't make me shoot you!"

"Go ahead. I don't care!" She swung at Shannon again.

Shannon fired her last bullet. It plunked into the middle of Cassandra's face, turning her nose inside out before it bored its way through the back of her head.

Cassandra blinked, rubbed blood from her eyes, and lunged at Shannon, throwing half her body over the desk in an all-out frenzied attack on Shannon's skull.

Shannon dropped the useless gun, then grabbed a sharp pencil and jammed it into Cassandra's neck. Blood squirted out, but Cassandra didn't even yell. Shannon stabbed her opponent in the hand with another pencil, making Cassandra drop the statue, which bounced on the rug and rolled out of reach.

Cassandra growled and set upon Shannon with her bare hands, trying to rip into her skin. Shannon doubled up her fist and smashed in Cassandra's mouth. Shannon's knuckles were cut up and the other woman's teeth were dislodged, but Cassandra kept pressing on Shannon, trying to find a place to dig in with her fingers. They rolled around on the top of the desk, Shannon underneath—being bruised by the various hard objects on the desk—Cassandra on top, clawing at her.

Shannon managed to get a good grip on one of Cassandra's wrists and jerked it back violently. The crunch of bones snapping told her she had broken it. But the injury did not slow Cassandra down. She continued to flail at Shannon with the other hand.

Shannon saw a pair of scissors off to her right. She stretched her hand out and clutched them in her fingers; then she thrust them deep into the base of Cassandra's throat, ignoring the rush of blood on her own face. She was getting used to it.

Cassandra tried to pull Shannon's hand away; Shannon responded by twisting the scissors back and forth and using them to saw around Cassandra's neck till her head was attached only by bone.

Shannon's attempt to decapitate her distracted

the redhead momentarily, as her head fell backward, and Shannon took the opportunity to get her legs up and kick Cassandra squarely in the stomach, throwing her to the floor. Then Shannon bounced off the desk and aimed a solid kick at Cassandra's head, which broke loose and rolled across the floor screaming.

Although Cassandra's head continued to scream, Shannon put the sound out of her mind. She sat on an overstuffed chair and panted.

Then, to Shannon's horror, Cassandra's headless body flipped over and started crawling toward her, the one broken hand flopping wildly as the body moved. Shannon sprang up and jumped on the body, stomping on the joints of the arms and legs, making them crack under her weight. The body kept twitching.

"Die, you motherfucker! Die!" Shannon spun into the air, then came down with all her weight on Cassandra's spine, splintering it in several places. At last, the body stopped moving forward.

Shannon jumped on the decapitated body until her feet were covered with gore. Finally, she stepped off. She turned her face and puked all over the chair. When she turned back, she saw the body still twitched, even if it couldn't move forward. At least, even if Cassandra wasn't dead, she wouldn't do any more damage. Shannon could get away from her.

Shannon wiped perspiration off her forehead

with the back of her hand, but she had more than sweat on her brow. Most of the moisture running down her face was blood.

"I must look like shit," she said.

"Have to kill, have to kill, have to kill," Cassandra's severed head mumbled.

"Why?" Shannon yelled. "For Christ's sake, why?"

Cassandra became silent.

"Now you shut up. Thanks a lot."

Shannon returned to the desk, took a big wad of tissues out of a dispenser, and wiped herself off as best she could. A couple of times she thought she would throw up again, but there was nothing left in her stomach. Another session like the one just finished, however, and she would get the dry heaves.

Shannon calmed down after a few moments, breathing normally and starting to think again. Two people had just died for real. And she herself had been forced to kill. Maybe the party had taken a twisted turn and the game had become a blood sport. If so, whoever was in charge had a hell of a hold on the players. How else could she account for a rather drab woman like the redhead becoming so intent on killing?

It could be one of those cult things she'd read about in the tabloids and seen on *Oprah.* There were a lot of those nut cases around, killing people for Satan or whatever they believed in. Cassandra had become one of them and had gone totally out of her mind—which was why she was so hard to kill. How many more like Cassandra were in the building?

Shannon would have to be alert constantly for the remainder of her shift. If she failed to remain vigilant for even a second, she might bite the big one herself.

She bent down and picked up the empty gun, figuring it had some intimidation value. She deliberately kept Cassandra's head and body out of her sight as she went over and checked McHenry's pulse.

The son of a bitch was still warm. But his heart wasn't pumping, and his eyeballs were already starting to dry out.

Shannon could do nothing for him or the woman. She could only move on. She walked across the lobby to the other side of the lawyer's quarters, where a staircase went down to the next floor. She descended slowly, trying not to make a sound.

Shannon's hatred for Sam—or whoever was controlling the general madness—was growing by leaps and bounds. She was a fighter, but she liked to pick her fights. Her hatred was further fed by having been forced to kill someone. Even though killing Cassandra was necessary, the gruesome act would be a terrible memory Shannon would have to live with forever.

That woman was a real person only a couple of hours earlier—probably a mother with children. But Shannon had killed her because Cassandra had been turned into a monster. Somebody had to pay for the horror, and Shannon vowed to collect on the debt that night.

04:28

McHenry's eyes shifted uneasily. He felt his brains oozing out the back of his head, yet there was no pain. He sat up slowly and realized he wasn't breathing! His flesh was growing cold.

"What the hell?"

A voice whispered inside his head. *"Get up, you son of a bitch, or are you as worthless dead as you were alive?"*

Chapter Nineteen

Wednesday, 22 November:
04:29

At the bottom of the wooden staircase, Shannon came upon a new trail of sooty footprints leading past the elevators on the twenty-eighth floor out into the hall beyond. At first she assumed they belonged to the presumably incinerated attorney Bowes, but it occurred to her they could also belong to whoever had set him on fire.

She didn't know where they would lead her, but she had to follow the footprints. She would also be very careful; she didn't want to encounter another murderously insane person like the redhead, especially since her gun was no longer loaded.

If she was to make it through the night, she would have to do something about weapons. She had been lucky in defending herself against the woman, but she couldn't count on there always being something handy. She racked her brain over where she might find some kind of weapons or something that could be used as a weapon, but nothing was coming to her.

It was pretty damn shortsighted of Jones Malone Security not to allow their guards to be armed. In this screwed-up world, guards should be armed everywhere. In fact, everybody ought to be armed. But guards were not allowed weapons at high profile posts, where the presence of a sidearm might upset tenants or clients. Some people were so gun-shy they didn't want to be around guns even if the weapons might be used to save their own lives.

Shannon was not allowed even to have Mace. Company policy said no Mace, no pepper spray, no nightsticks, no knives, and absolutely no guns. She should have followed Jack Landers' example and kept a secret weapon ready. After all, when a dangerous situation arose, it was her ass on the line, not her superiors', and they didn't know how dangerous things were becoming downtown.

Grousing about the company's policy was doing no good at the moment; she had to deal with her present situation. She went to the nearest desk, seeking scissors and other implements of potential mayhem, but could find none. And the desk was locked. She considered taking the phone. A slam upside the head with a phone might stop an attacker temporarily or at least stun him long enough for Shannon to escape. But as she reached to unhook the phone, it rang.

"Jesus!" A working phone and she had nearly disabled it! She grabbed it and held it up to her ear. "Hello!"

"Hi, Shannon."

"Mom, why are you calling me at work?"

"I was worried about you, dear. Because of the storm."

"Listen, Mom—"

"I've been praying for you, Shannon. I won't rest until you find God."

I didn't know he was lost, Shannon wanted to say, but this was not the time to try that line out on her mom. She needed help. "Mom, I'm trapped in this building. And I don't know how to explain it, but there are a bunch of other people trying to kill me. They already killed someone else. I can't handle it by myself. I need help. Call the police or somebody in case this phone doesn't work when I hang up."

"Call the police?"

"Yes, Mom."

"Call somebody?"

"That's what I—" A chill rippled down Shannon's body as she realized something was very wrong. "How did you know I was on this floor, Mom?"

"I"—the voice changed from the familiar whining tone of her mother to a man's raspy bass—"know where your tight little ass is all the time!"

"Who is this?"

"Wouldn't you fucking like to know!"

The line went dead. Then Shannon twisted the phone cord around her hand and jerked it out of the handset. "Son a bitch!"

It was another goddamn trick. A nifty one, too. The kingpin of the nut cases wasn't satisfied with attacking her physically; he wanted to play her mind over as well. She hoped she survived to make him pay for the torture he was putting her through.

Something stirred nearby making a noise that was not immediately identifiable. Shannon listened, tense as a cat, her senses keyed up as the adrenaline pumped into her system.

The sound became clearer. It was a scuffling noise, like someone walking while dragging one foot. Shuddering, Shannon held the detached phone close to her body, already regarding it as a blunt instrument of destruction. She took out the gun, too, intending to pistol-whip whoever might be her next adversary.

The scuffling sound started going away from her. The person making the noise was retreating or taunting her. She wouldn't let him get away; she'd track him down, get the first jump on him, and gain the advantage.

Determined and grim, she ran past the bank of elevators, following the sound of the dragging foot. It went down the hall, past the drinking fountains, then around another corner into a corridor between two walls broken up only by closed offices.

She skidded to a halt, her shoes almost squeaking. Standing at the end of the corridor was Jesus Christ.

04:36

Lilly Ann Zeto was a data entry clerk. She worked for the bank on the graveyard shift, processing the millions of dollars of canceled checks that cleared every day. She was 32, short, and a little overweight. Her hair was long and brown, and her face a pleasant oval actually enhanced by the stylish glasses perched on her nose. She always wore jeans and a sweatshirt to work. The yellow shirt she had on tonight was imprinted with the advice, "Leave Me Alone."

This admonition had not kept that terrible thing she had met on the twenty-eighth floor away. She had to think of it as a thing. It was certainly no longer a man, because no man could be burned that badly and continue to walk around.

For some twisted reason the thing blamed her for its condition, and it had set upon her with a cigarette lighter, trying to set her hair afire. She had only gone up there to get a snack from the lawyers' lounge; all the bank employees did that late at night. It was no big deal. She hadn't expected to have her life threatened. She didn't even know how to defend herself.

Fortunately, the monstrous thing had changed its mind about her; she didn't know why and she didn't care. Its stopping had given her the chance to duck into the stairwell, and the thing had not followed her out.

Unfortunately, she hated the stairwell. Its endless spiral of torturous metal steps gave her vertigo. She feared either that she would topple over the steel railing to plummet several stories to her death or that the whole thing would collapse under her.

The sound her own feet made on the metal steps echoed throughout the vast shaft where the staircase was anchored, adding to her feelings of apprehension. It was an unearthly, unnerving noise.

She wouldn't stop till she reached the nineteenth floor, where the bank's data-processing department was located. Nor would she feel even marginally safe till she was back with her fellow employees locked behind closed doors.

04:38

Shannon was caught in a glow that momentarily immobilized her. The glow came from the figure of Jesus about ten feet away. He was a very traditional Jesus with wavy brown hair and a full beard. He was clad in a white robe just like on a Baptist Church calendar.

Shannon's mouth fell open. She was reasonably certain she was not dead, and the twenty-eighth floor was a long way from her idea of heaven or any version of the afterlife. So what was Jesus doing there? Had He decided to return to earth that night or was He just passing through?

"Shannon."

She gulped. Jesus knew her by name!

"Of course I know your name. As I know everyone's. I saved your mother and your sister Linda." He opened his arms and beckoned to her. "Come to Me, child. Come and be saved."

Shannon was unable to move or speak. She wondered, however, what Jesus must think of the way she was soaked in blood. And He must know she had just killed a woman in self-defense.

"Your sins are behind you," He said. "Whatever you have done in the past is of no consequence. You are like a newborn child, innocent and unknowing. Come to me and be saved for eternity."

Shannon was starting to tremble. She needed to be saved because she was a sinner, and her mother had been right all those years. Otherwise, Satan would get her!

But she wasn't ready to go with Jesus. She wanted to see what else life might offer her. Wouldn't He understand?

Jesus smiled beatifically, compassionately. Since Shannon wasn't coming to Him, He glided toward her, like a vampire in an old movie. His arms were outspread. He enclosed her in them, and He was very cold.

Shannon smelled something strange, yet familiar. It was the odor of burned meat mixed with the smell of cigars.

Then Jesus extended a glowing hand and tweaked her right nipple. She slapped His hand away and veered away from Him. "Stay the fuck away from me!"

"Bitch!"

"You ain't Jesus!"

"Nice tits, toots." The visage of Jesus seemed to melt; then the glow dissipated and his heavenly robe disappeared. Standing in front of her was the badly burned corpse of Richard Bowes. "How about you let me massage those puppies for you? Better yet, let me cook them before I eat them!"

He had a cigarette lighter in his left hand. He flicked it on, and out blazed a long flame, which he aimed at her breasts.

Contact with fire would readily ignite Shannon's polyester uniform, even though it was somewhat damp. Shannon reacted quickly enough to avoid the flame, knocked the lighter from Bowes's grip with one hand and shoved the phone into his lipless mouth with the other, pushing it in with all her might. Bowes gurgled as spittle rimmed the phone, and he gripped it with both hands and tried to pull the phone out.

While he struggled, Shannon began beating

him with the gun. Every time she hit him, a puff of black ash rose. Soon the air was almost as sooty as Bowes's feet. Shannon choked and coughed, but she continued to rain blows on him. She soon saw her assault was doing little to harm him. If she had not jammed the phone in his mouth, he would be on top of her, possibly strangling her.

Bowes was literally tearing at his jaws, stripping away bits of muscle, but the phone was hooked in his esophagus. Only major surgery could extract it. So he stopped battling with the thing and turned his eyes toward Shannon. Bowes's eyes were scary, especially because the lids had been burned off. Had she not recently viewed the remains of the redhead, Shannon probably would have freaked out.

She couldn't tell if Bowes was attempting to express any particular emotion with his eyeballs, but she was certain he was pissed off, and he was coming toward her, bent on doing something she would regret later.

Fortunately, he was at a slight disadvantage, since he was basically in the end of the corridor while she had all of it before her. All she really had to do was run. She tucked the gun in her waistband and started to take off, but stopped herself. Running away would delay the inevitable. As long as the lawyer was able to move, he would probably keep pursuing her, no matter where she went. She had to stop him.

He wasn't that big a man since half his flesh

was burned off, so she decided to try a little of the judo she had learned in the service. It had proved useful a few times in the past when men she had dated went beyond certain limits.

As he lurched toward her, she took hold of his left arm and twisted it, intending to flip him on his back. Instead, the arm came off at the shoulder. She stared at the limb as it drooped from her hands. It was not substantial at all. She threw it aside. She guessed all that was holding him together was ash. She could rip him apart if she wanted. And she wanted.

Bowes was swiping at her with his right arm, while she nimbly ducked. As soon as there was an opening, Shannon gripped the remaining arm, neatly wrenched it out of the socket and tossed it away.

Bowes made an unintelligble sound and kicked at her. She caught his foot in midair, broke it off, and let it fall to the floor.

"C'mon, you mother!" she cried. "Is that the best you've got?"

Bowes almost fell over. He managed to keep his balance only by some miraculous defiance of the laws of gravity. He writhed with anger and frustration at not being able to do anything to her.

Shannon had to finish him off. From what she had learned from her skirmish upstairs, she knew she had to disable his head by tearing it from his neck. She didn't know if she was strong enough to do so because it might be more firmly attached than his limbs.

She had to try. She gritted her teeth and took a step toward Bowes, her hands outstretched to clasp his head. Suddenly, Shannon was thrown back by the force of Bowes's head exploding in a blinding flash.

Shannon instinctively shielded her face as bits of skull, brain, flesh, and ash peppered her. When she uncovered her face, Bowes's headless body lay on the floor, rippling in a final fit of small spasms that subsided almost instantly.

"What the hell caused that?"

"I did, Miss Security Bitch."

Shannon turned around slowly. A man in tattered clothes—a man with a terrible stink—a man wearing a mangled parody of Jack Landers's face was about two yards away from her. He didn't look pleased.

Chapter Twenty

Wednesday, 22 November:
04:45

McHenry had rather expected to get through the night alive. But circumstances beyond his control made him revise his expectations dramatically. At first, he had rejected his own death, denying it even after that strange voice had echoed inside his head, challenging him while confirming the fact he had ceased to exist on the mortal plain.

But he had not gone on to meet his Maker. Was there no Maker? Or was he experiencing yet another supernatural event? That meant, he supposed, the ealier encounter with things beyond the norm was also valid.

Things were not very clear-cut, however. He

felt forces tugging at him from different directions. The most insistent was that of the entity who had taunted him after he had killed Audrey. That foe apparently thought he should be able to control McHenry according to his whims.

But another force not immediately ascribable to any particular agency—human or otherwise—seemed to be vying for his afterlife self as well. McHenry guessed it was much more allied to the force that had made him a demonic monster than was the manipulative one.

Could it be the manifestation of evil he had speculated about before? Why had it not intervened to prevent his death at the hands of a stupid little secretary? McHenry had served it well. It owed him, did it not? Maybe its allowing him to continue to be—dead or otherwise—was its payment for whatever debt it recognized. Or it had further plans for him that death did not affect.

McHenry suddenly fretted about how long his strange, undead existence could be sustained. His body was a fragile organism. It was a complex of systems, most of which were shut down for him. Only his mind remained fairly intact, despite the loss of some brain matter.

Being and nothingness were two sides of the same dilemma. If that were the case, maybe it was possible for him to become alive again. It could be a mere matter of how he perceived reality. If all was illusion, then he must inevitably choose his illusion from moment to moment.

Maybe if he obeyed the proper forces, he would be rewarded with life anew.

McHenry certainly would not do anything his disembodied enemy ordered. As long as McHenry retained a scrap of his identity, he would have willpower and the indomitable volition to bolster it. McHenry might pretend to heed the wishes of his foe, but as soon as they met, McHenry would exact revenge.

He also wanted to get that snippy security guard. If she hadn't resisted him, he would not have been so easily killed by the redhead.

And there was the matter of Audrey's corpse. He needed to resolve that matter as well, though it was obvious that no one had just died that night. His murderess was herself severely damaged, but that had not kept her from whopping him on the head. He had taken a moment to inspect the redhead's remains and discovered she'd had no heart. All the same, her detached head had prattled on for several minutes after the guard left.

The only conclusion McHenry could make was that life and death no longer had any definition. The supernatural had taken over. And McHenry intended to find a way to use his altered reality to his own advantage. There was no situation he could not ultimately take control of.

For the moment, however, he would go along with his foe's orders and go to one of the places where many things were happening or about to happen.

04:50

Lilly Zeto banged on the metal door to the nineteenth floor, trying to get someone's attention. She had forgotten that the stairwell doors opened one way only as a security precaution.

Out of breath from her descent down the metal stairs, she felt desperate. It seemed she had been pounding on the door for a long time. Someone must have heard her, unless no one was on that side of the building. She was not sure which side of the nineteenth floor the door opened onto. A sign identified it as the south stairwell door, but she had never been able to keep her directions straight.

If no one came, she would have to go farther down the stairwell to a floor with an unlocked door and risk riding the elevator up. Just thinking about going down more of the metal steps made her whoozy. She was sure she would lose her footing and fall over the rail.

Finally, she heard the approach of footsteps on the other side of the door. She felt vastly relieved when the door opened, and she rushed in.

"What you want?" a male voice without inflection asked.

Though it was dark in the hall, Lilly could tell the man who had opened the door was not someone she knew. He certainly did not work in the bank's data-processing department.

"Who are you?" she asked.

"Sam."

"Sam who?"

"Sam. Just Sam. Plain Sam. Last name gone. You the security guard?"

"No. I work here. You don't. So what are you doing here?"

Lilly's gruff manner was only a pretense. She was actually scared of the stranger, but she knew showing any sign of fear would lead to trouble. She began to walk away from Sam, heading toward the nearest office she could lock herself into. She hoped she could keep the man distracted by talking until she reached it.

Sam did not respond to her question. As soon as she started to move, he followed close behind her, his gait slow and uncertain. Soon, the two of them came into a small break area where the tables and chairs had been overturned. There was a bad smell of burned coffee and urine in the air.

Lilly halted, looked down, and saw wet blood on the carpet. Under a table to her left lay something that resembled a pink sausage, except it had a fingernail. She gagged and pivoted as if to run, but Sam had stopped right behind her, a stony obstacle in her path.

Lilly could see him under light, and she gasped at the hole in his forehead. Sam's eyes were dull and vacuous. He looked dangerous, and Lilly was so frightened by his visage she couldn't speak. Sam didn't move. He seemed to be unaware of her presence, as if a switch inside him had been turned off.

Seeing he was not paying attention to her, Lilly merely turned around to head out in the opposite direction. Before she reached the door, another man had appeared. He had a T-shirt knotted around his waist, but it didn't totally hide the mass of gory intestines drooping from his body like a basket of slimy snakes.

"Hey, woman," Randall said, "you don't want to leave now. It's party time." He eyed the slogan on her sweatshirt. "And I ain't about to leave you alone. Hey, Sam, let's you and me take one of her legs and make a wish."

Sam was as motionless as a rock, but not as sentient.

"Sam?"

04:52

Audrey had worked her way down three floors in a frantic search for cigarettes. Then a man's voice ordered her to give up her hunt and kill that security guard and anyone else Audrey encountered. Feeling a need to do what she was told, Audrey sniffed the air like a dog, and she smelled a human nearby.

She was on the twenty-sixth floor at that moment. She followed her nose to a room in a corner of the building, where she came upon a young black man sleeping in a chair behind a big oak desk. He wore the badge of a

Clean Corps employee. Audrey uttered a shrill, animallike shriek at the sight of him.

Turner's eyes snapped open to view a naked white woman with a hole in her stomach. While she was not the sort of person he normally encountered, Turner always played it cool in any situation; especially when a naked woman was involved. There was no predicting what the woman might be up to.

"What you want, lady?" he asked calmly.

"You," Audrey growled, her hands held out like claws as she assumed a predatory stance. "I have to kill you."

Turner almost fell out of the chair. The lady sounded as if she meant what she said. "What you want to kill me for? I ain't done you no wrong."

As Audrey advanced slowly, drool dripping down her chin, Turner was reminded of a pit bull he had once seen moments before it had ripped someone's face off. He was also reminded of a chicken, because the skinny woman resembled a scrawny old bird more than anything else. He wasn't going to let a chicken mess around with him. He got to his feet and took a fighting stance, weaving back and forth as if he was going to spar with her.

"Come on, I got something for you right here," he said in what he considered a menacing tone. Unless the woman was drunk or crazy, she would comprehend he could whip her ass without trying, and she would get the hell out of there.

But she kept coming, and before Turner could strike a blow, she had hurled herself through the air and knocked him to the floor. She scratched his face with one hand, gouging his flesh with her long nails.

Turner cried out in pain. He punched her full in the face and heard the cartilage in her nose crunch. The blow sent her flying back. Before she was all the way back, she had twisted her body and locked her thighs around his head in a classic scissors hold.

Turner tried to yell at her, but Audrey's hold on his neck was already cutting off his air. He pulled on her legs, but he couldn't pry them part. She was strong for a chicken.

In response to his attempt to dislodge her, she shifted her body and suddenly her pubic hair was in his face. The smell of her crotch burned up through his nostrils. He was being suffocated two different ways at once.

Turner was never out of resources, however; he hadn't survived in bad neighborhoods without having had his wits always together. In his back pocket, he carried a home-made knife that was always with him. He let go of her legs, worked his hand behind his body, and managed to get the knife out. He held it up over his eyes so he could see which way the edge was turned, then began to slice at her calves, carving off bits of her flesh.

For all his efforts, Audrey didn't seem to care. All she did was tighten her hold on him. His blade hit bone without fazing her. His hand was getting so sticky with her lukewarm blood he lost his grip and dropped the knife. It was time to fight dirty, even if she was a woman. He reached up to jam his fist into the wound in her abdomen, figuring that would be sensitive.

It was sensitive all right, but the result of his hurting her was not freedom. Audrey yelped a little, shuddered, then tensed the muscles in her legs, tightening her thighs around his neck till his eyeballs bulged.

The last thing Turner saw was a piece of lint in her pubic hair. He thought how funny it was that little details became noticeable at the oddest times. Then he passed out.

Audrey waited a few seconds, then dismounted him. He was still breathing; he would come to shortly. To prevent that, she squatted, picked up his knife, and slit his throat from ear to ear, giving his neck a bloody smile. Turner snorted, his bowels and bladder let go, and blood seeped out of his ears, nose, and eyes. He kicked, trembled, and spasmed as life finally left him.

Audrey had made her first kill. She hoped it pleased whoever it was who was controlling her, though she couldn't imagine why she should care.

It was time to leave. She would have gone on, but her attention was arrested by the sight of a familiar bulge in the pocket of Turner's jeans. Her eyes wild as her true primal urge returned, she emptied the contents of his pocket, bringing forth a nearly full pack of generic menthol lights and a lighter.

She hurriedly fumbled a cigarette between her lips and fired it up. She sat on Turner's chest, quietly smoked, and idly scratched at her pubic area. She enjoyed two more cigarettes, tucked the rest of the pack in the hole in her stomach, and moved on, seeking more prey and more prizes as gratifying as the cigarettes. Hunting came naturally to Audrey.

04:56

Randall was disgusted with Sam. The man was just about totally brain dead, and he was offering Randall no help with killing the woman in the yellow sweatshirt.

"Why don't you do something, dude?" Randall asked, poking Sam in the shoulder while holding Lilly by one arm. "Ain't you got anything left at all?"

Sam's eyes were half rolled up into his head; he saw nothing. His lips moved erratically, but no sound came out. He just stood there, not reacting to anything.

"Let me go!" Lilly yelled for the umpteenth time.

"Shut your mouth. You ain't going nowhere." Randall threatened to hit her. As he was drawing back his fist to do so, Sam made a gurgling noise. "Go ahead, Sam. Say something!"

Gray ooze dribbled from Sam's mouth; blackish gore spit out of the hole in his forehead, pelting Randall and the woman. A gore-soaked head poked out of Sam's forehead, its tiny red eyes rolling nervously as its nose twitched. It was a rat.

"Damn, Sam!"

The rat chewed around the edges of the hole, freed itself, and jumped onto Randall, diving into his exposed intestines. Sam, his brain totally eaten out, dropped to the floor. Randall screamed as the rodent burrowed through his guts. He hadn't felt pain for hours; suddenly, intense, burning pain radiated throughout his body.

He couldn't hold on to Lilly. Free of his grip, she ran across the room to the exit. She heard Randall fall to the floor, struggling and yelling, but she had no wish whatsoever to stop and help him. He and his friend were beyond any kind of human help.

She turned a corner and jogged down a hall to the main computer room, where the bank's data processing was done. The door was on a digital-combination lock. It was supposed to be secured around the clock every day of the year. But it stood wide open. A din issued from the room that assailed Lilly's ears as she approached. Something was terribly wrong.

Lilly came to a stop at the door. Inside, she

saw six people—her fellow employees—who had been dispatched in various ways. Four of them were women. One had had her neck broken; another had been stabbed in the heart with a ball-point pen; another had been disembowled; the fourth lay face down across a computer console, the cause of her demise not readily apparent. One of the two men in the room had evidently been in a fight. His head was battered badly, and he was missing at least two fingers. The other had part of his arm sticking up out of his mouth, the arm having been torn from his shoulder. His other arm was stuck up to the elbow in the screen of a computer, the jagged edges of the glass rimmed with his flesh and blood.

Most of the awful noise was coming from the data-processing equipment. A check-processing machine was chewing up thousands of dollars of canceled checks, spraying the room with ragged confetti. Reels of tape on a miniframe computer were spinning wildly, much faster than ever intended, and the computer was starting to smoke. Two old adding machines were clattering, their keys being pressed by no one. Other nerve-racking noises came from different corners of the room. Everything was running too fast. The equipment would overload and explode if not stopped.

Lilly wasn't concerned about machinery. The state of her co-workers made her obey her first impulse: she fell to her knees and threw up right outside the door. As she finished heaving, she screamed.

Running down the hall toward her was a black rat, his coat slick with red and black stuff. The rat was bigger than a cat. It seemed twice as big as it had been when had it first popped out of Sam's head. The way its jagged teeth were bared, she guessed it was still hungry.

Lilly hurried to pull herself up along the door. When she was erect, she tried to pull the door shut, but it wouldn't yield. She noticed the top hinges were broken. While she told herself that it was impossible for anyone to have broken through a metal door an inch thick, the rat sprang up from the floor and dived between her legs.

It soon found a convenient way to chew up into her body, ripping through the crotch of her jeans with its sharp little claws and burrowing in with its needlelike teeth before she could react. She beat on her pelvis, trying to stop the rat as her insides splattered the floor. The rat was deep inside her, moving up. Her flesh bulged where it moved beneath her skin.

An open pocket knife lay nearby. Ripping off her sweatshirt, Lilly grabbed the knife. She started stabbing herself in the abdomen, trying to hit the rat, which poked its head out of her navel and stared at her. She pulled the knife from her stomach and aimed at the thing's neck. She missed the rat and hit herself in the breast bone.

Lilly let out a scream loud enough to wake the dead, and as she tumbled to the floor, she saw the dead around her awaken.

Chapter Twenty-One

Wednesday, 22 November:
04:48

The ugly thing with Jack's face and the body of a homeless street person seemed to be interested only in watching Shannon. He didn't seem inclined to hurt or kill her, as everyone else she had encountered lately had. Still, he effectively blocked her way out with not only his body, but with his stink. Shannon didn't know which would be harder to get by.

"I could do that to you, too. I can do anything I want."

His voice rasped inside her head.

"Do what?" she asked, innocent and wide-eyed, feigning interest. If he wanted to talk, she figured she would go along with him, delaying whatever mayhem he had planned for her. Her stalling tactic would also give her a chance to consider the best strategy to escape. She was nearly exhausted from her recent activities and needed time to get her second wind.

"Make your head go boom like I did him." Dead Ted pointed to the shattered remains of Bowes, whose corpse was completely still. *"I had to do that to him because he didn't do a very good job. Couldn't even kill a woman, but I guess you ain't just any woman."*

"You don't know anything about me. You don't know me at all."

"I know everything about you I need to know. And I know you keep getting away. When you going to let one of my people catch you?"

"Why should I?"

Dead Ted held up his hands in a questioning gesture. *"Why not?"*

"Because I'm not stupid." Shannon awaited a response, but Dead Ted made none. "You call them your people like you're their leader, so I guess you're the one who's making people act crazy."

"They ain't crazy. They're dead."

"What?"

"All dead. That's why I can make them do anything I want."

Shannon tingled. Though what he was saying was absolute madness, his explanation made sense according to the way things had been going. It had the ring of truth because she had seen things that could not be explained otherwise. Her main mistake had been thinking Sam Campbell was responsible for that night's mayhem. She should have realized only a totally insane wacko could be responsible for all she had experienced that terrible night. The hardest part to accept was that so many people she knew were dead. She would never see them again. Their deaths didn't seem right or fair, and Shannon was maddened that one person should create such havoc and get away with it.

"Did you kill them?" Shannon could barely contain the anger rising inside her.

"Not all. Some."

"Did you kill Jack?"

"Who's Jack?"

"You should know! You're wearing his goddamn face!"

"I didn't kill him. The building did. I just took his face because I didn't have one. I needed it more than he did."

Shannon had moved very close to Dead Ted. She could see how a jagged piece of metal was stuck into the top of his face, fastening it to his skull. She also spotted a couple of maggots squirming around the edge of the face. No wonder the dude smelled so bad—he was half rotten. Where had he come from then? Part of her wanted to know, but another part of her didn't care. He had to be stopped, and she would find a way. She had to go only a couple more inches and she would make her move.

"Who are you?" Shannon asked, more to

determine his awareness of where she was and what she was doing than from curiosity.

"You don't know me. Doesn't matter to you."

"Whoever you are," she said succinctly, "you are one sick mother."

"The name is Ted. Don't wear it out." He chortled behind his flaccid face. *"I just want to have fun."*

Shannon didn't like Ted's idea of fun. She would have told him that, but it was time to act. She had learned all she needed to know about the madman.

She doubled her right hand into a fist and slammed it against his face. The face ripped free from the piece of shrapnel holding it on and dropped to the floor with a squishy splat. The skull behind the face was a gory mass full of worms busily eating away.

Shannon would have been sick except there was nothing left in her to throw up and she didn't have time. Besides, she had accomplished what she set out to do. The madman was distracted and she ducked by him easily, running out of the corridor toward the lobby and elevators.

"See you in the funny papers, Teddy boy!"

Dead Ted stooped to retrieve his face, put it on upside down, and stumbled around until he realized his mistake and readjusted it. *"Go ahead,"* his voice echoed after her. *"I don't care. I got lots of people ready for you!"*

Shannon mentally thanked him for the warning. She made it to the elevators without incident, however. She pressed the down button on the wall, and an elevator opened immediately, as if it was waiting for her. She jumped in and hit the button for the twenty-fifth floor.

The elevator shot past that floor and kept going down. She hit other buttons, but they wouldn't even light up. Before she knew it, she was back on the ground floor.

04:58

Things were going according to plan. Dead Ted had wanted Shannon to get away. There would be no sport in his killing her when he could watch others do it. And although he had lost a couple of warriors, he had acquired more.

He focused his mental eyes toward the most recent additions to his killing crew, the people on the nineteenth floor. As he scanned, he came across the bodies of Sam and Randall, rendered useless because both their brains had been chewed out by a rat. When his dead servants did not have any brains at all, he could not control them.

Dead Ted should have anticipated hazards like the rat. Even at that moment, the little beast was attempting to destroy yet another of his people. He wasn't going to let a stupid little beast thwart him. He made the rat explode. Then he looked throughout the building for other rats, and blew up any he found.

It was very satisfying to kill the hideous vermin. In his days on the street, Dead Ted had encountered many of them and had grown to hate them. They always turned up where he was trying to sleep in abandoned buildings or searching for food in trash dumpsters. The little monsters deserved to die. All of them.

The only things more disgusting than rats were worms and maggots. Many a potential meal had been spoiled by the infestation of maggots. Although Dead Ted had forgotten about maggots, he began to worry that they might burrow into his brain. He would make them explode, too.

He started with one that was lodged between the place where his nose had been and the nose on his borrowed face. It made a little pop when it was snuffed out. Unfortunately, the small explosion blew backward, cutting into Dead Ted's skull. It even hurt a little.

If he blew up all the worms, he might damage himself too much. There had to be a way to rid himself of the squirming threats to his continued existence without messing himself up. But he could think of no reliable method at the moment. Something would come to him. Things had gone pretty much his way so far; the worms were only a temporary nuisance.

He wanted to go watch Shannon in the little

drama he had prepared for her. He had summoned up the headless body from the basement and guided it into place as she had asked him stupid questions earlier.

He went to the elevators. He wanted to be close by to see how Shannon handled the new challenge he had created for his amusement. Dead Ted plucked a worm from behind his left eyelid, smashed it between his fingers, then with a small sense of triumph, entered the awaiting elevator and descended.

05:00

The elevator opened in the main lobby, but Shannon refused to leave. She had guessed that the man upstairs wanted her to go into the lobby, and she was determined to resist anything and everything he tried from then on.

As if sensing her stubbornness, the elevator car began to shake up and down. At the same time, its doors opened and smacked closed over and over again, making a deafening racket. Shannon merely held onto the handrails inside; she felt as if she were atop a bucking bronco. She thought she could handle anything her enemy had planned—until blood poured from around the light fixtures in the elevator's ceiling.

"Stop it!" she screamed.

More blood sloshed over her. Choking from the smell, she backed into a corner and hunkered down, tucking her head down and wrapping her arms around her knees. She swore to hold out until the madman ran out of blood. But then the elevator doors slammed shut, and the blood started to fill up the elevator.

Shannon stood up, watching incredulously as the level of the dark red liquid rose quickly. As the blood touched her knees, she began to cough.

"What do you want?" she cried.

The crimson sea continued to rise. Gory bits of flesh floated on its surface. Her senses overwhelmed, Shannon went into a bout of dry heaves, coughing and hacking until she spit up her own blood.

"Enough! Okay?" she said. Her stomach ached terribly; her throat was raw. "Let me out. I'll do what you want."

She waited. The blood was an inch below her breasts. Soon it was spilling over them, trailing between her cleavage. She closed her eyes as the sticky warm liquid flowed under her armpits. With the last of her courage, Shannon cursed her enemy. She was not going to let Ted have the last word. Wherever he was, she knew he was watching and could hear her.

"Fuck you, Ted" she croaked in defiance. "You got me, but I still say you can go fuck yourself. I don't give a damn anymore. See you in hell!"

Gritty blood touched her chin. She tensed the muscles in her jaws so her mouth wouldn't open when the blood reached it. But just when Shannon had prepared herself for death, the gore coming from the ceiling abruptly stopped. A few seconds dragged by. Then the elevator doors burst open.

Shannon was washed out into the lobby, carried along in a bloody flash flood. She slid along uncontrollably, heading toward the security desk, certain she was about to smash her brains on its marble surface. She stopped herself by grabbing onto a large potted plant near the mail room.

The blood hit the wall at the end of the lobby and sloshed right into it, as if it were a giant sponge. The blood left no residue. Not a drop remained on the floor. The only residue was that which dripped off Shannon's body, and soon even that blood dissipated as if it had been vaporized.

The horrible scene had been a trick, an illusion. Yet she couldn't decide which part was illusion and which was real—the blood itself or the way it had disappeared?

"Neat, Teddy. Very fucking neat."

Shannon pulled herself up. She ran her fingers through her hair to straighten it, finding it was dry and unsoiled. Her hands and nails were clean, too.

Shannon realized she was clean because Ted was setting her up for something. He wanted her clean for a reason. The reason soon became evident.

"Hey, monkey nipples, wanna get it on?"

Stan Cork's head peered at Shannon from atop

the security desk. It seemed to have materialized out of the thin air. But Shannon was not surprised or shocked.

Stan tried to stick out his tongue, but he lost his balance and toppled down to the floor. His head looked much the same as it had before, except a lot of the blood had dried on the back of his scalp, giving him a kind of red-brown tonsure.

"Go away. You bother me." Shannon started walking towards the front of the lobby.

Cork's head inched along the floor on its own, leaving a wet trail. Then it turned around slowly until the battered features were facing her, and the lips crinkled in that familiar leer.

"A hell of a note, ain't it?"

Shannon ignored the talking head. She couldn't believe she would imagine talking to a severed head twice in one night.

You're not imagining anything, Shannon. God, I'm sorry about all of this. I didn't want any of it to happen, especially not to you, because I always kind of thought maybe some day you and me might—

"Get real." His phony remorse was almost as sickening as his face.

"Aw, you never took me seriously. I don't blame you. I was a jerk, I guess. Now there ain't any reason to even . . . I don't even have a dick!"

"Like that would make a difference!" Shannon was in front of the plate glass, trying not to pay any attention to Stan.

"Wow!"

"Nobody says wow anymore," Shannon said. She was caught up momentarily in watching the snow. Some of the drifts must have been six feet deep. And the snow kept coming down. Though she made a studied attempt not to care, her curiosity overcame her, and she turned around to see what could possibly excite Stan.

A body without a head waited in the middle of the lobby. Stan's head slid toward it like a fast little rat. Somehow his head propelled itself to the top of the body and landed with a splat on the jagged edges of the neck. There were squishing and slurpy noises as the head wriggled around, finally attaching itself to the neck. The familiar leer became a terrible grin as Stan Cork's head twitched and the body it had attached itself to shivered with new animation.

"This is great," Stan said with a voice not attenuated by a whistle. "Better than my own."

Shannon couldn't help but go toward him. The illusion was one of Ted's better accomplishments. He had given Stan a bigger body than before. It resembled a football player's hulk. The body wore a tight T-shirt and dirty slacks and basketball shoes. The skin of its arms and what showed of its chest was brown.

"Shannon, I'm whole again. And this body is a huge mother!" Stan's newly acquired hands probed down the front of the dirty trousers. He pulled the waist open, trying to display his prize. "Look what I got now! How about it, Shannon honey, let's bump uglies. Just once. Okay? I probably won't last long like this, but I can feel the juice running down to my dick, and you owe me at least one time."

As the newly incarnate Stan stumbled toward Shannon, backing her against the wall, Shannon said, "Get away from me, you crazy son of a bitch!"

"Shannon, c'mon. What will it hurt?"

She pried herself from the wall, pivoted, and ran to the end of the lobby, heading for the loading dock area. Behind her, Stan followed slowly, then picked up his pace. Shannon bounced the metal door open, pulled it shut, and grabbed a broom from the corner to jam underneath the edge so it couldn't be opened by Stan. She jumped to the outside door and threw herself against it again and again, but as before it wouldn't move. She had trapped herself, and Stan would pop the other door open. He was already pounding.

"Shannon! What's one little fuck to you? A wild woman like you? Why don't you treat me right?"

"Fuck off!"

There was a sudden silence. Shannon pressed her ear to the door and listened. There was no sound of breathing, but then something that was dead probably didn't breathe.

Shannon looked around frantically. To her right was the electrical room, its door locked.

Beyond that, the freight elevator, which, a glance at the elevator control panel told her, was up on the twenty-fifth floor. It was her only chance. She ran to the elevator door and pressed the up buttom, but it wouldn't stay lit. Dead Ted probably had all the elevators under his control. But she had a key. Maybe she could override his commands. After all, she knew the building better than he did.

She quickly inserted her elevator key into the control panel and called the freight elevator down. As she waited, she heard a tremendous thump against the outer door. She glanced that way just in time to see a hole appear in its center, followed by the protrusion of the head of a large, engorged penis.

"You like big ones, don't you, Shannon?" Stan yelled through the door. "This big enough fer you?"

She swallowed hard. She had never seen anything so ugly before, and the thought of it probing her insides caused her stomach to spasm. She turned and jammed her finger on the service-elevator switch. It stayed lit. The elevator began its descent. She watched the L.E.D. on the control panel count off the numbers of the floors.

Stan withdrew from the hole; then a couple of bloody fingers poked through and pulled. The heavy metal door snapped off its hinges and fell loudly on top of Stan.

"Dumb shit," Shannon muttered.

The body with San's head flailed its arms as it struggled to get out from beneath the weight of the door.

The elevator was on ten.

An arm was free.

Nine–eight. . . .

A leg.

Seven–six–five. . . .

Half his face appeared.

Four–three. . . .

With an abrupt rush of strength, the body bounced the door off itself, stood up quickly and jumped.

Two. . . .

Stan landed within inches of Shannon's face.

She screamed and pummeled the elevator doors.

One.

"Open up, goddamn it!"

Stan laughed wickedly. He had removed his pants and advanced on her, the taut, ugly penis bouncing erratically as he shambled toward her. As the doors opened, Stan sprang.

Shannon jumped into the elevator and held down the button to shut the doors, and they closed on Stan's engorged member. Shannon punched a bunch of buttons. She heard the motors grinding somewhere above her. Then the elevator finally began to rise.

Outside Stan shrieked with agony as his new penis was ripped from the roots when the car suddenly shot upward. Inside the elevator car, the disembodied penis slithered toward Shannon like a snake.

"Doesn't anything stay dead around here?" she asked.

The elevator stopped at the twelfth floor and the doors opened. Shannon leaped out. Before Stan's new penis could turn around and pursue her, the elevator doors shut again.

Shannon caught her breath and backed away from the doors, thanking God she had survived another of Ted's tricks. She tripped on something and fell with a jolt that sparked up her tailbone and danced on her spine.

"What the hell?"

Cussing inanimate objects was an art Shannon had mastered in the service. But once she identified the target of her rage, she felt more like shouting for joy. She had stumbled on a large metal box full of tools.

05:27

Stan could not believe how stupid he had been. Once again, he had no hope whatsoever of making it with Shannon. It was pretty difficult to do much without the proper tool.

At least the pain had subsided. Things were unpredictable that night. One thing caused pain while another didn't. And the pain was not in proportion either to what inflicted it or where it was inflicted.

Despondent, Stan wandered back out to the

lobby and put his trousers back on. As he zipped up, a misshapen shadow fell over him. He turned to face Dead Ted.

"Jesus H. Christ—you're the dude who chopped off my head!"

Dead Ted felt as if he was glowering at the kid, though his slack face betrayed no emotion. *"Damn straight, you piece of shit."*

"Hey, what did I do?"

"You could've tried harder to kill her. But you were more interested in pussy."

"I didn't want to kill her."

"I told you to!"

"Why should I do what you say?" Stan sneered. "Just who the hell are you, man?"

Dead Ted's body vibrated as a wave of suppressed rage rippled through it. He was tempted to rip Stan's head off again, but he also truly wanted Stan to know just who it was he was dealing with. Then Stan would have something to think about for the eternity he would be spending in hell.

"You want to know who I am?" Dead Ted picked a worm out of his nose and flicked it in Stan's direction. *"I'll tell you."*

Interlude Three: How Ted Became Dead

Ted Flanders was one of many regulars who used to hang out on the Wall over on Market Street downtown. The Wall was really a barrier only four feet high, a brick boundary at the end of a parking lot and between two old buildings. One of those buildings housed a few city and county offices; the other was occupied by bail bondsmen and dime-store lawyers who wore cheap suits. It was a good location for the latter, since most of the city and country courtrooms were located nearby.

The Wall's height was perfect for lounging, sitting on, leaning against, and hanging out. Its physical location was also excellent for panhandling. Many people walked down Market Street on their way to the city and county office building, and quite a few of them were willing to give a poor unfortunate a quarter or even a dollar. By the end of the day, the stalwarts who hung out on the Wall usually had both drinking and eating money.

Being a regular on the Wall required some finesse; not just anyone could use it. There were usually no more than four or five men there. If a guy was too brassy or demanding or foolish in any way, he was not allowed to share space with the others and asked to go elsewhere. Regulars on the Wall were a special breed. They were extremely polite to passersby, even if they didn't receive a handout. They never made rude comments to passing women, who, by general assent, were never asked for money. If anyone wanted to talk, they would provide good stories, offer opinions on current affairs, or chime in with agreement on any particular issue a stranger wanted to comment on. They studied to be colorful characters who deserved a person's spare change, and they were quite accomplished conversationalists, actors, and poseurs, according to the needs of an individual encounter.

The Wall people were also quick to point out they were not bums or feckless folk who refused to work. They were—all of them, it seemed—homeless unfortunates who were not the recipients of government aid or care and had no choice but to beg in the streets. Some of them even carried articles from newspapers and magazines about the state of homelessness and its perils and its sorrowful victims.

It also seemed that every one of the homeless

Wall denizens was a Vietnam veteran, no matter what his age. Some of them had been to 'Nam and probably had truly suffered as a result, but many had only memorized some facts and dates they used to convince strangers they had served in that war. Anyone under 60 did not remember World War II, and the Korean conflict had been reduced to a mere footnote in history compared to the moral outrage and sympathy one could expect from mentioning 'Nam.

Ted Flanders was not a vet; Willie, another regular who never revealed his last name, was. But Ted sounded more convincing than Willie when it came to talking about the war. He complained of a bad leg and bad back and having to take a lot of prescription medicine to control the endless pain he suffered. He hinted at being exposed to atrocities at the hands of the Cong or breathing defoliants like Agent Orange, which he claimed had burned away half his brain. If he had a particularly attentive audience, he would relate how he had seen whole villages wiped out by GIs strung out from the government's use of chemicals. The only thing he did not claim was being a pothead or coke addict; few people had sympathy for that kind of war experience.

Willie, who had been wounded in the butt, didn't have the imagination to embellish his true experiences into an elaborate story. But he had the general manner down pat and received his fair share of handouts.

The previous summer had been peaceful on

the Wall. It was a warm summer for Indiana and it had rained often, but the regulars still found enough time in every day to beg enough to get through the night. Then, as fall came, someone new moved into the office building adjacent to the Wall and started complaining about Ted and Willie and the others, saying they were pestering people and posed a threat to commerce on Market Street. So the police started rousting the regulars at least once a day, forcing them to scatter and try to find other places where they could hang out profitably.

Ted and Willie didn't see each other often after that. Nor did they see their fellow Wall buddies much. Every man was suddenly on his own, having to walk the streets and confront more and more people to get the money that had been so easily obtained before. By winter, Ted had become half crazy. He didn't have anyone to talk to. He had to beg too much. He didn't always get enough money to buy a bottle and often had to sleep with his DTs.

Life became hellish. Ted, who had before been too proud to ask, even sought sanctuary in one of the city's shelters, but was turned away because there was no room for him. Even the shelters run by charities and churches were full. In desperation, Ted approached a work agency, but he was physically unfit to do any of the hard labor jobs they offered him. He had never liked to work anyhow.

Ted spent his nights huddled in doorways

or curled up in dumpsters—wherever he could get protection from the cold—and thought and thought and thought. He thought about how he had once been a real person, not one of countless homeless wretches nobody wanted to help. He thought about how he had family in Louisville and wondered if they would ever take him back—even though they were too poor to feed themselves adequately. He thought about how, deep down inside him, there was another Ted—a Ted with imagination and talent and ambition who was good with tools and machines, who could fix things and be a good husband and father if given the chance. But that Ted had died one day.

One day was all it took to turn a man's life inside out. Ted had had a good job, one with a future, but then the factory he had worked in was bought out, and Ted was laid off indefinitely. He was past 40 then and found that no other factory wanted him.

Quickly, his life began to fall apart. His unemployment ran out; he could no longer pay his rent; his car was repossessed. He had to take the bus or walk everywhere. He couldn't make child-support payments and was receiving threatening phone calls from his ex-wife's lawyer. His girlfriend started seeing someone else. His few remaining friends soon stopped returning his phone calls; he had borrowed from them too often.

Something inside him snapped. He could no

longer go to the state employment agency. They never had anything for him anyhow. He was unemployable.

He started shunning people. He began to drink. And in the bottle, he found solace and numbing release from his problems. After a while, he found that enough alcohol could wipe out certain memories. He didn't have to think about the past at all. And his present was laid out for him: life in the streets.

It was fortunate for him that he had become one of the homeless hordes at a time when people were feeling sorry for them in general. It was a matter of definition. Ten years before, he would have been a vagrant or a wino; 20 years before, he would have been a bum or a hobo. But in the present, he was homeless—a pitiable state that no one could blame him for. The streets of most big cities had come to accommodate the homeless. So they in essence provided homes for them.

Ted took to the life easily. All he had to do was be one of the good homeless. And to do that effectively, he merely had to lose his identity. But that was before. Now he was less than the sum of his former parts. He retained almost no identity, and his overall health had begun to wane.

He never looked at himself, except to shave once or twice a week. Even then he had learned not to see the face behind the stubble; it was too frightening. It was the face of a very old man who was ready to die. He probably already had many diseases. He should have died. But he didn't die.

He thought death would come easily if he gave up, but the booze and what little food he ate managed to sustain him. Strangely, he had no thoughts about deliberately taking his own life, because he realized deep down inside that being alive at all was something. There might not be any hope of dragging himself up from the gutter, but as long as he was able to stand and walk, there seemed to be a reason to go on.

For a while, the reason was the camaraderie of the bums hanging out on the Wall, shooting the shit all day while kind pedestrians dropped money in his hand. But when that was gone, he had to face the realities of his first winter in the streets.

He could, he knew, do as some of his buddies had done and get himself thrown in jail for the duration of the cold weather. Just throw a brick through a big plate glass window when the cops were watching. That crime would get him six months in a place that was much warmer than the streets. Some guys did that every winter. But Ted couldn't bring himself to do it. It was too much like giving up and admitting he needed someone to take care of him. He had a scrap of pride, after all.

So he had decided to brave the winter on his own, fighting through each day. Ted would have been angry about his situation, if he had any energy left after his daily struggle, but winter sapped it all.

Yet Ted survived. He might have survived the entire winter, but he made the mistake of invading the wrong turf. Someone should have warned him. Had he been warned, he would have happily thrown a brick through the front window instead of going around to the back of the skyscraper that housed the Metropolitan National Bank.

It was late in the evening when Ted wandered into the loading-dock area. The dumpster there was large and full of carpet scraps, which made excellent bedding. He planned to snatch a couple of the larger pieces, wrap himself up in them, and sleep curled up against the building's outer wall, out of the wind. It was a week or so into November then, and winter was pretty much settled in for the rest of the year.

As Ted was reaching up for a piece of carpet, he noticed a security guard come out of the back of the building—a young guy with freckles. Ted's stomach rumbled at that instant, urging him to do something he normally wouldn't have done to anyone who wore a badge. He decided to put the touch on him.

Security guards fell into two categories: those who tolerated homeless people and looked the other way when they slept in a dark corner, and those who treated them like shit, sometimes even hitting or kicking them. Young guys usually had more feelings. They weren't as tough and mean as the others. So Ted tottered toward the guard, a practiced smile on his face.

The guard was checking the locks on a station wagon and didn't see Ted right away. When he did, his expression became a dark scowl. But Ted was undaunted. There was nothing to lose. He was too close to just back off.

"Hey, buddy, can you spare a quarter for some coffee?"

"Get the fuck away from me," Stan Cork snarled.

Ted didn't take the hint; his brain was too fuzzy from the cold or his judgment clouded by imminent delirium tremens. Any other time, he would have turned tail and run. But his stomach was insistent. "Just a dime. I ain't had food in days."

Stan came from around the other side of the car, his arms at his side as if he might pull a weapon. "I don't give handouts to bums. And you're a fucking bum."

"I'm not a bum. I'm a—"

"You ain't shit. Get out of here before I call the cops."

Ted was offended. "I was in 'Nam, you snot-nosed brat. I gave my balls for this country!"

"Who gives a fuck?" Stan said. "Nobody made you go to 'Nam. It was a stupid goddamn war anyhow. My dad told me all about it, and people who went to it are assholes."

"You mean people who didn't go were chickenshit draft dodgers!"

Stan's face reddened, heightening the contrast between his skin and the freckles, which seemed to become three dimensional. "You calling my Dad chickenshit?"

"No, sir," Ted said, hoping to avoid a fight. "Don't mean to offend. I'll be moving on now."

"You piece of crud." Stan unlocked the back door of the car and lifted a baseball bat out from under the seat. He waved it in Ted's face. "You want me to fix your balls for you? C'mon. I'm tired of all you homeless motherfuckers and your bullshit. You're nothing but bums who live off people. You don't deserve to live."

Ted took a step backward and found he was up against a concrete wall. The kid advanced, holding the bat at a dangerous angle.

"Kid, I'm sorry. I'm sure your dad is an honorable man."

"You don't know my dad."

"Okay. Okay. Let me move on, man. I won't come back."

Stan let the bat hang loose at his side. He was breathing heavily, but much of his rage seemed to have passed. "Bum." He turned sideways, as if to give Ted a clear path out of the loading dock area.

"Thanks, kid," Ted said, taking a step forward.

"Your ass!" Stan yelled.

Before Ted could turn or run, he felt the bat's impact on his skull. He even heard the bone cracking inside his head before he went down.

He didn't feel the second blow. Or the third.

After he hit Ted several times, Stan suddenly realized what he was doing and stopped himself. The back of the guy's head was mush. His face lay in a widening pool of bright blood. Stan forced himself not to look too closely. He couldn't let himself get emotional about what he had done. Since he had no intention of turning himself in, he had to get rid of the guy's body.

It would be too messy to put him in the back of the car. Since it was a station wagon, the dead man wouldn't be hidden very well anyhow. Even if Stan covered the corpse up, anyone would be able to tell he had a body in his car and not the week's groceries.

Stan thought hard. Then the solution came to him. It was so simple he didn't know why it hadn't occurred to him immediately—the compactor.

The compactor could crush a giant wad of boxes, trash, and garbage into a small cube. It was almost as powerful as those machines at junkyards that reduced scrap cars to blocks of metal.

Stan had checked the level of the compactor recently, and it was only a third full. There was plenty of space for an old rummy. By the time the body was mashed along with all the trash and garbage from the next few nights, there would be almost nothing left of it. Even if someone discovered the body later, people would be assume the guy had crawled in there. Such an accident had happened a couple of years earlier at another building downtown. Those old drunks were liable to do anything.

Stan examined his plan and pronounced it flawless. So he set about putting it into action. First, he took a large carpet scrap from the dumpster and used it as a shroud for Ted's body and to keep blood off himself. Luckily, the way Stan had smashed the guy's head in, very little had splattered on him. Having wrapped the body, he tied the carpet in place with telephone wire he found in the dumpster and started dragging the corpse toward the compactor.

The metal door to the large compacting apparatus was at the level of Stans eyes. He had to wrestle Ted's body up over his shoulder and into the hole. When it finally dropped in among the trashbags and boxes, it folded almost in half and slipped down in front of the massive metal plunger that compressed the contents of the compactor into nondescript oblivion.

Stan slammed the door shut. He took the baseball bat, wrapped it up in his jacket, and tossed them both under the front seat of his car. It was dark and no one would notice anything unusual. When Jack arrived, Stan would just say he had forgotten to bring his jacket to work and let the old man make fun of him.

Stan went into the building and brought the key to the compactor out. He inserted it in the small black box attached to the machine by long thick cables. A sign warned the operator the machine used 440 volts. He flicked the key to the right and pressed the compact button. The cables jumped as power surged through them. He heard the metal plunger grinding into place, then moaning as it crushed the evening's trash. It applied tons of pressure for close to a minute before it shut itself off. Whatever was in there would no longer be recognizable as a former human being. It was just more trash.

Stan's last task was to clean up the blood on the floor. Fortunately, the floor had been surfaced with a slick latex coating designed to repel oil stains, so the blood didn't sink in. All Stan had to do was soak the blood up with about 100 paper towels, then wipe the last few traces away with a wet sponge. He discarded the towels and sponge in the compactor and turned it on again.

He didn't feel any guilt until much later. In the middle of the night, he awoke in a clammy sweat. Only then did it occur to him that he had committed murder. After a few days, he gradually convinced himself it was a justifiable homicide. Though there were moments when the specter of the dead man loomed in his thoughts and made him feel queasy, Stan learned to live with those small discomforts. It was not as if he had killed anyone who had meant anything to anybody.

Inside hell:

Ted's face was all bloody, but he couldn't move

anything to clean himself. His arms and legs were numb. His brain was numb. His eyelids wouldn't function. Then someone wrapped him up and lifted his body. He could not speak to protest.

The person carrying Ted didn't seem to care if he was hurting him or not. But it did hurt. Everything hurt. Then the carrying stopped, and he felt himself being manhandled and maneuvered into a hole. His body dropped, but only a couple of feet.

He was in a metal box. He could smell it. He thought at first it was a furnace, then he realized there was garbage around him. He heard a door clang shut, and a few seconds passed.

Then came the awful, ominous sound of machinery coming to life. The wall Ted was leaning against started moving against him. He couldn't get out of the way. The wall pressed him against another wall—one made of compressed garbage that didn't yield. He tried to cry out, but he still could not talk. No one would be able to hear him over the sound of the motor that propelled the wall against him.

As the wall pushed harder and harder, Ted felt his bones crush inside his body from inside. Blood shot out of all his orifices. His head popped like a melon. Then his body parts were mangled in among the garbage, but he didn't feel that part because he had been dead for several seconds.

* * *

A few hours later, maybe a day, even a week—time meant nothing in the dank dark confines of the metal prison where he dwelt—Ted regained partial awareness.

He didn't wonder too much about the strange limbo in which he existed. For all he knew, everybody who died lingered around the spot where he had bought it. Ted had accepted the fact that he was irrevocably dead. He knew his physical self could not have survived the impact of the initial crushing. And since people continued to add more trash and compact that, too, it would probably be impossible to sort out the shreds of his flesh from the coffee grounds.

At first, he wallowed in self-pity. He had come to a most hideous end, and there was no one to mourn him. Probably no one even knew or cared that he was dead. He was just a worthless ghost who was as worthless as he had been when he was alive. He couldn't even get out and scare people. Ted was apparently doomed to haunt the compactor, his spirit trapped in the metal cell forever. But that all changed when his old friend Willie had come along.

Chapter Twenty-Two

Wednesday, 22 November:
05:47

The toolbox Shannon had discovered was around the corner from a space in the building that was being remodeled. She had not seen the box during her rounds because she had no reason to go into that area. But since she had discovered it, she would make good use of its contents. The box was too heavy to carry around with her, so she was choosing the tools she thought would be most effective as weapons.

She had lost the gun during the bloody deluge in the lobby. She replaced it with a cordless power drill, tucking it in the same place the .38 had occupied. The bulge it created made her feel almost as secure as the gun had. She took out the biggest screwdrivers and stuck them in her belt along with a claw hammer and a short metal pry bar that was curved on both ends and forked on one. She put a small utility knife with a sharp blade in one back pocket of her pants and a pair of pliers with thick, heavy jaws in the other pocket. Finally, she took out a small propane torch. She would have to carry the torch in her hand, but she felt its possible value was worth the hassle, if she could find a way to light it.

Once armed, Shannon was ready to do battle with Dead Ted and his warriors. She had determined the only way for her to survive was to wipe out all his minions. They were no longer people she knew. She could no longer think of them as human beings. If God existed, she hoped He would be forgiving and understanding. If she got through the night alive, she might just check out the church her mother kept urging her to go to. She wouldn't be working down at the bank anymore, so she would have Sundays off.

Whatever God thought, Shannon knew she had to destroy the others before they destroyed her. It was the only way to weaken Dead Ted and ultimately stop him and his servants. Of course, she had to find them first. If she did not go looking for them, they would find her. Dead Ted would see to that. She was not certain how many there were, but they probably did not number many. There hadn't been a lot of people in the building to begin with since it was the third shift. The few who had remained had been trapped by the blizzard.

She realized her search-and-destroy mission might already be doomed. Dead Ted might be watching her, already making plans to counteract her own. But she knew he also liked the fun of watching her fight. He might be saving her for a horrid murder at his own hands.

In any case, she had to get a move on and keep moving. She would go up. She was on the twelfth floor. She was reasonably certain the few floors below her were unoccupied, though she knew Dead Ted or his crew could turn up just about anywhere. She could always go back down if her search proved futile.

She started to get back in the service elevator, then changed her mind. It was too chancy. Dead Ted had probably figured out the trick she had pulled with her key, and he would have taken control of the elevators again. She would use the stairwell, which would give her access to every floor. And she didn't think Dead Ted could manipulate the stairs.

She stepped out of the service area into the hall. Quickly getting her bearings, she remembered the south stairwell was down the hall and to the left. She set out in that direction. Before she was a third of the way there, she stopped, seeing something she should have noticed before—a fire alarm box.

She smashed it with the hammer, and alarms screamed throughout the building. Electric fire doors slammed shut, cutting off access to the elevators. When the fire alarm was activated, all the elevators automatically descended to the first floor.

She hoped her actions had given Dead Ted something to worry about. By the time he regained control, she would be on her way to screw up more of his plans.

She rushed to the stairwell door, and again she came to an abrupt halt. She smelled cigarette smoke.

05:51

Stan had little to say after Dead Ted's revelations. What could he say, after all? It was all true. He had let his hatred for the bum cause him to commit murder. And because of his crime, he faced retribution more hideous than death itself. Dead Ted would certainly not allow Stan to be released from the torments he had already suffered or would continue to suffer.

Stan could not help but wonder where Ted's power had come from. There was certainly nothing magical about a trash compactor. Maybe since Dead Ted had suffered a violent death, his soul wouldn't rest until the guilty party was punished. Stan dreaded what Dead Ted might consider a fitting punishment for him. Dead Ted had already demonstrated how easily he could control not only Stan, but anything else he desired.

"What is the best way to get my revenge on you now?" Dead Ted mused aloud. *"I want you to suffer a long, long time, just in case there isn't any hell."*

"Why couldn't you give me another chance? I'll kill Shannon for you. Look what she did to me!"

"That silly little bitch doesn't mean anything to me. She's just part of the fun. I could kill her anytime I want."

"Why don't you then? Kill us all! Let us go."

"No, no, no! You won't cheat me that way."

Ted's wrath was cut short by the noise of fire alarms, followed by the mechanical din of all the elevators coming down at once.

"I didn't do that."

He heard another alarm go off at the security desk—a piercing electronic horn that was louder than the fire alarms.

"What's that?"

"The alarm for the nineteenth floor," Stan said. "The computer room must be overheating."

05:53

McHenry prayed—not to God, but to the essence of evil he knew was visiting the building tonight. He prayed that it would give him the strength to overcome Dead Ted, reasoning that he did not deserve to be bested by such an inferior soul.

He prayed over the body of a woman he had just killed. She had been asleep on the couch in a rest room on the seventeenth floor, and McHenry had been guided to her presence by Dead Ted's mental prodings. He'd killed her by snapping her neck as if it were a twig. She was a fairly attractive woman, no more than 30, with long bleached-blonde hair and cantaloupe-size breasts. She had evidently come to sleep in the rest room because she knew she could not get out of the building in the blizzard.

McHenry recognized her as one of the owners of a travel agency on that floor. He had seen her in the offices upstairs; the bank had provided financing for her business. She probably would have been a good lay, but McHenry had suppressed his lust, reserving his strength for the important tasks he hoped lay ahead—such as killing the security guard and taking power away from Dead Ted, so McHenry could destroy *him.*

He prayed his reward for all his efforts would be the return of his natural human life. His brain still worked; if his body was restored, he could live. His imprecations were interrupted by the sound of fire alarms.

"Goddamn it," he muttered. "What in the hell is happening now?"

05:51

Audrey opened the fire door. It was held in place by an electromagnetic lock and easily disengaged even without the strength she possessed. In the hall, she regarded Shannon with distaste as she puffed on a cigarette.

Shannon didn't like her either. No one liked Audrey Masters because she was such a petty bitch who always found something to pester people about. She was dead, of course, and not the same. She surely would not go around naked if she had her senses about her, for her body was not one to be proudly displayed.

"Well, it's the security guard," Audrey said, raising her voice over the sound of the alarms. "How lucky of me to find you."

Shannon waved the torch at her. "Keep away from me."

Audrey dropped her cigarette on the rug and ground it out with her bare foot. "You don't mind if I smoke, do you?" She reached into the hole in her midriff and extracted the pack of cigarettes and lighter she had stashed there. "I only have a couple left. I guess I should cut down." She lit up, took a drag, then stared at the end of the cigarette. "You know, I think it would be fun to put this on your tits. What do you think?" She replaced the cigarettes and lighter, showing no sign of discomfort from probing her gaping wound.

The alarms suddenly went silent. The ensuing quiet made Audrey's threat seem more real to Shannon because there was nothing to distract her from carrying it out.

Shannon had hoped to fake Audrey out with

the torch, but it wasn't working. Maybe the woman knew she didn't have a way to light it. While she was considering which of her new weapons to use on Audrey, the scrawny woman had leaped into the air and came down hard on Shannon, shoving her face to the floor.

Shannon felt Audrey's legs tighten around her head. Something wet oozed out of the dead woman's crotch and ran down Shannon's chin, creating a mighty stench that would have caused her to pass out if her nose were not already accustomed to terrible odors from her previous travails.

Audrey hunched on her face a couple of times. "Like that, sweetie? Are you a lesbian?"

"Fuck you," Shannon said through gritted teeth.

"That's what I had in mind!" Audrey puffed on her cigarette, then aimed it at Shannon's face.

Shannon's arms were pinned, but not totally immobile. She felt around until her fingers came to rest on the handle of the power drill. She stretched her hand to get a good grip on the drill, put her finger on the trigger, and pulled it free. As she pressed the trigger down, the drill spun to life, and she jammed it into Audrey's lower spine. The sudden shock made Audrey growl. Hoping the drill would stop the other woman, Shannon held the trigger down, speeding up the drill. Blood and ground-up bone sprayed on her hand.

"Stop that!" Audrey plunged the hot cigarette toward Shannon's face.

Although Shannon was able to avoid getting the cigarette in her eye, it made contact with her right cheek and she screamed. But she kept drilling. The end of the drill bit whirled into view as it came through the other side of Audrey's body, just above the stomach wound. Shannon closed her eyes to avoid being blinded by the blood.

Audrey felt pain at last. She yelled and fell over, clutching at the drill, the trigger of which Shannon had locked into place.

Shannon didn't have much time. Drilling a hole in a dead person would not stop her, and it would surely piss Audrey off. Before Audrey could get the drill out of her back, Shannon reached into her gaping wound and plucked out the lighter. She wiped it on her shirt and lunged for the torch, which had rolled a couple of feet away.

The drill hit the floor as Audrey wrenched it from her back. Its motor still whirred.

When Shannon had the torch in her hands, she turned on the gas and flicked the lighter, which only sparked.

Audrey was coming toward her, her hands stretched out before her bloodied body, her long, already bloodstained fingernails ready to dig into Shannon's flesh.

Then the lighter lit. Shannon held the flame to the head of the torch. The gas ignited.

Audrey was standing over her, gloating. "Too late, bitch!"

Shannon thrust the torch into Audrey's crotch, lighting her pubic hair. Audrey paused to swat at the flame, and while her head was down, Shannon torched her hair and held the fire in place when Audrey looked up.

Her face was combustible, too. Already blistered in places, it caught fire easily, and Audrey screamed. The fires on her head and on her crotch spread rapidly. She dropped to the floor and rolled around.

Shannon had a sudden, dreadful thought. What if the fire didn't destroy Audrey? She remembered that the attorney Bowes had been badly burned, but he still had been dangerous. She had to make sure Audrey didn't survive. She knew that the head was the key component that kept Dead Ted's group mobile and seemingly alive.

She took the pry bar from her belt, went over to Audrey, and plunged the bar into the top of the burning woman's skull. Then Shannon jerked on the pry bar to create a wide, bloody fissure. Finally, she stuck the end of the torch in the hole.

05:53

Stan showed Dead Ted how to silence the alarms by taking him to the control panel behind the service elevator and sliding the alarm-override switch into place. He did that not only to buy some time for himself, but also in the hope that Dead Ted might feel more kindly toward him.

Dead Ted said nothing. He saw that the L.E.D. for the alarm on the nineteenth floor was still glowing and making noise. He jerked his head toward the L.E.D. to indicate to Stan that it needed to be taken care of as well.

"I have to silence that at the security desk."

Dead Ted followed him out to the desk, where Stan quietened the alarm by flipping a toggle switch.

"That doesn't mean the trouble's over," Stan said. "You still have to go up and check it out."

Stan stopped talking because he saw several people standing in the lobby. Judging from their physical condition and stance, they were dead, too. They had been in the elevators that had come down to the first floor.

Dead Ted was frustrated. His warriors were not in useful positions. Shannon had also just removed one of his most fierce—that skinny woman—from among them. And the banker was not heeding Dead Ted's orders at all. He didn't like the way things were going. There was more to come.

At that moment, there was a massive explosion on the nineteenth floor. The whole building rumbled and shook, and everyone was thrown to the floor.

Chapter Twenty-Three

Wednesday, 22 November:
06:01

Shannon could barely hold on to the metal railing in the stairwell when the blast went off. Above her, a metal door blew loose at the same time. Caught up in the confusion, she couldn't decide if the explosion was Dead Ted's work, a real disaster, or an accident brought on by Dead Ted's screwing around with the building's various systems.

She was curious, but she would have to wait to find out later. She had to keep going up. She had already quickly checked out the thirteenth floor and found no one living or dead.

She went into the door for the fourteenth floor, then crept through the offices quietly, searching. No one there either. Where the hell was everyone?

06:02

Dead Ted got to his feet. His mind was almost as jolted as his body was from the concussion of the explosion. He was disoriented and confused. Then he saw the others in the lobby. They were watching him and waiting for his next command. Their expectant stares brought his plan back to him. He would get them moving soon after he took care of Stan.

But to Dead Ted's surprise, Stan had disappeared. Dead Ted swore and vowed to get Stan yet. There was no place he could hide where Ted would not find him.

For the moment, however, he needed to do whatever was necessary to restore his position as primary power in this building. He had not counted on the security guard being so clever. She had used things he hadn't known about. But he was back in control. His mind penetrated all the electronics in the building, and no switch could be touched without his knowledge.

He strode down the lobby to inspect his troops. Many were replacements for those he had lost to Shannon and other unforeseen causes. The rest were stalwarts who had managed to avoid being destroyed.

Goddamn that Shannon! He should have killed her when he had her close by. Maybe he should just make her explode. He could do that. He knew where she was. No, he wanted to see her die. That was the only way he'd be sure she was permanently out of commission.

Occupying an equally high position on his hit list was the banker McHenry, who had somehow tapped into the power that animated Dead Ted himself. McHenry had even deluded himself into thinking he could match Dead Ted's powers! To prove the banker wrong, Dead Ted would set his followers on him as well. Then both Shannon and McHenry would taste his revenge.

Before Dead Ted took his troops up into the high rise with him, he had them gather various body parts that had been caught in the elevator doors when they shut during the alarm. They collected three hands, a leg crushed off just below the knee, and some fingers. All the parts were still moving as they were tossed in a pile. Dead Ted made them disappear, sending them somewhere they would be very useful. He didn't notice that Stan's penis was not among the severed parts.

06:10

Continuing her upward search, Shannon met no one on the fifteenth and sixteenth floors. That was good and bad. She couldn't stop the forces of the dead if she couldn't find them.

On the seventeenth floor, she went into a

lounge. She sat on a chair to rest a little and realized how thirsty she was. There was a Coke machine handy, so she dropped a couple of quarters in its coin slot and took out an icy can of pop.

As she chugged the drink, she caught sight of a sandwich machine. She was out of change, but she could break into the machine with the hammer and grab a sandwich. She stepped over to the machine and drew back the hammer.

What Shannon saw changed her mind about having a sandwich. Instead of sandwiches and snacks, the machine was filled with hands, feet, fingers, ears, noses, and various internal organs. The sight made Shannon choke on her drink; it burned her nostrils as it spat out of her nose.

Ted was sick. Very sick. Or was this display merely an illusion—another challenge to her senses designed to drive her crazy? Ted liked to play that way.

She decided to call his bluff. She smashed the front of the machine, ducking to avoid flying pieces of glass. A pair of eyes in a slot marked for bagels with cream cheese stared at her. The illusion was still holding.

Shannon reached into a slot where there was supposed to be a ham-and-cheese sandwich on rye. In its place was a white breast about the size of a grapefruit. Refusing to believe the breast was real, she pulled it out. It was spongy yet firm like one of her own breasts, except it was cold. It even looked like one of hers.

Shannon held the breast close to her face, expecting it to become a sandwich. Then, without warning, warm milk squirted from the nipple right into her eyes. She dropped the breast, and it skittered away across the floor like a small animal running for cover.

"I'm not impressed, shitface," Shannon said boldly, wiping the milk from her face. Oddly enough, the milk made the cigarette burn on her cheek feel much better.

"How do you like this?" She lit the torch and touched it to a few body pieces, then held it on the plastic frame around the slots that held them. The plastic smoked and started burning, sending smoke into the air. Shannon finished her drink and watched to make sure the machine would continue to burn.

When she left the room, she ran into a blonde-haired woman whose head was cocked at an impossible angle. The woman did not hesitate. She threw herself on Shannon and went for her throat. Shannon kneed the woman in the groin, which didn't do much except distract her long enough for Shannon to take a screwdriver from her waist and stab it into the place where her eyebrows met. The woman fell backward off Shannon. Both hands pulled on the screwdriver. Shannon had to do something else. So she reached into her back pocket and took out the utility knife. Then she knelt down and cut the woman's throat. The woman didn't even yell when her blood flowed over her neck and soaked into her long hair.

Since the knife wasn't sharp enough or long enough to cut off the woman's head, Shannon would have to torch her. When Shannon turned on the torch, it wouldn't light because the gas cannister was empty.

06:12

McHenry had barely missed getting his arm caught in one of the elevators. He had a bad feeling about entering it and jerked his arm clear just in time. He had also foreseen the coming explosion and crawled under a table to avoid being hurt. Though he could not be injured, he wanted to keep his body intact in case he should return to life.

He was gaining more confidence in that idea. The fact he had been forewarned told him someone—or something—was watching over him and offering help and strength. He could feel himself growing stronger from minute to minute.

He had gained mental power as well. He had effectively blocked all of Dead Ted's intrusions into his mind and was thinking entirely on his own. He was sure he could take over the building if he wanted to. He could conquer Dead Ted. In order to do that, McHenry sensed he needed to lure his enemy up to the top of the building—to his office suite—where McHenry judged he would have the most power. There he would make sure his enemy joined the ranks of dead forever.

He was climbing the steps in the north stairwell and had reached the nineteeth floor, where the outside door lay on the landing. He smelled smoke interlaced with the acrid pollutants plastic gave off when burnt. This was not a place he wanted to explore. He did not want to singe the lining of his lungs. Besides, why should he try to save anyone?

McHenry stepped on the door and continued following the twisted stairs toward the top of the building he considered his dominion.

06:15

Dead Ted had looked throughout the building. He had filled the vending machine with the body parts gathered by his followers. He thought it was a nifty effect, but he should have known the trick would not keep Shannon at bay very long. At least it had provided some temporary amusement.

He took a worm from his right ear and rolled it between his fingers absentmindedly. He looked beyond the waiting dead at the snow piling up outside. It looked different somehow.

Then he realized the sun was starting to come up. Though its light was diffused by deep cloud cover, the sun was beginning to penetrate enough to brighten the snowflakes.

For some reason, the imminent arrival of daylight filled Dead Ted with a sense of dread. The powers of darkness did not fluorish in the light—that was a common belief among all those who dabbled in the supernatural. But Dead Ted had never believed in any of that bullshit. Then again he wouldn't have believed the dead could walk either—until that night.

He felt abysmally ignorant. For all he knew, he and all the dead around him would fall over at dawn—like in the movies. How foolish of him to have thought he could go on indefinitely suspended between life and death. He crushed the worm between his fingers and wiped the goo on his pants.

If time was running out, he had to make the best of what remained. All he asked was enough time to destroy the woman and the banker. Then he'd die satisfied. He just hoped he didn't have to haunt that goddamn trash compactor any-more!

He ordered his forces into the elevators. Shannon and McHenry were getting close to the twentieth floor. Dead Ted and his followers would get off there. As he dragged himself in after the motley dead, he wondered what he had ever done in his life to deserve such an afterlife. But then, no one had ever told him that the afterlife would be any fairer than life itself.

06:18

Shannon had thrown the empty torch aside. It was not heavy enough to do the kind of damage necessary to stop the blonde-haired woman for good.

She might hammer the woman's head into mush. That would work if the woman would just cooperate with her. Then she remembered the power drill and decided to drill the blonde's brains out!

Before Shannon could get the drill ready, however, the other woman finally extracted the screwdriver from her skull. She rose from the floor and held the tool at her side. Undaunted by the new threat, Shannon turned the drill on, hoping the sound would intimidate her enemy.

The blonde was not even marginally afraid. She kept advancing on Shannon, raising the screwdriver, preparing to plunge it into Shannon's heart.

Shannon jabbed the drill into the woman's arm, and she dropped the screwdriver. But she still went for Shannon's neck with her other hand. The blonde pushed Shannon up against the wall roughly, banging her head and causing her to lose the drill. As Shannon's eyes darted about frantically, searching for something that would serve as a new weapon, the blonde tightened her grip on Shannon's throat, then punched

Shannon in the stomach with her other hand. Her next blow was to Shannon's crotch. Then she pummeled Shannon's breasts.

Extreme pain tore at Shannon's senses. Every fiber of her being was hurting. She tried to fend off the blows with savage counterblows, but no matter where she hit the blonde, Shannon couldn't hurt her.

Shannon's breath was being cut off; soon the blonde would succeed in crushing her larynx. Shannon thrust herself forward, rolling over and over with the blonde, but Shannon couldn't break her adversary's grip. They came to a stop next to the wall, and the blonde was on top, bearing down with her full weight.

Shannon twisted under the stranglehold. She tilted her head in an attempt to break free, but she failed. Then she spied something she hadn't thought of before. Above her on the wall, encased behind a glass and metal door, was a fire extinguisher.

Shannon thought of one of Dead Ted's tricks, and her body surged with renewed strength as hope of winning the fight returned. She tucked her chin down against the other woman's hand, clutched it with her own fingers, and managed to get her mouth along the edge of her attacker's palm. Then she bit down hard and chomped a piece out of the woman's hand.

Surprised, the blonde let go, sat back on Shannon's stomach, and viewed the ragged bite on her hand as if she couldn't understand what had happened.

Shannon spat out the chunk of the woman's hand, then bucked and turned at the same time, heaving the blonde off her. She was up on her feet in an instant. She whirled on one foot and kicked the vicious woman in the face, splintering all the bones in her nose and cheeks and sending her sailing backward across the floor. Before the blonde could get up, Shannon had yanked open the small red door and pulled the fire extinguisher in her hands. She jerked out the pin, flipped the extinguisher upside down, and aimed the hose at the woman.

The woman was halfway up. Blood from her nose and cheek bones obscured her features. Shannon knew where to stick the hose to do the most good, however. She rammed it between the other woman's lips, ripping her mouth wider by the force of her action. Then Shannon squeezed the lever down.

Some of the gunky foam from the extinguisher cascaded down the blond woman's chest, but most of it clogged up her throat and filled up her head. The blonde tried to get up, but Shannon sent her back on her ass with a kick to her shoulder.

Having gained the advantage, Shannon used her body weight to press the hose deeper into the woman's head. As she did, foam sputtered from the blonde's nose and ears. The blonde's eyes flew out and bounced off Shannon's stomach. Although the effect was horrifying, Shannon kept the lever down. Within seconds, the blonde's head exploded.

Having defeated her enemy, Shannon should have felt victorious. Instead, she was exhausted. Shannon took a quick break in the rest room. She had to pee, but she also wanted to clean some of the muck off her body. Her uniform was stained with so much blood its original color was obliterated. Once distinctly brown, the uniform was decorated with smears of red and yellow and purple.

Shannon wiped her skin off with wet paper towels. Then she tried to get some of the remnants of the blonde's head out of her hair, but without a brush or comb, her efforts were worthless.

Shannon looked terrible. The cigarette burn on her cheek was a livid dot of black encircled by tender pink flesh. There were dark bruises everywhere she looked. She also feared some of the cuts and scratches she had received would become ugly scars she would have for life. She ached all over, too. The woman had hit her in every tender spot she had. If she made it through the night, Shannon would be sore for weeks.

At least she had learned something important from that encounter—something that might prevent further bruises and injury. She had learned how to make Dead Ted's followers explode. There were at least two fire extinguishers on every floor, and as the security guard, she knew where every one of them was located.

Dead Ted no longer had the upper hand.

Chapter Twenty-Four

Wednesday, 22 November:
06:25

Jerena was not adapting to death very well at all. Sure, she knew that Dead Ted had said she and he were just in an accident. But she had studied on their condition, and nothing really explained how cold or unfeeling she was, except being dead. Besides, any fool knew there was no way she could get her head and hand cut off and have them put back on, unless she was dead. Well, hands could get sewn back on, but heads couldn't.

After Ted left, she had stood there for a long time, feeling stupid because she had actually believed what he'd told her. But when she kept getting colder and colder and saw that she didn't bleed after the vacuum cleaner blew up, she

v she couldn't be anything but dead.
nd dead was not very exciting. It was down-
ht boring. It was nothing like she had been
d it would be by her mama and all the
reachers she had ever heard in her life. There
idn't seem to be any heaven or hell, or any
angels or devils either. There were no streets of gold and no heavenly choir singing and no glory. And none of her loved ones to meet again. It was just a bunch of nothing. Boring nothing.

In fact, it wasn't that much different from being alive, except she had kept hearing that man's voice inside her head telling her to do things she didn't want to do, such as finding Shannon and killing her.

Why would she want to kill Shannon? Shannon had never done nothing wrong to her. Jerena thought Shannon was good people and didn't deserve a hard time from anybody. It was that dead guy's idea—the guy who had slammed her so hard she thought she was just going to fall apart. He was the one talking in his head.

He had said his name was Ted, but maybe he was the devil and not a man at all! He even had a mask on to make him look like that old security guard who was on the shift before Shannon. The mask had fallen off, though, and she had seen that ugly face behind it that had to belong to a real devil.

Whoever that strange guy was, Jerena wasn't doing anything he said. She'd stay right there on

that floor until she was good and ready to mo
So far, she had not been ready. She had thoug
about it when the fire sirens went off. But sh
hadn't smelled any smoke, and she knew if ther
was a real fire, Shannon would make sure she
got out okay.

Nearby, Jerena heard the elevators moving again. She wondered what all those people were doing, going up and down like yo-yos all night long. Why didn't they stay put or go on home?

Jerena thought about going down to the lobby to check things out. The man hadn't spoken inside her head for a while, so maybe he'd forgotten about her. Maybe she should try to find Shannon. Shannon would tell her straight; she was a woman who didn't take any garbage from anybody. Shannon was good people, all right. But Jerena didn't really feel like bothering Shannon. She probably had enough problems of her own.

Jerena decided not to go anywhere until she had done some more thinking. She sat down in a swivel chair, put her elbows up on the edge of a desk, and let her chin rest on her palms. Jerena lost herself in her thoughts for a moment. Then her stomach made a bubbling sound, breaking the uneven flow of her thoughts.

"What you talking for?" Jerena asked her stomach.

It made no reply; then the rumbling moved down, rippling through her abdomen and settling in her womb. The sound subsided and ame a feeling—like cramps at first, then an hing sensation inside her.

"Son of a bitch!" She scratched the surface of er abdomen, having to unzip her jeans to get ner fingers in. That provided no relief, and the itching soon became a burning feeling.

Jerena hesitated. Dead or not, she had some modesty about digging around in her crotch when there might be people around somewhere. Somebody could come off the elevators and find her there, and if she had her hand in her pants, she'd *really* look the fool! Of course, she'd been with that guy out in the open, so she might as well scratch that itch real good. What did she care who saw her? She started scratching herself so hard her right hand came off again and landed on her stomach.

"I'll be damned!"

There was no pain and no blood. Her hand looked stupid, lying there unattached, but it didn't hurt. Then, all of a sudden, her hand jumped down the front of her panties, just about tearing them off.

"Stop that!"

The hand ignored her. It pulled on her jeans, and Jerena saw what it was up to, so she helped it. Soon she was sitting there with her panties and jeans down around her ankles and her right hand rubbing her. She kicked her panties and jeans all the way off, then propped her legs up on the desk and let the hand do its stuff. All the while, she was getting warmer and warmer. Soon, however, the burning became more intense, and blood seeped from between her legs.

Jerena jerked the hand away, stuck it on her wrist, and peered down at what was becoming very messy. More blood bubbled out of her, followed by slimy pink mucus, then by a small head. For a moment, Jerena thought she was having a miscarriage.

But what was coming out of her didn't look very dead. The head popped out and the shoulders and arms and the rest of the body, and the thing was very alive. It squeaked as a tiny baby would. And it was a boy, no doubt about that. Its penis was about four inches long.

Jerena was afraid to touch the baby, because it didn't seem as if it was a normal child. In addition to it being hung like a horse, it wasn't brown or white or any other natural human color. It was more yellow than anything, and when it turned to look at her, it had green eyes. Then it opened its mouth, revealing a set of sharp teeth, which it used to bite off the umbilical cord.

"What kind of baby are you?" Jerena asked her child.

Her newborn, whatever it was, didn't hang around long enough to answer any questions. It bit Jerena on the left breast, its teeth easily penetrating the thick fabric of her sweatshirt. Then, while she was yelling, the child ran across the floor, shrieking as if it had been bitten.

Jerena just about threw up, but couldn't because she was as dead as ever. What if she wasn't dead, but was having some terrible dream? How could a dead woman have a baby?

The answer to that question didn't amount to much either. For a few seconds later, another head appeared between her legs.

"I'm having twins!"

It wasn't twins. Or triplets. There wasn't a regular name for the number of little monsters that clawed their way out of her womb, leaving her body ravaged. Every one of them ran away the second it was clear of the womb and had bit its cord off—except the last one. It stayed behind to eat its mother.

Chapter Twenty-Five

Wednesday 22, November:
06:39

Shannon had strapped a fire extinguisher to her back with a makeshift harness fashioned from her belt. The extinguisher was so heavy she could only lug one with her at a time. She hoped she would only need one at any given moment. Each extinguisher should have enough chemicals in it to stop at least two of Dead Ted's people. When she emptied one, she would immediately get another, the only problem being the possibility of running into someone before she made it to the next fire-extinguisher case. If that happened, she still had her tools; she could stall an attacker with one of her improvised weapons.

Shannon had come to the nineteenth floor and ventured a few feet beyond the fallen stairwell door. She choked on the smoke and fumes in the air, but covered her mouth in order to explore. It didn't take long for her to discover a real fire was in progress on the floor. Anyone caught in it would have perished completely. She was only a few yards away and the heat was stifling.

She also realized the fire was gradually eating into the ceiling above, which meant it would spread to the next floor and possibly keep spreading upward. The only question was how long it would take to travel to the top. The fire should have been put out or retarded by the sprinkler system. The sprinklers should have been on throughout the floor, but they were not functioning at all. They were not electronic; heat set them off. Only the lack of water would render them ineffective.

Dead Ted had probably done something to the water supply. He wouldn't care if the building burned down. Why should he? He could be burned up, too. Didn't he know that?

There was no use risking asphyxiation by going any farther. She returned to the stairwell. The fire would take time to get up to where she was headed. She hoped it was enough time for her to do what she had set out to do.

In the meantime, however, the fire might spread down as well. Getting back to the ground floor might become impossible. She could go back before the fire created an impasse. But Dead Ted would still come after her with his killing hordes. None of her choices was appealing. She could die at the hands of Ted's loonies or die by fire.

Whichever way she went, she would die fighting. Let them put that on her tombstone, provided there was enough of her left to bury. If she took Ted with her, she'd be happy. He had turned her friends and other normal people into monsters, and it was only just that he should perish for that. That thought was enough to keep her going up.

Before she started on the next flight of stairs, she was chilled by a distinct sound above her. Someone else was climbing the stairs. The sound of footsteps echoed down to her.

Who else would be in the stairwell? No one who was a friend. She had only enemies left. Whoever it was, she would meet him up there somewhere. And then it would be party time.

06:45

McHenry had never been so glad to see the door marked 30. It had seemed he would never get there. But he didn't feel tired. If he were his former self, he would probably be huffing and puffing. In his present state, he wasn't even fatigued.

But he was aware of time's passage, and he was anxious to get things over with. He wanted his living self back.

He was certain his nemesis would know where he was and be up there shortly. His foe's desire for confrontation—and revenge—was as strong as his own.

McHenry opened the door and hurried to his private office suite, where he would prepare for anything his nemesis might try against him. McHenry would win, though, if the essence of evil provided him with the extra powers he needed.

He sat on the sofa bed and waited anxiously.

06:47

Dead Ted and his group filed off the elevators on the twenty-ninth floor. He knew where McHenry was, but he also expected the banker to be prepared. Dead Ted wanted to surprise him.

Before he confronted the banker, Dead Ted wanted to get rid of Shannon, so she wouldn't get to do anything to spoil his revenge. The banker wasn't just another enemy. He represented all the uncaring forces in the world that had squashed Dead Ted in life and ultimately fomented the hatred that caused his death. The people with all the money were the source of true evil in the universe; Dead Ted was convinced of that. And ridding the world of one of the worst, as he imagined McHenry to be, should give him a foothold in heaven.

Compared to McHenry, Shannon was a minor nuisance. She was only defending herself. Admirable, but still annoying. She had to be removed. And she had to suffer for all the trouble she had caused him. She would be arriving soon. Dead Ted sensed her approximate wherabouts in the stairwell.

Dead Ted dispatched a man and a woman to wait for her at the stairwell door. He had warned them not to kill Shannon right away, so he could participate in her final demise. But if his servants got carried away and killed her anyhow, that was tough shit.

06:52

Shannon was weary. Though she was not in the worst physical shape, she was no longer 18, and the added decade had robbed her of much of her stamina. It was hard to continue on adrenaline alone, no matter how dire the circumstances.

But she was close to the end of the night. In fact, it was already morning. It was unfortunate that the stairwell had no windows. The sun would be trying to shine through the snow by now; the coming of morning after a long third shift was always a special moment.

Shannon had been through every floor up to the twenty-eighth. She had found a headless body, an arm crawling around on the floor by itself, and nothing else. Dead Ted and the others all had to be on one of the next two floors. And whoever had been on the stairs above her had reached his goal at some point, because she no longer heard his footsteps.

She plodded up to the twenty-ninth floor and took a few deep breaths before opening the door. She had to be totally prepared for whatever waited beyond it. She had to psych herself up. Get the attitude right. Kick ass.

She undid the harness and swung the fire extinguisher in front of her, removing the pin and turning the whole thing upside down. With her hand on the discharge lever, she was ready to terminate all enemy personnel. Military talk; it was great.

One, two, three—

"Bonzai!"

She jerked the door open, ran in, hit the floor, rolled over, and rose into a crouching position. A half-naked woman with most of her guts torn out and a man with his throat cut stared at her from either side of the door. She recognized the man; it was Turner, his throat a bloody mess. The woman was a new player.

Shannon pointed the hose in their direction. "Who wants to go first?"

Lilly Ann Zeto rushed at Shannon while Turner held back a little, probably to see what his partner would do. After the woman leaped at her, Shannon ducked and stabbed Lilly in the neck with a screwdriver.

Turner pressed down on Shannon now. In one fluid movement, she stuck the hose of the fire extinguisher into Turner's mouth and turned it on before he realized what was happening. Foam bubbled from the cut in his throat first; then it filled his head, which soon exploded. His body folded to the floor.

Shannon couldn't look. Turner was a good guy. They'd been joking only a few hours ago. Now she had had to kill him.

It wasn't Turner, she reminded herself. Not anymore. The Turner she'd known was really dead. That creature was one of Ted's boys.

She had no time for sentiment; there was still the woman to deal with. Lilly Ann had recovered sufficiently to mount another attack. Shannon barely had time to remove the hose from Turner's mouth and jam it in the woman's. Lilly Ann tried to hit Shannon, but the foam filled her head too quickly. She lost control of her body as her brain became numb just before it blew out the back of her head.

Shannon emptied the extinguisher in Lilly Ann. She left the hose in the woman's mouth and stepped over her body, as foam oozed from the jagged rip going from her pubis up to her collar bone.

Shannon hustled. Following a mental map, she turned into the first hallway she came to, at the end of which was another extinguisher. There were three more extinguishers on that floor—the bank's attorneys had more than most. She prayed they would be enough.

She went out toward the lobby, the extinguisher at the ready in front of her, her hand poised on the lever.

"Ted!" she yelled. "Hey, come out, you mother! I got something for you!"

Dead Ted had witnessed what Shannon had done to his people. It was so damn easy for her, too. He had vastly underestimated her because she had big breasts. He realized he'd been stupid. If Shannon reached him with one of the extinguishers, she could actually destroy him.

Then it occurred to him that her method of dispatching people had a major disadvantage. She could only take on one at a time; two was more of a challenge, though not impossible. Three or more would make it really rough for her. So he sent five after her.

06:58

McHenry was getting hot. He was perspiring so much he had removed his shirt, and he was still uncomfortable. Yet only a moment before he had felt nothing from climbing hundreds of metal steps. Maybe it was the anxiety of waiting. Maybe he needed a drink. He wasn't thirsty, but the alcohol might provide a little relief and calm his nerves.

He went to his wet bar and started to pour a glass full of scotch, then dropped the bottle as he swooned. He felt weak at the knees, but that feeling was gradually replaced by one of growing strength.

It was happening again; his prayers were answered. He was becoming the demon! His features drew up into a frozen grimace as the skin on his face tightened. His eyes turned yellow green. Cold sweat broke out all over his skin. His fingers lengthened; his nails turned dark as they became long and sharp.

He shed his pants. The transformation had taken place there, too; standing out from his groin was the demonic penis with its green eyes and jagged sharp teeth.

McHenry was ready for Dead Ted. He would rip him to pieces, chew him up, and spit him out in the toilet. He was also ready for the security guard. He was going to do to her what he had done to Audrey—only he planned to take his time and enjoy every minute of it.

Chapter Twenty-Six

Wednesday, 22 November:
07:00

The lobby on the twenty-ninth floor. The arena of battle. The location of Shannon's last stand.

She heard them approaching, the walking dead. Dead Ted's warriors. Dead heads.

Terminate.

I can talk the talk, and I can walk the walk!

A woman with one arm peeked around the corner at her.

Terminate with extreme prejudice.

Shannon started for her.

Then another woman's head jutted into view on the opposite side.

Kill.

A man appeared behind her.

She turned as a fourth rounded the corner.

Kill!

Then came another one.

Too many.

Kill, Shannon, kill. Terminate. Off the mothers!

07:04

Dead Ted no longer felt the need to watch Shannon die.

It was getting late and too much time had been spent on her. The people he had sent would finish her off soon enough.

His greatest imperative now was to face off with the banker. Even if he were to cease to exist when the sun was up, Dead Ted wanted to make sure the banker went with him. No scumbag banker deserved to survive!

He went out to the stairwell and ascended as quickly as he could.

07:05

Shannon set the fire extinguisher on the floor. She had to save it until she had no other options. She could not get by Dead Ted's people to get another.

They advanced slowly. Unevenly. Not organized. Their only advantage was numbers. Shannon could be faster.

She had to be a hell of a lot smarter.

Goddamn Ted!

"All right, shit-for-brains, come on. Get it over with."

A new surge of adrenaline pumped through her body; it lit up her brain, too. She was a fighting machine, not a woman. She was Bruce Lee, Van Damme, and Schwartzenegger all in one! And Wonder Woman, too. Men weren't the only ones with killing force!

Two men came at her simultaneously.

She drew the power drill.

Man Number One grabbed her around the waist.

She jammed the drill into the base of his skull, as Man Number Two clutched her legs.

One held on.

The one-armed woman stepped forward.

Shannon threw a screwdriver, which plunked into the top of the woman's head.

It didn't stop her.

She pressed the drill harder, hitting brain. Gray matter spun out of the hole, wetting Shannon's face.

Number Two was trying to bite her on the leg.

She tried to kick at him and tumbled backward to the floor. Now she landed a strong kick on the side of his head, stunning him momentarily, while she fumbled to grab the pliers from her back pocket. Number One lay next to her now, trying to get the drill out of his head.

She opened the pliers, snapped them around

the bridge of his nose, crushed the bone between the heavy jaws, twisted, opened them again, and plunged them farther into his skull, turning them to gouge out a deep hole.

She jerked most of his brain out in a gory wad and threw it over her head.

So much for that asshole.

The woman had removed the screwdriver and was getting ready to use it on Shannon. She stood over Shannon, her legs spread, holding the tool overhead, about to stick it in Shannon's face.

Shannon yanked the drill from the man's head and thrust it up into the crotch of the woman's pants. She kept pushing the drill upward and inward, until her arm was buried to the elbow in the woman's guts.

The woman thrashed around. She lost the screwdriver, but pounded on Shannon's head with her one fist. Shannon grabbed the fist with her free hand and held it away, as Man Number Two came up and wrapped his arms around her middle, trying to squeeze her breath out.

Yet another woman advanced.

"Damn!" she gasped.

Shannon withdrew her arm from the woman, leaving the drill on inside her and letting go of her fist. As the drill ate into her lungs, the woman fell to the floor again, writhing as she tried to get her one arm up into her innards to remove the tool.

Shannon clawed at the man's arms. Though

she ripped his flesh to the bone, he wouldn't loosen his grip.

How could a bunch of dead sons of bitches be so strong?

But not invulnerable, Shannon reminded herself. She was just able to get her hand under one of the man's arm and grasp the pry bar. She twisted her body and inserted the pry bar in the joint at his shoulder and pulled back on it with all her remaining strength.

The joint popped and the arm, held in place by only a few strands of muscle, was rendered useless. The man lost his grip around her waist, but smacked her with his other arm.

The blow knocked her into the pool of gore. The momentum created made her slide across the floor next to the fire extinguisher.

Thank God for little favors!

The extinguisher in her hands, she went for the new woman, poked the hose into her mouth and engaged the lever.

While her head was being filled with foam, the woman with the drill in her joined the man with the dangling arm to mount a frontal assault.

Two on one again—no fair!

Shannon threw the hammer at the man; he ducked. She had one screwdriver left. She rammed it into the woman's ear, sending her to the floor one more time.

The other woman's head exploded.

Shannon removed the hose, but there wasn't enough time to stick it into the man's mouth. So she slammed it against his head. He dropped to his knees.

Swinging the extinguisher reminded her how heavy these industrial units were, even half full. She hefted it over her head, jumped, and brought it down full force on the man's head, cracking it open to expose his brain. She lifted the extinguisher again and smashed the brain into oblivion.

The woman on the floor was up again.

The last of this group, another woman, was coming, too.

Shannon squatted and kicked this woman's legs out from under her, then quickly fed her fire extinguisher foam while she lay on her back.

The other woman was a true bitch—a drill up her crotch, a screwdriver in her ear, and only one arm—but she still wanted to fight.

As the other woman's head bulged, then went to pieces, Shannon got up.

The fire extinguisher was empty.

She threw it at the one-armed woman.

The woman bent down and the extinguisher rolled off her back.

Shannon's tools were scattered all over, out of reach.

She'd tear the bitch apart with her bare hands!

She waited.

"C'mon. I ain't got all day."

The woman went into a squat and deposited the drill on the floor between her legs. It lay there humming, then slowed down and died, finally out of juice.

Shannon held her hands out, working her fingers, looking for the best place to get a hold on the woman.

The woman took one step, stopped, tilted her head as if listening to something, then abruptly turned around and headed in the opposite direction.

"Hey! Come back! You can't run away!"

But the woman had left, disappearing into the labyrinth of offices. After a few seconds, Shannon heard a metal door open and shut.

She knew what she had to do and where she had to go. She gathered her tools together, placed them in her waistband and pockets, and went to the northwest corner, next to the stairwell on the other side of the building. There she equipped herself with another fire extinguisher.

07:10

Having reached the thirtieth floor, Dead Ted proceeded with caution.

McHenry was no easy target. He was a powerful adversary who had successfully resisted all Dead Ted's efforts to control him.

Maybe he could sneak up on the banker, though Dead Ted didn't think that would make much difference.

"It's about time," McHenry said in a voice that rumbled.

Dead Ted saw the banker standing in the doorway to his suite. McHenry had become the demon again—and now Dead Ted knew there was a force at play there that was equal to whatever had bestowed power upon him.

Maybe it was the same force.

Maybe it had planned this confrontation all along.

Maybe it didn't care who won.

A lot of maybes and only one certainty—there would be only one winner.

Fortunately, Dead Ted was not stupid. He had not sent all his warriors to do battle with Shannon. The rest had come up the other side of the building.

They gathered across from him, and their dead eyes shifted in the direction of the demonic banker.

Chapter Twenty-Seven

Wednesday, 22 November:
07:12

The thirtieth floor of the Metropolitan National Bank building, downtown Indianapolis. Outside a blizzard pounded the building, shaking the windows. Inside, hell was in session.

McHenry glared at Dead Ted and his newly marshaled forces. His eyes glowed orange with unmitigated, unfathomable hatred.

Dead Ted's face was immobile, but beneath it he felt as if he might be smiling.

He had McHenry outnumbered. He could—would—win.

Maybe.

The crowd of dead beings across from him awaited Dead Ted's command. Their bodies were in various stages of disfigurement. Some lacked limbs. Some had been burned. One man had a giant hole in his chest, oozing blood and pus. A woman's torn mouth gaped open showing stubs of shattered teeth. Another man's head was oblong from being crushed. A former secretary for a travel agency watched expectantly, her breasts bare, one hanging lop-sided about to drop to the floor, both nipples impossibly erect. There were more than McHenry had anticipated, for Dead Ted had always had more followers than anyone had known. He had stored them in places around the building where they would be out of harm's way, summoning them together only when he needed them.

McHenry was apparently stymied.

There was a moment of hesistation; neither Dead Ted's forces nor McHenry moved. Then, as one, obeying the mental orders of their leader, the horde of the dead advanced slowly toward the banker, some of them dragging on one foot or a stump.

"Who's got the last laugh now, sucker?" Dead Ted plucked a worm from his ear and flicked it toward the banker.

McHenry didn't answer the taunt. Instead, he shut the door to his suite.

What did he hope to accomplish by hiding? Doors meant nothing to Dead Ted's troops. Neither did walls.

Dead Ted set his forces to breaking through the flimsy plasterboard walls of the suite, using their fists and feet. A woman kicked down the door. Dead Ted came forward to watch.

"Rip him up! Tear him apart!"

The dead tore up the furniture. They heaved things through the windows, letting in frigid air and snow from outside. They broke into the bathroom and trashed it. They overturned the huge desk. They splintered chairs. They shattered bottles of expensive liquor.

But McHenry was no longer inside.

07:16

Shannon heard a terrible din when she stepped through the stairwell door. Then a rush of cold air whipped by her. She crept toward the source of the noise and was astonished when she saw how many warriors Dead Ted still had.

There was no way she could survive an attack from them. Nor could she get through them to Dead Ted himself.

She had no choice but to turn tail and run.

But someone else had plans for her. A scaly hand covered her mouth from behind. Another hand reached around and gripped her left breast so tightly it hurt.

She felt something like a baseball bat pressed up against the cheeks of her butt.

McHenry laughed softly in her ear as he pulled her away.

07:17

Dead Ted used his mental power to survey the thirtieth floor. McHenry could not be far away.

In fact, he was in a copy room behind his suite, having apparently escaped there via a secret door. He must have envisioned a day when he would need an escape route—the mangy son of a bitch.

Dead Ted also saw that McHenry had somehow captured Shannon. He didn't know which surprised him more—that Shannon had managed to survive an attack by five of his warriors or that McHenry was thinking about sex when he was about to be destroyed.

For a banker, he wasn't very smart.

07:18

Behind the closed door in the copy room, McHenry had laid Shannon atop one of the cabinets that lined the walls. He had to shove a paper cutter off on the floor to make room for her.

He didn't care about Dead Ted at the moment; his mind was too occupied by demonic pleasures. Shannon was too great a prize to be wasted. He intended to waste her, all right. She was the reason he was dead.

Shannon tried to get up. She tried to stab McHenry with a screwdriver. She slit his wrist with the utlity knife, but he didn't even bleed. She even hit him in the forehead with the hammer and didn't raise a bump. She didn't think the fire extinguisher—which he had dragged along and set in a far corner of the room—would be effective against him either.

He wasn't the same as the others. He was not even half human. Nothing human had a penis with a face and hungry jaws.

It was clear what he meant to do to her.

She didn't know how to resist. She had run out of energy.

She thought about ways to stop rapists: yell, scream profanities, urinate, defecate—make herself undesirable.

None of that would work with McHenry. It might make him madder—if that was possible. As long as she drew a breath, she had hope, however small.

She would cooperate. That was best. It would give her a chance to think.

McHenry growled like a bear. He had one knee up on the top of the cabinet and both arms braced on the sides of her shoulders. His demonic penis worked its jaws, dripping with brackish spittle.

Shannon closed her eyes. She heard—and felt—the head of the thing starting to chew into the seam of her slacks. She urinated involuntarily.

The sharp teeth of the penis grazed her skin.

It would be over soon.

Then McHenry was interrupted by a sudden racket. One of the copy machines, a big floor model, had come on by itself. It was spitting out sheets of paper.

Shannon opened her eyes when a piece of paper landed on her face. On its surface was the visage of Dead Ted.

McHenry roared. He slid off Shannon and beat his chest like a gorilla.

Shannon rolled to the floor. She picked up the paper cutter, lifted its handle, and pushed it at McHenry's groin. She snapped the handle down and the demonic penis was cut off.

"Goddamn bitch!"

"Fuck you, too." Shannon jumped on the banker's unattached penis, mashing it to pulp. Then she went for her fire extinguisher. She swooped it up and opened the door, diving out into the hall.

McHenry was on her heels. Blue-black gore gushed from the hole in his crotch as he chased after her. But he was stopped when he ran into a whole congregation of dead.

07:22

Dead Ted's forces carried McHenry aloft on their arms, conveying him back to the general office area where their master waited. McHenry struggled and fought all the way, but his supernatural strength did not match their combined might.

By the time they set him down in front of the dead man who had become his greatest enemy, he had lost much substance from the wound inflicted by Shannon.

He was even a bit light-headed.

Dead Ted could not help but gloat. McHenry was not even in the same league with him. He was a mere mindless demon; he didn't possess the street smarts that had allowed Dead Ted to survive in a hostile outside world.

Behind McHenry was another goodie: Shannon had been taken by one of the men, who held her now by one arm.

It was strange that she didn't try to get away. Or maybe she was as interested in seeing the destruction of the banker as Dead Ted was.

The only disturbing aspect of her presence was that the dead man who had abducted her had failed to take away her fire extinguisher.

Dead Ted hoped she didn't think she could use it on him. He would have her torn into a million pieces if she tried.

The whole floor was cold now, because the heating system was not strong enough to offset the air pouring in from the broken windows in McHenry's suite. The cold seemed appropriate, however. It might even be preserving the dead in what could be their final moments before the sun rose completely.

That was of no consequence. Only Shannon

would feel the effects of the cold air. Everyone else was insensitive to it, except maybe McHenry.

Dead Ted could feel McHenry's strength starting to wane. Shannon had screwed him up good.

McHenry's orange eyes betrayed no emotions whatsoever. He had not said a word since he'd been standing there. He uttered no oaths of defiance, no curses. Nothing.

What a disappointment.

"Cat got your tongue?" Dead Ted inquired. *"She sure got your dick!"*

McHenry's eyes changed color. Now bright red, they glowed with an intensity that could melt metal. He lunged forward, breaking the arms of two of Dead Ted's troops who had been holding him. He snatched Dead Ted's face off and shredded it in his massive hands.

"Get him!"

The dead warriors descended on McHenry, burying him under their bodies. For a few seconds, it seemed he had been bested. Then, the bodies started flying—along with ripped off limbs, heads, and anything else McHenry could get his hands on.

Dead Ted was pressed up against a wall. He could not see, but he sensed Shannon was standing placidly at the periphery of the melee, just observing.

"Help me!" Dead Ted implored.

Shannon started laughing so hard her stomach began to hurt. Dead Ted had made a joke!

"I don't want to spoil your fun!" she said as her laughter subsided. "It's your party, dude."

Dead Ted growled and the flap of flesh hanging over his throat fluttered. *"I'll get you."*

"No, you won't." Shannon had taken advantage of the confusion to work her way around to the other side of the room. She now had the hose to the fire extinguisher only inches from Dead Ted's head. All she had to do was stick it into his sinuses—if she could find the damn things under all the worms.

McHenry suddenly emerged from the bloody battle. Many of the warriors had run off. The rest were mangled pieces under his feet. None of them posed any further threat to him.

"You can't have him, bitch."

"I don't like people calling me a bitch." She aimed the hose at McHenry's face and held down the discharge lever. Foam pelted his features.

He flailed around blindly for a few seconds as the foam ate into his eyes.

Shannon shoved Dead Ted at him.

Now the blind would be fighting the blind.

McHenry and Dead Ted locked arms, fell over, and tumbled around on the floor, each trying to tear into the other's head.

Shannon was watching closely; it was almost as much fun as wrestling on television, except she didn't want either of them to emerge the victor.

Finally, the two monstrosities were on their

knees with their hands dug into each other's throats.

This was it.

Dead Ted let out a mighty sound that gurgled up from deep within his body, and he tore McHenry's head off triumphantly.

Gallons of gore erupted from the banker's neck, splattering the ceiling, splashing over Dead Ted, and showering Shannon.

Dead Ted stood erect, and McHenry's body fell forward, the gusher at the end now pounding the wall. He held McHenry's head above him—the bloody trophy of a battle well fought. Dead Ted made a guttural cry of victory.

Shannon stepped back a little to avoid bumping into him. She was dangerously close to being trapped in a corner. She didn't have much time to act before Dead Ted thought about bringing his troops back.

But she was curious about what Dead Ted was doing now. She put off acting until he was finished.

He had wiped a bunch of worms from his head, then stooped down and set McHenry's head on the floor. He pulled a small pocket knife from the pocket of his ragged pants and opened it. Working by touch alone, he inserted the blade at the edge of McHenry's face and cut around it.

She understood now.

He pulled the face loose—it was weird how little held a person's face on—and set it down on the bloody front of his skull, restoring to himself eyes, nose and mouth.

"Peek-a-boo!" Shannon cried with glee and pushed the fire extinguisher into Dead Ted's new mouth.

"No!"

"Yes, yes, and yes!"

She was going to empty the entire extinguisher in him. She was about to jump astride him and ride him like a horse as she pumped the foam into his head, but the floor beneath them suddenly shook.

Shannon was thrown against the wall. The floor buckled, rippled, and blew apart, leaving behind a hole 12 feet across.

A deafening sound followed—like a hundred freight trains, or an atom bomb exploding—and a pillar of flame shot up through the hole, gouging its way through the ceiling above and out through the roof. Heat radiated from the fire, and it was spread outward.

Dead Ted spat out the hose and a mouthful of foam. He had been heaved to the other side of the hole and was basically unscathed. Now he crawled around its edge, going for Shannon.

"Now, I'll see you in hell." His blistered hands reached out for her.

Shannon pulled herself up, cowering against the wall. The heat was becoming more intense.

Dead Ted almost had her. The tips of his fingers touched the bottom of her feet.

Then they were whisked away.

McHenry's body had risen and grasped Dead Ted around his chest. It turned around swiftly and threw itself into the column of fire.

Dead Ted's scream seemed to rise from the pit of hell. It echoed throughout the building and shattered glass on the thirtieth floor.

The inferno became a fiery tornado, spinning around, sucking things into its vortex.

Shannon gripped the edge of the wall and was lifted up by the swirling forces of the fire. She kept holding as the rest of Dead Ted's followers were consumed by the fire.

Then it suddenly went out. The ensuing silence was eerie and unreal. Shannon's feet drifted to the floor. She went to the smoldering edge of the hole left by the fire and peered down. It seemed to go all the way through the building, cutting through every floor.

Experiencing vertigo, she stepped away.

A chill descended on the area now, brought on by the artic air pouring in through the roof. Snow began to fall inside.

Shannon glanced up into the sky. For a second, she thought she saw a hole in the clouds, but it must have been an illusion. They formed a solid ceiling in the sky, interrupted only by a spot of yellow—the sun trying to shine through.

She sighed and walked wearily to one of the elevators. She pressed the down button and was surprised that the elevator actually responded.

As she rode down, the fire alarms went off again.

07:48

Since the building was in fire alert mode—probably because Dead Ted was no longer in control—the elevator took Shannon all the way down to the first floor without stopping. She got out, then took the stairs to the basement part of the parking garage.

When she got there, she saw what she expected to see—a large hole approximately where the pillar of fire would have been. The fire on the nineteenth floor hadn't caused the explosion. Something else had. Something beneath the building. A portal to another dimension? A gateway into hell?

Shannon couldn't guess. She didn't want to know. She didn't even want to see how deep the hole was.

Behind her she heard something fall over. She turned and saw Jack Lander's body, his face completely gone, on the floor at the end of a wooden bench.

Why shouldn't he fall? she asked herself. After all, there was nothing around to keep him moving now.

Not Ted, anyhow.

When she looked back, the hole was gone. So was the hole above it in the lobby floor.

The building was a living thing, with a circulatory system and a heart. It was healing itself.

And hell had two new recruits.

Shannon hadn't noticed at first, but now she felt very cold. A gust of chilling wind bit at her neck, and she wondered where it was coming from, since the hole that went up into the sky had closed over.

She changed direction, and as the wind flowed over her face, she realized its source. To make sure, she went around to the ramp across from the basement entrance—the ramp where she had tried to help Richard Bowes, the attorney, get out of the building.

At the top of the ramp, the metal door had been ripped open, providing a ready exit to the loading dock. Judging from the amount of snow collected inside, it had been open for hours.

And Jack's truck was parked only a few feet beyond the door.

She could have avoided all the carnage, all the pain and suffering, if only she had checked the garage—as she was supposed to every goddamn night.

Chapter Twenty-Eight

Wednesday, 22 November:
07:57

Shannon Elroy was sitting behind the security desk, her head resting on her folded arms. She was almost asleep.

A mental alarm clock went off in her head, and she glanced down at the digital clock on her control console.

It was almost eight o'clock—time for her relief to show up so she could go home.

Where was he?

Why were the fire alarms going off?

She stared at her hands. Why were they so scratched up? What the hell had happened to her clothes? And she stank like she had been rolling in a pigsty.

She heard someone banging on the doors. She got up and ran to the front of the lobby. Fire trucks were parked outside, their lights flashing off the mounds of newly fallen snow lining both sides of the street. Firemen had dug through the snowdrifts on the walk out front to get to the entrance. One of them had a heavy tool, and he was getting ready to smash the glass in at the side doors.

"No, wait!"

Shannon would have opened the door for them. She had keys. She had keys to everything. She was the security guard there. She watched over things.

Glass blew inward from the blow of the tool; then the fireman reached in and released the safety bar on the door. He held it open as several of his fellow firefighters filed in.

Shannon was going to ask them where the fire was, but she heard the creaking of the metal door that opened into the other end of the lobby from the loading dock.

"Hey, Shannon!"

It was Stan Cork's voice. Her relief had arrived at last. She could go home.

Shannon turned to greet him.

Stan stood in the door, clutching his penis in one hand, and holding his head under one arm. Around his feet were dozens of monstrous small beings—demon babies with wild eyes, ugly gray skin, and sharp teeth. They shrieked altogether—like diminutive banshees—then ran past Shannon to meet the firemen.

"Stan?"

"What's up?" he asked, leering.